DATE DUE

WITHDRAWN

GAYLORD   PRINTED IN U.S.A.

Blind Singer Joe's Blues

ALSO BY ROBERT LOVE TAYLOR

Loving Belle Starr

Fiddle and Bow

The Lost Sister

Lady of Spain

Blind Singer Joe's Blues

A Novel by Robert Love Taylor

Southern Methodist University Press

Dallas

This novel is a work of fiction. Names, characters, places, and incidents are either the product of the author's imagination or are used fictitiously.

Requests for permission to reproduce material from this work should be sent to:
Rights and Permissions
Southern Methodist University Press
PO Box 750415
Dallas, Texas 75275-0415

A portion of this novel, in slightly different form, previously appeared in *The Ohio Review* and in *New Stories from the South*.

Cover illustration: "Riley Puckett," by Steven McNalley

Jacket and text design by David Timmons

Library of Congress Cataloging-in-Publication Data

Taylor, Robert, 1941–
    Blind Singer Joe's blues : a novel / by Robert Love Taylor. — 1st ed.
        p. cm.
    ISBN-13: 978-0-87074-511-9 (acid-free paper)
    ISBN-10: 0-87074-511-5 (acid-free paper)
        1. Rural families—Fiction. 2. Blues (Music)—Fiction. 3. Blues musicians—Fiction. 4. Appalachian Region—Music—Fiction. 5. Bristol (Va.)—Fiction. 6. Bristol (Tenn.)—Fiction. I. Title.

PS3570.A9518B56 2006
813'.54—dc22
                                                                2006044386

Printed in the United States of America on acid-free paper

10   9   8   7   6   5   4   3   2   1

For Tom and Jina, musicianers extraordinaire

Once again, for my everloving guitar-playing companion Sue

And in memory of Blanche Nichols and Earl Burris

Prelude:

Singer Joe

DALLAS, 1939

He had seen all he needed to see before he was born. In darkness, some sounds you could almost touch, smell. Color curved back into itself, the shape of sound. The world went on and on, twisting deep, in and out.

He didn't care to be reminded of what he could never see.

All the same, Pink Miracle said, your mama, she loved you, son.

I'm not your son.

Pink Miracle's breath came a little quicker. He was so close you could smell the candy he sucked on, peppermint, favored by cowboy fiddlers to hide the smell of whiskey.

I got no right, I know, Pink said.

That's correct. I didn't ask you to come here, didn't even know you were coming.

It's just—I was in the neighborhood, so to speak, playing over at the Baker Hotel, and jawing with our guitar player—Henry Witmer, maybe you heard of him, from right here in Dallas, used to play on the WBAP *Barn Dance* with old Captain Bonner—and he remarked as how there was a hot guitar player down on Deep Ellum, a white boy name of Singer Joe Crider that was blind, and I said to him, Henry, says I, I know that boy—

You don't know me, though.

Well, son—sorry, I know you don't like being called son—but I did know you when you was a lad in East Tennessee, and I married your mama, which makes me, in the eyes of the law, your stepdaddy, and so, naturally, I thought I had some knowledge of you.

I expect I've changed some.

I expect so. Yes. We are all of us changed. It's a whole different world. But I had to see, don't you know. I felt a powerful calling, like it was your mama's voice saying to me, Go see my son and tell him I never once forgot about him and loved him to my dying breath.

She never thought no such thought.

It's a feeling I had.

I have a different feeling.

It was late summer, long about dusk. Outside, crickets clicked and whirred in the skimpy trees that endured on Deep Ellum. You had to pay attention you wanted to hear them above the voices, all the jive-talking and shuffling feet and somebody singing downstairs. Close all that off, easy enough for him to do, something he'd done all his life, and you could almost imagine you were back in East Tennessee, that dark lonesome place of lost kinfolk, brothers and sisters gone every which way, his mother and all her sweet grieving music long gone for good.

He didn't want to think of that place of his birth and the music he'd breathed with his first breath, the mountains humming, every ridge and holler beating its own time, mixed in crazily with his mama's voice and, though he did not like to think it, with Pink Miracle's fiddle. He was in Texas, he told himself, city of Dallas, down on Deep Ellum, and even though Blind Lemon was long gone, Blind Norris McHenry was still around, and Papa Chitlins, and once in a while Arizona Dranes, blind too and a woman to boot, stepped out of the Holiness meetings and made your heart shake. Oh, music was thick from everywhere, and everybody came from someplace else, going someplace else: New Orleans, Oklahoma City, Kansas City, Memphis, Chicago, New York.

He meant to stay put. He wasn't black, no. So he'd been told and made to understand why for some folks that made a difference, but he was blind, wasn't he, and didn't he play the guitar and sing the blues. The people he moved among on Deep Ellum didn't care to know about his hillbilly mama, who after all had made only half a dozen records with this man Pink Miracle, and that was fifteen years ago, an eternity in Deep Ellum time.

These days were bad, the WPA hardly making a difference at all down here, but if you had music in you, you could get by, you could always eke out a living. He was twenty-two years old, on his own for six years now, the last five in Dallas. You could get by anywhere as long as you had a guitar and sense in your head.

Listen, Pink said, it's just, well, after Henry Witmer told me about you, I came down here and heard you and I thought, damn it, that is some voice, and some fine guitar. Never heard nothing quite like it, and I've heard some good ones in my day—even played with Eddie Lang and Lonnie Johnson once upon a time.

I heard you play, he told Pink. Heard you fiddling to my mama's singing before I knew what I was hearing. Then I listened to you on the Victrola. Auntie Lewetta bought all your records. Pink Miracle and Argenteen Dupree, she said, why, she said, that ain't no Argenteen Dupree, that's your mama, honey, Hannah Ruth Bayless. Can't she sing up a storm, though!

She surely could, son, Pink said. A nightingale, a meadowlark, a thrush in the woods, a songbird of Old Tennessee—

I know her voice.

But you, now. Son, you sing like you see!

I don't see.

Surely. But you heard the blues, I reckon, somewhere along the line, and some of that Lonnie Johnson jazz. I'm white like you, but I been on Beale Street, learned from Sonny Boy Jimson, made my way. Maybe you hear some blues in my fiddle, listen hard enough.

I hear my mama's voice in it, you want to know. I get the feel of my daddy's skin.

I knew your daddy. I had nothing against your daddy. He was as good as he knew how to be, like anybody else.

Not good enough.

He remembered even less about his daddy than about his mama. Auntie Lewetta never would say much. Just you never mind about Dudley Crider, she said, her footsteps quickening, the door slamming behind her. Once an old woman whose shoes thudded against the floor like a man's came to see him, said she was his daddy's mama. A man came with her, said he was his daddy's brother. They wanted to know how his soul was getting along. Said they'd babtized him and therefore took an interest. He was seven, eight years old when they came to tell him this. Auntie Lewetta, who hauled him to the Holiness church all the time and to the big camp meetings during the summer months, told them his soul was doing fine and he might make a preacher one of these days.

Ain't that a wonder, the man that called himself Daddy's brother said.

Hush up about wonders, the old woman said. She was his grandmother, Auntie Lewetta told him, Dudley Crider's mother. Don't you worry, Auntie Lewetta said. I ain't going to let them two crazy people take you away.

He was never studying to be a preacher. It was his singing that made Auntie Lewetta say such things. Gave you the shivers, she said, why, she said, it might have been Jesus setting his tongue to quivering. They all said it. He heard their whispering, knew what it meant when they patted his head, touched their fingers to his shoulders, stroked his cheek, squeezed him in their spindly arms, men and women alike, praising Jesus, kissing his hands all over with their dry little lips. He had to get out.

Pray for our souls, they said.

He prayed that the day might soon come when he could escape. Lord give me the vision, he prayed.

Sent him to the School for the Blind in Nashville. This wasn't what he'd prayed for, but it beat staying put.

And then one night during the summer of his fifteenth year the Lord gave him a girl good as any vision. Came to him, she did, after a camp meeting, slipping through his window. Hearing the rustle of her dress before feeling her touch, he thought it was a hant, maybe his mama herself, but he knew better soon enough. She came to him every night that summer while Auntie Lewetta slept. If you're Jesus, she whispered, I'm the Queen of Sheba. When I touch you, touch me back.

She was seventeen, biding her time same as he was. Her daddy passed the collection plate at the meetings. Singer Joe went back to school in the fall, found another girl there, but in his mind the girl with sight, his Queen of Sheba, wouldn't go away, and the next summer she was still there, as if she had been waiting for him.

Let's get away from this place, she said.

All right, he said.

She led him a long ways from Bristol and then one day, some months later, a chilly damp day in Louisville, she was gone without a word. He supposed she had taken up with someone else, somebody with finer prospects. After all, he could take care of himself, blind or not, by then, playing his guitar on the street, singing, his case open for the take. She had taught him as much and more with all her touching, and though he missed her and to this day thought of her fondly he knew it was better to be his own man and pay as he went for whatever services he required.

He headed south, was in Oklahoma City awhile, down on Deep Deuce. This was where he first knew he was not the right color for the music he meant to play. He had to prove himself through his music. And he did. Have mercy, he did.

In his hands the guitar had eyes to see for him. He stroked it into song. The song was not as his mother had sung it, though it was the same song. His mother's voice told him what he had to know about her. In his memory her voice rang out, singing, always singing some ditty or another, nonsense, most of it pure-dee nonsense, the way some folks might run on at the mouth, afraid of silence, afraid of what they might hear. This voice of his mother's that he remembered was not the voice heard on the phonograph records. He had heard that voice, too, and it was not the same, it was a voice out of some other life. He liked the silence when she stopped singing.

But it was never any silence, truth be told, save in song. Shut your mouth, listen, you hear something, a train whistle, a tree frog, a creaking floor, the wind, the swish of silk, release of breath. No one soul could hear it all.

His mama's song wasn't in the words she sang. The words lay upon something deeper, they scratched and burrowed, and sometimes hit a kind of paydirt, but they was not the main thing. Sometimes when he sang, he heard her voice, but this did not happen often.

His daddy was the one in the deepest silence, the place closest to being no place at all. You could not hear his daddy, no, sir, that was one quiet son of a bitch, was his daddy. Old Dudley that must have slipped up on Mama like a noose. He liked to imagine it, liked to see it, as if it was burned onto the back of his eyelids, Daddy's lips and Mama's pressed together, her hand on his hardness.

She went away with Pink Miracle after old Dudley played out, was last heard from in California, but she was long gone before that. That's what his Auntie Lewetta would have had him believe. And so Lewetta gave him herself instead, improbable, miraculous. He liked the word miracle. It did not mean what people thought. You couldn't imagine a miracle, that was the point, wasn't it.

Nor was there mercy. Not for Pink Miracle, nor Argenteen Dupree née Hannah Ruth Bayless nor Dudley Crider nor for himself, Singer Joe.

No one would carry his merciless self into the future.

Oh, but someone who could touch you deep inside yourself, that would be something. That was a longing that would not go away. It was in every song he sang, as well as the certainty that there was no such person, neither woman nor man, with sufficient reach. His mama had that longing, too, yes, he'd heard it in her music and longed with her before he knew what he was longing for. So he hunkered down, deep as he dared, reaching for the sound that would tell him who he was at last, what mother's son, what father's boy.

You have a brother and sister, Pink Miracle said.

That ain't nothing to me.

Brother's rich—a Holt, you know. Your sister's my own little daughter. She's the spittin image of her mama, right cute in cowgirl boots and a fringed skirt. Now, she don't have her mama's voice, but I tell you she can play the accordion right well.

What do you want with me?

Pink was slow in answering. The chair squeaked. The singing downstairs had stopped, replaced by the breathy sound of a clarinet in slow time, a guitar plunking along. Smoke from cigarettes and reefers seeped up through the floorboards.

A fellow needs to know where he's been, Pink said at last. And he grabbed Singer Joe's hand, tugged at it.

Feel that? he said.

The hand was rough, but a hand like another until he felt the stubs, two of them smack in the middle of the hand, smooth at the tips and round and hard like marbles.

That's how it is with your mama, Pink said. It's a part of me that's gone, sure as those two fingers on my right hand, but I tell you, son, some days comes a tingling in those fingers, a powerful itch, and that's how it is with your mama, only it never goes away. I feel her presence every day of my life. Lord God a-mercy, I miss that woman!

I wish I knew her better, Singer Joe said.

It's what she would have wanted.

I appreciate your telling me that.

It's the truth.

I'd like to believe it.

Yes. A fellow's got to make his peace.

Pink let go of his hand then.

I'll be listening tonight, he said and left without another word, closing the door hard behind him, his footsteps quick in the hallway. Singer Joe sat still for a few minutes, gathering the silence into him, and then went downstairs with his guitar. It was none of his business who listened to him. His business was to listen to the guitar, let it take him into the dark where seeing was just a word and his mama's mystery was his own.

Part One:

Hannah Ruth

1

Hannah Ruth was likely to remember, waiting her turn to sing, sitting to one side of the band beside the big upright piano while Pink Miracle stroked his fiddle, how her father had moved across the room, his long arms rocking, his chin held forward, such a large chin in her memory of it, above such a slender and sinewy neck. He wore a collarless blue shirt, and his chest hair, black and wiry, bloomed out and up thick and unruly, like mangled weeds.

I'll be going then, he said to Mama.

All right, Mama said.

He did not even carry a satchel nor look at Mama, who sat in the straight-back chair stiff and pale, nursing Little Lewis. It was early evening, May 1907. Hannah Ruth was seven. Her brother Alvin, who would have been nine, had gone chasing after Daddy, but came right back, sniffling, his head hung down. Hiram, just two, was asleep, and her younger sisters Esther, Chloe, and Lewetta were playing with spools on the floor, quiet for a change. You could hear Little Lewis sucking.

She was Daddy's favorite, she knew, because he asked her to sing for him and called her honey lamb. Yet he hadn't even told her good-bye.

Where she had been left behind was in the town of Bristol, which sat square on the state line, half in Virginia, half in Tennessee. She lived on the Tennessee side, but Virginia didn't look a lot different—just a word on a sign.

Born January 19, 1900, she was the second child and eldest daughter

of Lewis and Rachel Bayless, named for her two grandmothers, dead a
long time. On the mantel their pictures stood in egg-shaped gilded
frames. Mama's mama had long hair piled high in braids atop her head.
It was red hair, Mama told her. You got her hair, I reckon, she said, but
her eyes was the prettiest blue ever. There was no picture of the grand-
fathers because they wouldn't sit still long enough, Mama said.

Hannah Ruth didn't especially like having her grandmother's red
hair, though she wished her eyes were blue and not green. Mama's eyes
were blue, as well. Daddy's were brown. Did her other grandmother
have green eyes, she wondered. She asked Daddy once and he didn't
remember for sure, but he didn't think so. In the picture, her other
grandmother's eyes looked black, her hair was white, and she wore a
dark shawl with long fringe.

The picture of Daddy's white-haired mama disappeared after he left.
She looked for it, but never could find it. Daddy's clothes, though,
Mama saved in a box for Hannah Ruth's brothers to wear when they got
big enough.

Until Daddy left, the four girls slept in a pallet in one corner, the two
boys in the other, and baby Lewis with Mama. Mama's bed was in the
room back of the kitchen. It had a curtain across the doorway made of
feed sacks stitched together. Daddy slept in that room, too, of course, for
there wasn't any other room for him to go to then, just those three
rooms each one back of the other, a shotgun house, a name she didn't
learn until many years later. The house had plank siding, but it was not
painted white like the big houses up on the hill on the Virginia side. It
was not painted at all, the wood gray and splintery.

A year or two before Daddy left, he built on another room, making
the house L-shaped and taking up some of the space where he planted a
garden in the spring, a few rows of corn, some tomatoes, pole beans, col-
lards. Like many families in Bristol in those days, they kept a few chickens in a roost to one side of their garden. They wouldn't have to give up
the chickens, only a few rows of corn and a little apple tree that didn't
produce much, but Mama didn't like that. It's a growing family, Daddy
said, and he set to building that room, which took him a long time, for
he could work on it only in the evenings and on Sundays. The rest of the
time he took public work at the mill, grinding cards.

The room he built was for him to sleep in. Mama stayed in their old room off the kitchen, which was connected to his by a door that closed and locked. You didn't dare set foot in his room unless he said you could or he'd take a switch to you. But he never took a switch to Hannah Ruth, his little sweetheart.

Sweetheart, sing a song for your old daddy, he said.

And she sang. She liked to sing, knew even then the sweetness she could command, the pleasure she might call up and give out like it was hard candy at Christmas.

It wasn't enough to satisfy Daddy, though. He went to Texas, Mama guessed. She let Hannah Ruth and Esther have her old room and bed, and she moved into Daddy's room. Hannah Ruth sometimes woke at night, hearing the floorboards creak in the front room and then seeing a dark shape come through the curtains and pass quickly across the room and go through the door into Daddy's old room. It scared the daylights out of her at first, but then she got used to it. Mama was a handsome woman and it was natural for a man to admire her and visit now and then. Once one of them tried to crawl into the bed with her and Esther. He smelled like buttermilk and whiskey and was easy to push off. Esther never even woke up. The man was still asleep on the floor in the morning but gone by dinnertime and no trouble.

It wasn't that many of them, really. Three or four, maybe, spread over a period of a half-dozen years, and never more than one fellow at a time. For Mama was religious, too, in her way, especially during the big revivals and camp meetings, which to Hannah Ruth felt like parties, such a lot of singing and yelling and dancing around in the spirit.

Herself, Hannah Ruth had not given a lot of thought to boys. One time when her Fugate cousins, the sons of Mama's brother Nimrod and his widow-woman, were sent down from Roan Mountain to visit, the older boy Roscoe took hold of her hand and pulled her off behind the lilac bushes that grew tall and unruly in the backyard. Hannah Ruth, he said, do you want to feel how big I am. She did not. Well, then, he said, do you want to have a look. She reminded him that she had three brothers and had seen all she needed to see. She must have been twelve or thirteen and he was two years older and ought to have known better.

Hey, he said, what makes you think you're so smart!

The likes of you, she said.

But afterwards when he looked at her with his big blue eyes, sad and full of want, she thought she might have been kinder.

She began to look at her brothers in a different light. She studied their long legs, their bony feet, considered their angular shoulders and the awkward way they had of holding their hands, as if embarrassed not to be employing them for some good purpose. Alvin, fifteen years old, walked with a swagger. Already he had hard, firm muscles in his arms and shoulders. Some girl might find him pleasing enough, she imagined, with his quick broad smile and sly disposition, as if he knew some things that he might or might not tell you. There was a difference, of course, and a big one, in a boy of Alvin's age and boys her age.

When Dudley Crider came along on a hot summer day midway through her sixteenth year, standing before her, all lit up by the sun, tall and slender and with big brown eyes like her daddy's, he took her breath away. She was sitting on the front steps with Chloe and Lewetta, snapping beans into a bucket and singing to pass the time, wearing a hand-me-down gingham dress of Mama's. Esther was with Mama in the kitchen, and the boys off somewhere as usual.

It wasn't any particular song she was singing, snatches of one melody or another, no words attached to it unless now and then to say "snapping beans with Chloe and Lewetta" or "Ain't we doing fine, sitting on the steps together, and not a cloud in the sky, Hannah and Chloe and little Lewetta."

Sweetheart, the man that turned out to be Dudley Crider said, whatever you say is okay by me. I hear a choir of angels in your voice.

She blushed and quit singing. He walked on, but not an hour later was back.

They teach you to sing like that at school, he asked.

She reckoned not.

I went to school once, he said. But not no more.

Well, she said.

What they teach you there ain't worth learning.

I don't mean to go back, she said.

It surprised her a little when she said it, but she understood it was true.

He's a handsome feller, Esther said when he'd gone away.

Chloe giggled, and Lewetta frowned mightily.

You like him? Esther said.

No, she said. I don't even know his name.

But the next day he told her that. He took her for a walk up to the graveyard at the end of town and they sat beneath a shade tree and he said he was Dudley Crider, age of eighteen, been all around the world and meant to keep going until he came to the end of it.

Mama said he was twenty-five if he was a day.

Well, but so what.

On the third day, she slipped out of the house carrying a change of clothes in a poke and met him at the train depot. Three hours later she was made his wife by a justice of the peace in the Knoxville City Hall.

Solitary, single to the soul of his being, he was the lonesomest man Hannah Ruth ever came across, before or since. What on earth did he have in mind, wanting to marry her. She was sure she couldn't say.

She sang to him and at first it pleased him. Soon enough, she saw him looking away. He sighed, fidgeted, yawned.

She knew she liked his long legs with the soft hair on them, and she was fond of the way his voice was always on the edge of a whisper, and how the warmth and hardness of him took her deep into the secret of herself where the songs resounded. But in Knoxville he put her in a second-floor hotel room on Western with a view of the viaduct, just a little bleak, he expected her to stay there the livelong day, and when he came back from God knows where—he told her he was a night watch-man, but sometimes had to be gone in the daytime, too—he carried a bottle of whiskey in a paper sack and, right there in front of her, he drank that whiskey down without once offering her a sip.

You're my good girl, he said, such a good, good girl.

Maybe she was and maybe she wasn't.

2

Dudley wanted to cross beyond the locked doors, stand in the hall-ways, listen to the breathing from the rooms all around, and then step into the rooms. People didn't usually wake up, or else pretended not to because they were afraid.

They were smart to be afraid. He carried a Bowie knife in a leather sheath strapped onto his belt, kept sharp.

In the daytime he followed ladies from Gay Street back to their big houses and then went there at night, a bandanna stretched across his face. He liked to step softly through the dark hallways, into the bed-rooms, and pick up the purse laid on top of the chest of drawers, the necklace still warm from the skin, the scented handkerchief.

Sometimes a lady had her own bedroom, and here the main pleasure was just to keep watch over her. If she was to wake up, he reassured her. When she saw the knife, quickly unsheathed, she kept quiet.

He felt no regret. His mother had tried to make a good Christian out of him, but it didn't take. His daddy, a logger and blockader who died unsaved in aught-two, when Dudley was twelve, beat something into his head, not godliness.

Uncle Crockett, one of Daddy's brothers, treated Dudley a little nicer, sometimes slipping him a little chunk of sweet gum or chaw of tobacco, on account of he had only one boy that died some time ago, run over by a train, and a half dozen daughters that didn't count. Heartaches, he called them.

The still was up on the ridge, behind a tangle of laurel slicks. A hog still, Uncle U. S.—another of Daddy's brothers—said, which meant it sat at ground level with the furnace dug into the hillside instead of setting out in the open. Water from a spring even higher up ran into the still from hickory troughs set into the ground and covered over with branches and leaves. It was a pretty thing to behold.

You can't never relax, Uncle Fremont, Daddy's third brother, said whenever revenues were rumored in the vicinity. It was always something coming after you in this rotten old world. He told about the hants of dead Indians in the woods that liked to scalp little boys.

Dudley had a brother O. T., which stood for Olden Times, but if you once called him Olden he would look at you as if he might cut your throat. Dudley had seen him cut a cat's throat once.

Mama and O. T. studied the Bible together. O. T. meant to start up a church some day. Sometimes he took to babbling—it was God talking, he said—and he was fond of finding snakes to drape on his shoulder or coil on the top of his head in order to prove the power of his faith. They were only black snakes, though, so shy they were almost polite.

Uncle Crockett showed Dudley how to lay out corn to sprout in the summertime, putting it in tow sacks and covering the sacks with sawdust for the heat. When it sprouted, this corn would be your malt. He showed him how to grind the corn up fine in a sausage mill and then stir it into the still and fire up the water to make mash. After that, you took the sprouted corn, ground it, and mixed it in with the mash. Eyes glowing, his hands working in the air, Uncle Crockett spoke of the worm and the dead devils and the goose eye, the slop and the dog heads, the faints and the thumper, the runs and the proof, and Dudley paid attention for a while, but the words began to sound like dogs yipping and howling and it was easy to lose the drift.

The first time he sampled the product, he was sick for a week, his head a-throbbing and stomach churning. He snuck back, though, and tried a sip at a time until he could keep it down and then increased the dose.

One summer evening when he was about nine years old, he set out for the still. Daddy and O. T. and all the uncles were down in Johnson City spending their paychecks and his mama dozed over her Bible. It had been a hot day and hadn't cooled down much. Pretty quick, though, you were in the deep cool quiet shade of the woods, and in a little while he heard a rapid knocking: a logcock up high on a tall dead elm. He wished he had Daddy's rifle to shoot that bird.

Then he heard a shrill cry that made him think of Uncle Fremont's Indian hants. He hunched down and held his breath and heard the yell again and then leaves rustling not so far off, and through the tangled peavines and saw briers he saw a flash of something that looked like skin. He thought it might be a wild hog rooting in the mast. But, no, sir, it was two naked people, a woman and a man, lying on a pallet, grabbing at one another, the man atop the woman. His bare back had black hair all over it and he was breathing deep. It was the woman making the howl.

He had seen dogs at it like that, chickens and mules, but never two human beings. Naturally, he wanted to rescue the lady, and the man's back was an easy target for a rock, but before finding one he noted how pink her skin was, how smooth and soft it might be to the touch.

Then the lady gave out such a screech that he jumped back, stepping on a branch that snapped in two, loud as a gunshot, just as she stopped yelling. He froze. The naked man jumped up and Dudley saw the face of his own daddy.

He turned and ran and tripped on a root and, next thing he knew, there came a sharp pain in the back of his neck. Daddy had given him a good sharp thump, then another.

Millard, the lady was calling. Millard, what is it.

It was the voice of his schoolteacher, Miss Markham, that had taught him to read and write and was doing her best to learn him arithmetic, calling out his daddy's name.

Finally it got quiet and dark. He lay still for a while. Crickets begun to chirr. He hurt all over.

But when he got back home in the dead of night and stretched out on the pallet beside O. T., who was snoring like a house afire, he thought about Miss Markham's skin, how it shone, how fine it would be to touch—he would touch softly, not the way Daddy did—and he forgot his aches and pains.

At school he began to work at making his handwriting pretty for Miss Markham's sake, for she would stand right close to him, guiding his hand and helping him with the curlicues, and he liked the smell of her.

Mama wanted him to stay in school and do good like O. T., who had stayed all the way until he was twelve, but when Miss Markham left— for reasons unclear, her place taken by a tall, gangly fellow who liked to swoop down on you and whack you good with a ruler—he quit school and was with Daddy on the logging crew at the age of ten years.

By sunrise, he and Daddy and O. T. were on the narrow-gauge railway, swaying and bumping along, rounding curves and mounting hills, all around them the deep woods taking shape, the broad trunks of pine and oak and beech and maple and chestnut, the dark good-smelling branches of hemlocks along the creekbanks, the rocks along the creeks brightening in the first rays of the morning sun, and then the big clearcut that made him feel proud and sad at the same time.

Sometimes, watching Daddy working up a sweat at the band saw, he would remember Daddy rubbing against the naked skin of Miss Markham, and it helped him get through the day.

3

The room in Knoxville that Dudley put her in was hot and stuffy. The floor sloped and dipped and yelped if you stepped on it wrong. There was a small gas stove and a tiny icebox tucked into a corner. The bed had a thin, lumpy mattress. At the foot of the bed, Dudley kept a trunk that she was always banging her foot against. She didn't know what was in it. He kept it locked. Sometimes when he came home she saw him put things into it, but couldn't make out what they were in the dark.

When he was out, she moved one of the two chairs over to the window and watched the automobiles and carriages pass over the viaduct on their way down onto Broadway, where the Southern Railway Station was, or else up the hill to the courthouse.

The courthouse was where they got their marriage license. It was a pretty building outside, made all of red brick, but inside it smelled like mud or sobby wood. When the woman at the desk had doubted that Hannah Ruth was old enough for a marriage license, Dudley told her they were country people, born without certificates. The woman had black eyes that looked like insect eyes behind the thick lenses of gold-rimmed glasses, and black hair wound up into a cone on top of her head.

It was plenty we had to do without, Dudley told her.

Well, the lady said. I'm sorry—

And this little lady, he said, his arm tight around Hannah Ruth, this little lady never knew her daddy, killed by a tree while cutting wood to build his little girl a house.

A tree—

Ma'am, worse things happened every day.

Dudley hung his head and shut his eyes, still squeezing her tight. It's a lie, she wanted to say. No tree never fell on my daddy. He run off to Texas.

Dudley began to wipe at his eyes with his bandanna.

I'm sorry, ma'am, Dudley said, looking up at the woman. I looked at you just now and I swear I thought I was seeing my dear old mama.

Listen, the woman said, I'm no man's dear old mama. Here's your license. Can you sign your name? If you can't, put your mark right there, and then take your girl bride and get on out of here.

Hannah Ruth hadn't even known if he could read and write. She found out then. He wrote his name in handwriting as pretty as a girl's, all in delicate strokes and graceful loops.

That afternoon he took her to the room and pushed her onto the lumpy bed. He started out okay, kind of soft and sweet, but then hurt her. You're mine now, he said, and he never even noticed the blood.

At night the room was a long time cooling off from the day's heat. Noises came from everywhere, squeaks and hisses, rapping sounds from above, sudden thumps from below, voices—distant, quarrelsome—and, from outside, the occasional clopping of hooves on the cobblestones, the clatter of an automobile on the viaduct.

For a time she liked to be awake when he came through the doorway. Some nights she watched at the window and could see him from the streetlamp as he neared the hotel, walking slowly, always, his long legs slightly bowed, the paper sack clutched in his hand or held tight against his chest, the duffel bag thrown over his shoulders.

Then she started falling asleep before he came back. Once she woke up in the middle of the night to a sudden noise. Light streamed in from the streetlamp and she saw him plain as day unlocking the trunk at the foot of the bed. He took from the duffel bag what she'd swear was a corset, folded it up carefully, and put it into the footlocker.

The next day she took a hairpin and fiddled with the lock on the trunk until it clicked open. The corset, lace-trimmed, heavily boned, lay on top of an assortment of clothing, male and female, and flatware, boots, bracelets, fobs, spectacles, framed photographs, tintypes, combs, jackknives, finger rings, thimbles, hairpins, buttons, playing cards. There was a gourd-shaped mandolin with no strings and a hairless fiddle bow.

That evening when he lay down beside her and pulled her to him, there came a pleasurable trembling instead of the hurting, just the sweetest tingling when he laid his rough hand upon her breasts. Touching herself when he was gone, she imagined his hand lightly upon her, his fingers gently encircling the nipple, his tongue following. She wanted him then, hard and deep inside her.

Alone or not, she heard melodies in her head, mostly wordless tunes of things, but sometimes words came right along. Sometimes it was hymns she'd heard the Holiness brethren sing and other times it was ones shouted out at the camp meetings her mama took her to during her religious spells. But mainly it was her own music.

One morning that fall, she woke up and saw him sitting there beside the bed in the straight-back chair, looking at her. He was looking at her funny, and he had his hands behind his back. Morning, he said. Sweet dreams? And before she could answer, he was putting something smooth and silky in her hands.

It was a nightgown, with lace at the hem and bows at the top.

For my baby girl, he said.

When she put it on it felt smooth, though in truth a little snug, for she wasn't such a baby after all, her nipples pressing up against the silk.

She looked at herself in the dresser mirror, and she looked at Dudley Crider looking at her. She saw the desire in his brown eyes and felt her own desire strong.

She took to waiting up for him again, putting on the silk gown, walking from the mirror to the bed, working herself into such a longing, thinking that surely this was what she was supposed to do, rehearse, practice up, get herself ready, so that when at last she heard his footsteps in the hall, his key in the lock, all of the things she wished he might do at the outset—the soft, slow touching—would have been already done.

As often as not, she fell asleep waiting.

By the time the mornings grew cooler, she was as eager for him to leave as to come back. She sat in the hard chair and watched him stretched out in the bed, spread-eagle, the thin gray blanket pulled to his chin. She might scrape a fork in the skillet, raise and lower the window. Or even sing: Oh the mornings, oh the long long mornings, will it rain or will the sun shine, will the wind blow or will it be fair. Once awake, he was sure to stretch himself even longer, his legs pushing his long pale feet from beneath the covers, the great toes curling and straightening, the covers at last slipping off him, and then with a moan he sat up.

Woman, he said, wiping his eyes, I've had such a awful night.

She warmed up coffee for him, made grits, and, when he had given her enough money, fried him an egg in butter.

A man deserves better, he said. The world is wrong.

Leave me some money, she said, if you want better.

It don't grow on trees, he said, frowning mightily.

But he drew up a dollar bill from his pocket and laid it on the table.

When he was gone, she waited awhile, and then checked his trunk to see if he had added anything of interest to it. More of the same. Then she went out herself, leaving the door unlocked, for he had not given her a key and she did not want somebody in the hall to see her fooling with the lock and a hairpin.

She walked across the viaduct and up Summit Hill to Gay Street, studying the ladies who walked in and out of the stores, packages in their arms, purposeful expressions on their faces, their lush dark skirts raised gingerly, their tiny booted feet clicking upon the plank sidewalk. Surely these fine ladies did not have husbands like Dudley Crider.

One day she followed a lady onto the trolley and got off at the same stop, a neighborhood of two-story houses with broad front porches and tall shade trees all along both sides of the street. She watched the lady step up onto one of the broad porches, her silhouette lost in the shadows except for her hat, a wide-brimmed straw hat tied at the chin with a big white organdy bow.

After the lady had gone inside, Hannah Ruth walked to the front of the house, put her own plainly booted foot upon the first step. This is how it might be, she thought, I am that woman who has just closed the door. This spacious house is where my soul lives.

A man stood on a lawn across the street, a brass spigot in one hand, watering the dead grass.

Back in the room above the viaduct she put on the silk gown, and when Dudley came back that night, she was wide awake.

You think I'm here, she wanted to say to him, but, honey, I'm long gone, I'm not even in the next county.

I could sing you such a song, she might have said, that would set your heart a-thumping.

The gown was like a membrane between them, smooth and slick as egg white. He came alive, her Dudley Crider, her sad besotted husband, quick in his blood even if sluggish and dark in his spirit. Bless her, his loins knew her, his skin remembered, and, almost as if in spite, something like love blossomed forth between them that night.

But when she woke in the morning, he was gone.

That is the way it went, and that is how it would go, until one morning she woke shivering and sick in dim light, the December wind shaking the window in its pane, and she knew without having to unfold the note he'd left, written in those delicate strokes and ladylike curlicues, tucked beneath his coffee cup along with a brand-new twenty-dollar bill, that this time he was gone for good. All that week she was sick and cold and glad he was gone, glad to be alone day and night with the knowing he'd left her, glad to keep to herself the certainty of what they'd made together, the other life she knew curled up inside her, growing.

She went home while she still had train fare, the very next morning. The rails hammered crisp as drumbeats, the car swaying in its speed through the dark hill country along the Holston River and into the darker mountains of upper East Tennessee. The Bristol depot smelled of dust and coal oil.

She resolved to stay a few weeks at the longest, only long enough to rest, to gather her wits, to think what she could do next. She would need money, but she could work, do what had to be done, and be on her way in a few weeks. Her baby girl—she was sure she would give birth to a daughter—would be born far from here and come into herself in another, brighter country.

4

Along about Easter Hannah Ruth felt her baby kick, and she woke Mama to feel it. They shared the big bed in Daddy's old room.

That ain't nothing, Mama said. Feel this, you want to feel some kicking and thrashing.

She took Hannah Ruth's hand and placed it over her stomach.

Why, Mama. Are you—

I ain't dead yet.

Mama wouldn't say who her beau was, but Lewetta whispered that he was a railroad man and not likely to return anyways soon.

Some nights before going to sleep they talked about whether they wanted a boy or girl. Mama said a boy was easier to raise, but Hannah Ruth still wanted a girl. They got a laugh over the idea that Mama's baby would be an uncle or aunt to Hannah Ruth's baby, even though he might be born after hers.

The winter had brought no word from Dudley. She didn't miss him much, only now and then remembering some way he had of touching her and then putting it out of her mind.

Her time came before Mama's, on a hot day in July. Mama sent Alvin for the granny woman and made Chloe, Lewetta, Hiram, and Little Lewis go next door. Esther she let stay. It would be a good lesson for Esther, Mama said. But when Hannah Ruth lay sweating and heaving, certain she would die from the pain, she didn't see Esther anywhere. Later, Mama told her Esther had run and shut herself up in the privy.

The time came before the granny woman could get there, and it was Mama, close though she was to her own time, who pulled the baby forth from Hannah Ruth.

She cried when Mama told her it was a boy. He looked just like Dudley, though bald, looking at her as if there wasn't a thing in the world worth seeing. She cried again, holding that tiny ugly thing close to her, and then she sang to him.

That baby wanted to be up all the time. He was hungry. He wanted something else, too, but he couldn't tell her what. She sang herself hoarse. Sometimes he listened and then fell so silent she thought he had stopped breathing. Then he took a deep breath, as if he had to suck in the air like milk. She laid him in the crib and he went right to sleep, but in five minutes—ten, if she was lucky—just as her eyelids grew heavy, here came a whimper and then a loud crying. It seemed she'd never sleep the whole night through again, and those first few days she cried almost as much as the baby. Mama worked herself to the bone, walking him, changing him, bathing him, cooing at him, rocking him, just so that Hannah Ruth could get some rest. Her sisters weren't any help.

An ungodly heat set in. When Mama's time came, the air seemed about to burst into flame.

Mama's labor, like Hannah Ruth's, was long and hard.

Is she going to die, Little Lewis asked.

She's going to have a baby, Esther said.

But is she going to die?

Did Hannah Ruth die?

I don't want her to die, Little Lewis said.

She ain't about to die, Esther said.

Well, but she might have. She didn't scream or holler a lot, but you could look at her face and see the pain and the weariness, her eyes glazing over one minute and the next flaring up, and she'd grab hold of your hand and squeeze it hard, saying, I love you, honey. You know I love you.

The granny woman sat beside the bed, her shoulders slumped, eyelids half shut. Hannah Ruth did not trust her. Shouldn't she be looking on closely? The woman's head lowered, her breathing deepened. She began to snore. When it was time, though, the granny woman, her arms thick as Hannah Ruth's thighs, was wide awake and bending to Mama, reaching, her big hands tugging, the long yellowish braids of her hair swinging, brushing against Mama's belly.

All the time, Hannah Ruth's own baby boy sucked at her breasts until they were sore. Lewetta stroked Mama's sweat-soaked hair, and Esther stood there all fidgety, itching to go somewhere, her cheeks rubbed with rouge, eyelids darkened with kohl.

The granny woman lifted up a sleek, pinkish thing and held it up by its feet.

It's a girl child, the granny woman said, frowning.

It looks like a skinned rabbit, Lewetta said.

Esther ran out of the room, her hand cupped over her mouth, the front door slamming behind her.

The baby girl lay still as a turnip in Mama's arms.

What are you going to name her? Chloe asked.

There's plenty of time to ponder on that, Mama said.

But on the second night of that quiet child's life, Hannah Ruth woke to her mama's scream, and they buried the baby two days later, still calling it Little Sister.

The night after the burial of Little Sister, Hannah Ruth woke suddenly. The room was light as day, the moon full, the air cool and brittle. Mama, wide awake on the other side of the bed, smiled, her head propped on one elbow, her nightgown pulled up, the boy child sucking and tugging at her breast.

Mama, she whispered. What on earth.

I've got the milk, she said. It won't go to waste.

After that, if he so much as stirred in his sleep, Mama picked him up, took him to her breast. This was a relief to Hannah Ruth and the boy seemed not to care which nipple he sucked on.

Daytime, a quietness settled upon him. He looked like he was mad about something, even after Mama had nursed him to what was surely his heart's content. It frightened Hannah Ruth to look in his face, hardened like an old man's face and him just a tyke. She didn't want to go to him.

One night while she and Mama were in their nightgowns, brushing out their hair, the baby asleep in the big bed, Mama said it was time they gave the child a name.

You never named Little Sister, Hannah Ruth said.

I did, though.

You never did!

Yes, I did now. In my heart I named her. I gave her my name. Rachel.

You never told a soul.

Mama turned out the lamp and they climbed into the bed, snuggled up to the boy child.

All right, then, Hannah Ruth said, for it came to her there as if on the breeze that blew in from the window off the mountains and the hillside of Little Sister's grave.

I'll call him Singer, she said, for he did sing, even if he looked sad about it.

Singer, her mother said. That's no name.

That's what I'm going to call him, though. Singer.

If you say so. Singer. But make his middle name Joe. I knew a man named Joe once. He was a good man. It was before I knew your no-count daddy. It would please me if you named that child Singer Joe.

And so he was Singer Joe, and she sang to him about how his daddy was gone but he had two loving mamas. Sometimes she'd swear he seemed to sing along with her as she held him, but often as not he just looked at her, grim like an old man.

It's the best I can do, she told him. Take it or leave it. His expression told her clearly, said: I don't need you. I don't need a thing in this wide world.

Well, then, she said to him. Maybe I need something you don't have.

And she sang whether he listened or not, as if the music would tell her what she needed.

Something's wrong with that child, Mama said. He don't act like any child I ever saw. Look here, she said, waving her hand in front of Singer Joe's eyes. It don't faze him a bit. Sits still as a stump. I never saw a baby look so sad and not even give out a whimper.

He sings sometimes, though. We gave him the right name.

He ain't right, Mama said. I'm trying to tell you. You take him down to Doctor Chapman. I'll pay for it. You let that doctor look at him. Maybe that poor boy's daddy give him a disease.

She took him, and after just a few minutes Doctor Chapman, a tall thin man with long hands that shook until he put them in his pockets, told her that Singer Joe was blind, most likely from birth. It was no fault of hers, he said. She might have another child and it would be perfect.

Crider blood, Mama said.

That night as she lay in bed with her baby boy beside her, she sang that his daddy didn't mean to hurt him. She sang softly so as not to wake Mama.

And she thought: My blind Singer Joe will have powers of sound and skin, he will know the smell and taste of his darkness.

Still later, unable to sleep, she touched herself the way Dudley Crider had done. It wasn't that she missed him. She imagined somebody she didn't know yet, somebody who would love her and stay with her, somebody with music in his soul as well as in his fingertips.

5

By the time cooler weather came, Mama was doing almost everything for Singer Joe, and Hannah Ruth, feeling useless, went to work in the big houses on the hill where Mama had worked, going now to one, now another, doing housekeeping chores, kitchen work. At least she was needed and the pay was tolerable. The houses she worked in, with their broad porches, some of them curving all around front and sides, reminded her of the ones in Knoxville in the neighborhood where she had followed the elegant lady. The lawns sloped up into small hills of their own, with rows of steps leading to still other steps, until at last you faced the dark-stained door in its columned frame, the double doorknobs of polished brass.

At the house of the banker Amos G. Holt, she followed a narrow walkway around the side to the back door, stepped first into a dark passageway damp as a cellar and then into the warm bright kitchen with its great enameled iron oven and stone fireplace and thick smell of roasted pork and melted butter.

In the kitchen she took orders from the cook, a small black woman with a tiny chin and a husky voice. Hannah Ruth sliced and chopped, she husked and shelled and peeled and scraped and grated. She seasoned skillets, polished silver. Music sizzled and hissed and steamed from the black kettles, but she did not like to hear it. In the laundry room the piles of freshly cleaned clothing smelled sweet as cake, and sometimes she wanted to sing, but did not for fear of being heard.

She tried to put Singer Joe out of her mind. Her mama was taking care of him, and this seemed fine with him. When Mama called his name, he reached out. He almost grinned.

Then one day in that spring of her second year away from Dudley Crider, in the kitchen of the Holt house, she heard a singing from upstairs somewhere. It felt close, a single tone, high and clear, one tone giving way to another, lower but softer, then high again, held a long time without wavering, unfurling like a ribbon of silk. It was no human voice.

You watch yourself there, the cook said. You gone scrub the seasoning out of that skillet, girl!

She was not back in that house until the first of the next week. It was May and very mild, the day after a thunderstorm that had washed clean the cloud-thick sky and made the new grass glisten. She paused at the top of the steps to look out on the distant purple ridges, their sleek sharp summits and slopes and humps. The strong warm wind seemed sent straight down from those mountains, and it was Dudley Crider's distance she tasted in the blue of the mild air.

In the kitchen, slicing potatoes, she heard the sound again.

What is it, she asked the cook, whose name was Virginia.

What is what.

That sound.

Oh, that just Miss Amelia.

Miss Amelia?

Her clarinet—you know what a clarinet is, don't you, child?

She did, though only from books.

Like she don't got a thing better to do with her time, Virginia said, lowering her voice. Once I mighta had me something to sing about, but that was a long time ago.

It's pretty.

Plenty loud. She play the piano, too. I like that better.

Home that evening, Hannah Ruth asked her mother about Amelia Holt.

Honey, I don't know her and don't care to. You worry about your own. There's Our Alvin a soldier boy, going off to kill folks in a foreign country. That is burden enough.

Our Alvin was not gone yet, though he swaggered about and talked big of killing Huns. When he came in that night, banging the door behind him, smelling of sweat and whiskey, she asked him about Amelia Holt.

I don't know my ass from a hole in the ground, he said, looking at Hannah Ruth solemnly. Then with a deep sigh, he stretched out, belly down, dead drunk, on the floor. She rolled him onto the pallet alongside Hiram, and then went to the back bedroom. Moonlight shone in through the small window, and a breeze played upon the gauze curtains, tied to one side with pieces of string. Her mother lay in the middle of the bed, as always, asleep on her back, her legs spread apart beneath the sheet. Singer Joe was about to fall off. He was getting big now, ten months old. She gave Mama a little push, then pulled Singer Joe away from the edge. He whimpered and drew his thumb to his mouth. She wondered if he saw in his dreams, thought he probably did.

She undressed and stood for a moment at the bedside, letting the night breeze, cool and full with the scent of blossom and leaf, wash over her. Only a year ago she had been herself swollen with life, a good time, the long lazy wait for her Singer Joe like a wakeful dreaming that had nothing to do with Dudley Crider, a matter of her own soul, her own body.

She took the silk gown from the dresser, slipped it over her head. Night sounds were fine this time of year, the beat of the crickets and then the silences, when they came, deep and faraway, a dark hush, and now and then the hiss of a barn owl and the whish of her mother's soft, steady breath, and the quicker breathing of Singer Joe, so that the room seemed full of breath and the thrum of her skin.

Always men watched her, she knew they did, they looked at her as she brushed past them in front of the shops on State Street, they came into their wives' kitchens and stared at her while she polished their flatware, they saw her in their secret thoughts and they lay down beside her in their hidden bedrooms. They could never hear the darkness humming in them, and their denseness pleased her, wrapped itself around her like arms.

She slipped into the bed as quietly as she could, the gown cool against her skin. Singer Joe stirred, but Mama quickly took him to her breast and he never woke.

On a pleasant June morning not long after Alvin left, full of himself in his soldier's uniform, Hannah Ruth stepped softly up the long staircase of the Holt house, into the dark hallway, listening to the singing of the clarinet, meaning to follow it to its source. It was a dreamy walk, the polished floorboards slick, almost slippery, the banisters cold, the silvery sound now here, now there, no end of doors in the hallway.

She didn't expect the playing to stop, a door suddenly to open, light flooding out into the dim hallway, a tall woman stepping swiftly through the light, the clarinet clutched in her hand. She had dark and shining eyes and wore a lavender satin dressing gown. Hannah Ruth, ashamed, exposed in her ugly gray servant's dress with its stained white apron and cap, turned away quickly, plunged headlong down the stairs.

In the kitchen again, she was still catching her breath, trembling, scrubbing at the frying pan, when the woman appeared at the door.

Come with me, please, she said.

The room upstairs had mirrors everywhere, framed in corners and resting on tabletops.

You don't need to be afraid of me, the woman said.

I heard your music, Hannah Ruth said. That's why I came to your door.

And did you like what you heard?

Yes. I was sorry to disturb you.

I was not disturbed.

She extended her hand.

I'm Amelia Holt. Tell me who you are, please.

Hannah Ruth, giving her name, clasped the hand quickly and released it.

Amelia's eyes were deep and blue like Singer Joe's unseeing eyes, but they did not tell you to keep out the way his did.

I'm the kitchen girl, she said.

Kitchen girl? You're no kitchen girl. You mean to do other things, don't you.

I mean to do other things, yes, but just now I'm a kitchen girl.

Go to your kitchen then.

There was no more clarinet that day, nor any the next, and when it did begin again, it had a hardness to it, almost an ugliness. You could shut yourself off to it though. She felt that she could shut herself off to anything. It was a power she always had. She could listen to the windows moan and sigh, and the kettles' and skillets' endless screaming, or she could listen to nothing at all.

Or she could sing herself, as in the evenings, when she sat on the front stoop of her mother's house, Singer Joe on her lap, and later when she bathed him, soaping his soft skin, and still later when she at last drew herself down into the warmth of the bathwater in the tin tub, her breath quickening.

You mean to do other things, Amelia Holt had said, and it was surely true. Her life was her own, to do with what she pleased.

Amelia took her from the kitchen, giving her chores upstairs. Early in the morning she dusted and swept, cleaned mirrors, polished crystal doorknobs and pretty drawer handles shaped like little mouths. Sometimes Amelia led her downstairs to the parlor, where there was a grand piano in a highly polished black cabinet with sturdy carven legs, its handsome top opening onto an array of gold wires. Alongside the piano stood several high-backed chairs, cushioned and with curved legs, and opposite it a lectern with a fat Bible on it. There was a small sofa that Amelia called a fainting couch, and rows and rows of books in dark covers, all across the walls, in bookcases with glass doors.

Listen, Amelia said, touching her fingers to the piano keys, sounding a doleful chord. Learn to listen beyond the sound.

She heard the sounds in her mind long after Amelia had made them, but it seemed that she could never make them herself. Sometimes she slipped into the room alone, sat at the piano and let her fingers play what they would.

My lover's gone, she sang. My baby boy's blind.

Singing, she lost track of time and could not have said where she was: in the music, maybe, or at a camp meeting with her mother and sisters, the hymns ringing out all around.

What I once was, she sang, I'm not anymore.

And sometimes Amelia took out the clarinet, insisting that Hannah Ruth stop whatever she was doing, sit across from her in the cushioned chair, and listen. Or she asked to be sung to, which Hannah Ruth did, finding this, to her surprise, a pleasure, especially when Amelia played along with her, making up melodies to go with the ones Hannah Ruth found to sing.

Once during one of these odd, made-up duets, Amelia's mother appeared at the door. In her white silks, long strands of dark-colored beads, and shiny, white thick-heeled shoes, she looked solemn, as if displeased. They did not stop playing, and soon she was gone. Another day, when Amelia was away and Hannah Ruth sang alone in Amelia's bedroom, changing the sheets on the big bed, she was surprised to see Mrs. Holt enter. She beckoned Hannah Ruth into the big front room, sat her down in a mahogany rocker between a white statuette of Rebecca at the Well and a potted plant with curving, spiky leaves as long as arms.

She has spoken to me about you, Mrs. Holt said, standing in front of the rocker with her arms clasped behind her back. She has told me you have a gift and that she would help you to develop it. Do you think she will?

Hannah Ruth could not say.

No, of course not. I believe you said, when you came to me for employment, that your education was limited.

I went to school.

But then you got married.

Yes, ma'am.

That is an education of sorts, I suppose.

Yes, ma'am.

I've heard you sing. Your voice is extraordinary, I believe.

Thank you.

She wanted Hannah Ruth to know that her children had modern ideas with which she was not in sympathy. Her son Emmett cared for nothing, it seemed, except gallivanting around the countryside in an automobile absurdly called a Bearcat. As for Amelia, well, Amelia had a good heart, but it had been a mistake to send her North for her education.

Well, she concluded, I will not oppose my daughter. Once I might have, but it will do no good now. She will have her enthusiasms.

Shortly afterwards, Hannah Ruth was given a room in the back of the attic, at the end of a narrow hallway made even narrower by the presence of steamer trunks and dress forms, once a servant's room, Amelia explained, though no servants lived in the house anymore.

Except me, Hannah Ruth said.

Oh, you're no servant, Amelia said.

Though small, the room had a dormer window at one end looking out on the long, downward-sloping yard behind the house, with its well-trimmed tall hedges along both sides, a pair of willow trees and a curing house beside a stream at the far border. On sunny days, the curing house shimmered in its white paint, and the stream, its banks glowing with thick ranks of flame-colored lilies, flowed silvery and swift. Hannah Ruth could easily fancy herself happy.

Coming out of Amelia's room one morning she heard footsteps behind her in the hallway. Glancing over her shoulder, she saw it was a man, a young man, tall and lanky, with a great shock of yellow hair. Before she could reach the door to her staircase, he stepped quickly to her side.

Allow me to introduce myself, he said. Emmett Holt. The prodigal son. The ungrateful brother. The wastrel. The ne'er-do-well.

He bowed deeply, one arm behind his back, his thick yellow hair falling forward. No man had ever bowed to her before, and she didn't know what to make of it. She guessed it was all right. When he stood straight again, she saw that he had blue eyes like Amelia's and full lips. He was not smiling. There was something like merriment in his eyes, but it was not merriment. He seemed out of breath, a little unsteady on his feet. She didn't smell whiskey on him. He might have just stepped from a haystack—that was the smell, like country boys—and he spoke in a deep, clear voice, not slurring his words the way her brother Alvin or Dudley Crider did when full of whiskey.

And you, he said, are Amelia's handmaiden, I believe. The former kitchen girl.

She nodded and walked on. He didn't stop her. He might have followed her if he chose to, but he did not. She shut her door swiftly and closed the latch. Handmaiden! She was trembling, standing by the door, listening. But there was no sound, and when she came out later, she did not see him anywhere.

Most evenings she went home for supper, afterwards holding Singer Joe, singing to him. Blind or not, there was an alertness to him, as if his sight turned inwards and he saw what was worth seeing. He cared little for her, she was sure, and would need her less and less. He preferred Mama or Lewetta or Chloe to her. They cared for him, too, and even Esther, turning away from her mirror, sometimes could be caught saying sweet things to him. Hiram and Little Lewis pretended indifference, but she had seen Hiram pulling Singer Joe up, encouraging him to stand, and Little Lewis, when he thought no one was paying attention, talked to Singer Joe like an old friend, telling him all about the people in the train depot whose shoes he'd shined that day. Singer Joe sat motionless, with that stern look on his face. Maybe he was listening and maybe not. Seeing him so still, never moving towards a sound, as if nothing were real, nothing out there at all, she was afraid of him.

On his first birthday, July 4, 1917, she was sitting on the front porch with her sisters, brothers, and Mama. Singer Joe sat on her mama's lap. The girls had made a little cake and put a candle in the middle of it. Chloe held the cake on a tray, and Lewetta was going to cut it. Singer Joe scowled and kept rubbing his eyes. She did not like him doing that, as if he could rub the darkness out. She had told him many times not to do it. He knew it would do no good.

Happy birthday, everyone sang, Happy birthday, Singer Joe.

Still, he kept rubbing his eyes.

She snatched the candle from the cake and put it in his hand, squeezed his fingers around it, and held his other hand up to the flame.

Feel it, she said.

He screamed, threw the candle down. Little Lewis grabbed it, and Mama pulled Singer Joe to her.

Lord, girl, Mama said. What in God's name.

You're a mean one, Hannah Ruth, Chloe said.

He's not hurt, Hannah Ruth said. See. Look at his hands. He's not hurt a bit.

Still, he'd felt it, she knew, he'd felt the fire. She wanted him to know heat and flame. He didn't need vision if only he knew heat and flame.

We might ought to be thinking about weaning this child, her mama said, baring her breast. He's getting his teeth.

6

The quiet in the Holt house was different from anything she had known. And how fine to have her own room, a bed she shared with nobody, a chest of drawers, a dresser and mirror.

She liked watching Amelia play the clarinet, her mouth tight around the black mouthpiece. The sheet music rested on a music stand made of varnished red maple, the grain swirling like veins.

On the day after Singer Joe's birthday, Amelia was away, Mrs. Holt had gone with her husband to Nashville, and Hannah Ruth ventured into the parlor alone, the best room for singing in. She sang softly at first, but her voice felt strong, and it was a pleasure to free it. When she stopped, it was as if all time had stopped, and this too was a pleasure. The great curtains hung motionless, tied with a golden rope alongside the window frames, letting sunlight pour through the tall windows. Sunlight flashed from the silver vases. The black Bible on its stand lay closed. She heard something, a slight rustling from the hallway. It could be no one but Emmett. She had not seen him since that afternoon he'd approached her so suddenly, three, maybe four weeks ago. It pleased her to remember the way he had bowed to her, though the pleasure embarrassed her.

But he was not in the hallway. She went upstairs, came to the door that she imagined had to open into his room. Now all was quiet, not a sound coming from inside. Was he hiding from her?

She knocked on the door—still no sound—and so she turned the knob, slowly. It was like a game now, hide-and-seek. Well, she'd find him. The door opened, just a crack, enough for her to peek inside. All she saw was a bulky chest of drawers with an oval-shaped mirror attached to the top of it. Then she heard the voice.

What is it, he said. What is it you want with me.

It was not an angry voice, but, as before, it frightened her, and the game was no longer amusing. She hurried back down the hall to the attic door. She could hear his breathing, his heavy footsteps, smell that peculiar scent as of hay, and before she could close the door behind her, whatever good that would have done, he had hold of her wrist, pulling her back through the hallway and into his room, shutting the door behind him, standing in front of her, shoeless, his long arms hanging at his sides, his large hands dangling, his yellow hair falling at an angle across his high forehead and down across one eye like a bright patch. He wore a white collarless shirt, thick black suspenders, and loose-fitting gray trousers.

What do you want from me, he said again.

Nothing, she said. I, I thought I heard you listening to me. Downstairs just now. I wanted to see.

I'm here, though. As you can see.

He was smiling. Had she said something funny? She didn't know what to say. She was embarrassed now, no longer afraid. He had obviously been dressing or undressing and could not have been sneaking up on her downstairs.

In fact, I was listening, he said. Your voice carries marvelously. You were singing for me, weren't you.

It was just singing, she said. It wasn't meant for anybody.

It seemed meant for me, aimed at me. It made me feel—known—though I doubt you even remember me, do you.

You're Emmett. Amelia's brother.

Correct, he said. Absolutely I'm Emmett Holt, brother of Amelia Holt—devoted son, furthermore, of Amos Gamaliel Holt and Violet Elizabeth Powell Holt. How sweet to be remembered.

What do you want with me.

Ah, that's my question to you.

Why did you close the door?

You knocked at that door, you pushed that door open. You must have wanted in. Now you're in.

It was a meanness creeping now into his look, not the meanness of a Dudley Crider, born of whiskey and loneliness, but a meanness with no reason to it. He was someplace else, far from here, long gone. Just where that place was, she couldn't say. Something in her wanted to know. Something in her wanted to be taken to that place and shown the scenery. He was right, after all: She wanted to come looking for him, she had wanted to find where he was hiding. It was no game.

Please, sit down, he said. Over there, on the bed.

She didn't move.

Maybe you didn't hear me, he said.

I heard you.

Sit down, sister.

She sat. The bedsprings gave a little squeak.

You wanted in here, he said. You were singing to me. It was me you wanted, wasn't it.

She shook her head no, but he was already reaching for her, and when he kissed her it was like a darkness falling. She swayed, grasping for something to hold fast to. There was nothing, of course, no wall, no door. He was here, in this weight that bore her down, in the air she had to breathe. She sucked that air in, and she bore that weight, willingly, God help her, down and down.

After that, she kept out of his way. When by chance they met in the hallway, her cheeks burned with shame—for she had wanted him. She knew she had wanted him and now he made her feel ashamed.

He had not hurt her. He had not been rough with her, not like Dudley had been on that first night in Knoxville. Neither had he given her pleasure. Finished, he seemed polite, oddly shy, sad. I'm sorry, he said. I shouldn't have presumed.

At home, she felt like a stranger. She talked to Singer Joe, sang to him, but he stiffened to her touch and always he seemed mad at her, resentful, that awful stern expression on his face.

Where was it she could go?

She put back the salary she received for her service to Amelia—

though Amelia said the money was not for housekeeping but for the sake of the music they made together, for the effort she made to sing the foreign words with Amelia's clarinet melodies. It was no effort, really, the meaningless words taking on meaning by virtue of Amelia's long fingers fluttering over the clarinet, her lips tight around its mouthpiece, voice, breath, hands making a music almost palpable in the room. Come with me, Hannah Ruth fancied the clarinet saying, and I will take you where the music comes from, a distant, lovely place. She believed the message, trusted the music, could not believe her good fortune in such a union, but then one day, in that downstairs room with the grand piano, the black Bible on its broad lectern, everything polished and smooth, hard and cold, she saw in Amelia's eyes the eyes of Emmett Holt, the blue eyes laughing sadly, calling to her. She could neither sing nor listen to the clarinet. She couldn't stop shaking.

It was a Sunday in late September, almost two months since she'd gone into Emmett's room. The trees outside the window still bore green leaves, and she could imagine—as she liked to do—that time stood still. But it had not. Time came for her to bleed, and she did not bleed. Emmett's child quickened and blossomed in her, wasting no time, she was sure of it.

Still shaking, she felt Amelia's arms encircle her, and she broke down then, told about Emmett, how he had thought she was singing for him, and maybe she had been, she didn't know, she didn't know what she meant, what she wanted, and it didn't matter anyway because he would think whatever he pleased about her, and now she would have his child, though she didn't want to, and it was in July when it happened, right after Singer Joe's birthday, when she put his hand to the flame.

Amelia led her across the room to the couch. It was easy to let her head lie snug against Amelia's breast, her cheek pressing against the softness and the warmth of the skin beneath the smooth silk.

The baby will be ours, Amelia whispered. It will have nothing to do with Emmett.

Hannah Ruth might fall asleep covered with a blanket, only to have to throw it off in the middle of the night, her skin slick with sweat. She showed no outward signs of the new child yet. She had been sick a few times, but that passed.

Afternoons she sometimes sat with Amelia for hours on a pallet near the curing house, the willow leaves gliding into the dark and shallow stream, clouds towering behind the calm hills, white and stately. A wind came up, clouds skittered all across the blue sky, and everywhere leaves shimmered. Emmett did not appear. Amelia said he'd gone away.

Music came, it seemed, as much through the eye as the ear, and it came through the brush of flesh upon flesh, the press of lips and tongue, the scent of a lover's hair, skin itself. Inside the dry, sweet-smelling house, she took joy in folding Amelia's airy summer lawns and organdies and crepes and georgettes, tucking them into the cedar chest, and unpacking the stout woolen waists, the serge skirts. Sometimes she would take out a silk bandeau and wrap it around her chest, then step into Amelia's knickers, her lacy petticoats, her fine French-heeled shoes. The skirts were too long, shoes too large, but that didn't matter. At the dressing table, she might unbraid her thick red hair, pull Amelia's ivory-handled brush through it, sweep it up and hold it in place with a tortoise-shell comb. Then she slipped out of the clothes and stood naked before the cheval glass, her heartbeat quickening.

It was a fine piece of luck to be pretty, no matter where you were.

7

It was a dream of his father that had made Dudley leave Hannah Ruth. In that dream his father was coming for him with a knife. The impulse to run stayed with him, and the next day he jumped a freight and went back home to his mama.

She still lived in the house he'd grown up in, a dinky three-room shack put up by the Dennard Brothers Company for the families of mill workers. When the mill went broke some years ago, pretty much everybody left, for there was nothing else there for them, too far from any town, in the shadow of Roan Mountain. The sawmill now was a heap of rotten boards and dust and patches of grimy weeds, most of the houses had fallen down, and the pond had dried up.

Mama didn't look so great either. Her dugs sagged low, her arms hung like sticks. She had teeth—he knew she had some because he had sent her a good set from the dresser top of a lady—but she didn't trouble to wear them. His brother O. T. still lived in the house though he ran a chili parlor in Elizabethton and a church a good three miles down the pike. O. T. slept in the front room, not on a pallet as in Dudley's youth, but on a makeshift cot. He had a dresser with his Bible and comb on top of it. He kindly suggested that Dudley, as the prodigal son, might have the cot while he visited, but Dudley wasn't above sleeping on a pallet.

Brother, O. T. said, have you been saved?

I reckon not. Still draping them snakes around you?

When the Holy Spirit comes down, yes, indeedy.

There was a rain barrel and a well out back and an outhouse that had seen better days. Beyond the outhouse the ridge rose up steep, thick with new pines and maples, some of them strung with grapevines and choked by shumake and greenbrier. Up the ridge would be the grave of his father and, a little ways beyond it, the still, unless it had required moving recently.

This was no place for Dudley Crider, never had been, and soon he wondered why he had come back to it. When he tried talking to his mama about his dream, she looked at him hard and spit on the floor. He felt low and sinking.

O. T. came in, laid a poke of greens on the table, and her eyes lit up like she'd seen a holy vision.

I could eat a horse, she said.

Not without teeth you couldn't, he felt like telling her. I give you a good set of teeth, and you don't even use them.

He stayed a week, and then he drifted from one town to another. Strange things began to happen. Over in Virginia, up in Gate City, he walked out of the hotel lobby one bright noon and something heavy fell onto his shoulders—a panther, he thought at first, but it was an alley cat, gray and mangy.

Another time, the weight came from inside him, rising thick to his heart. Air was tough to come by, and he sat down, breathing hard, in the middle of a street, a muddy street somewhere, and he could not sit for long, though no one seemed to take note of him. On the sidewalk a lady in a poke bonnet glided past while seeming not to move at all. He felt a glimmering of the old desire to follow her, but it was more like remembering the desire. He was tired and wanted to close his eyes. A buggy swerved around him, splashing mud, its wheels squeaking.

He took to drinking in earnest. He stole money from the houses he went into at night.

Two years passed before he saw Hannah Ruth again and time came back to him. It was in Bristol on an October day hot as summer. She was seated on a bench outside the bank on State Street, wearing a faded green dress that hung down to her ankles and black, thick-heeled shoes, dusty and scuffed. She held a baby in her arms and suckled it in full view of the general public.

Hannah Ruth, he said. Honey.

She looked up, squinting her eyes, and he saw his mistake. The woman was Hannah Ruth's mother.

You sorry son of a bitch, she said.

Ma'am, he said, tipping his hat. I thought you was your daughter.

You was mistaken.

The baby suddenly pulled loose from her nipple and looked at him, frowning. The eyes were like an old man's eyes, and a big foot stuck out from the tattered blanket. The child was surely a year old, maybe two. It cried and began to kick its feet and shake its arms. Mrs. Bayless cupped the back of its head with her palm and pushed its face into her breast. It went back to sucking.

There was reasons why I left, he said, seating himself beside her on the bench. He remembered Hannah Ruth pressed up against him, smooth and soft, and in the next minute his headless father in the darkness, crouching with a sharp knife.

It's some fellows, he said, does things for no reason in the world.

You're not telling me nothing, bud, she said.

She stood, flinging the baby across her shoulder, and walked away, her long skirt brushing the dust on the plank sidewalk. The baby looked at him with those shining bleak eyes.

He waited a minute and then followed them back to the little house on Mary Street where he'd first met Hannah Ruth while scouting for neighborhoods to come back to at nighttime. It wasn't a likely neighborhood, the houses little and mean-looking along a narrow dirt lane, bunched up on plots hardly big enough for an outhouse. Hannah Ruth's house looked a lot like the Dennard Brothers house he'd grown up in, in fact, leaning a little easterly, unpainted. And there she had sat, right on the steps of that puny porch, snapping beans and singing.

He stayed back a ways, remembering, and when Mrs. Bayless went inside, he waited awhile until the remembering stopped. The sun was going down. Up in the knobs to the north you could see flecks of white shining through the trees. Birds sang, and there was the smell of fresh cornbread in the air. A couple of boys in knee britches ran up to him, pushed at him, then jumped around him as if he was a tree. Watching them run off, he almost missed her. She was stepping down off that rickety front porch, Hannah Ruth, his wife. She wore a white dress and had her hair down and, by God, that red hair shone in the evening light.

He followed her across State Street, into the Virginia side of town, stayed with her as she walked up the hill to the white houses, saw her enter one of them, just about the biggest of them all. He wondered what her business might be in such a house. That pretty white dress didn't look right to work in. He'd never seen her dressed so fine, like a lady, he'd say, a regular lady.

He walked back down to State Street and sat on the bench where he'd found Mrs. Bayless and the large baby that had looked back at him as if it knew him and didn't care for him.

Maybe it was her baby and maybe not. A woman sometimes might suckle somebody else's babies. His mama had an aunt that was a wet nurse down in Johnson City. Then he had the sudden thought: Could it have been Hannah Ruth's baby? If it was, why, wouldn't that make him that grim little child's daddy?

If it was his child, he'd say to it:

Don't look at your daddy that way.

He rose from the bench and walked briskly back up the hill toward the big white house. If he was a father, by God, he would look out for his child. He felt sure Hannah Ruth would understand.

8

When Emmett Holt returned, he had a hangdog look, his thick yellow hair slanting across his forehead, his blue eyes watery. Slouching up the stairs or sidling along the hallway, he met Hannah Ruth with a grunt, as if clearing his throat of something nasty. When he looked at her, it wasn't for long. She wasn't afraid or ashamed anymore. She felt something like pity for him, thought he might actually be ill, but Amelia said what was wrong with him was all in his mind.

And then he was gone again.

Indian summer came, the warmth of the days continuing into the evenings. One warm night she slipped out of the house, walked the length of the long yard, and, at the stream, took off her clothes. She dipped her feet into the cool water. The air was warm, still, and the half-moon dipped into the branches of the tall trees, most with leaves clinging to them, quivering in the breeze. Her heartbeat raced, she felt strong, as if she might rise into the sky if she wanted to, but she did not, she wanted instead to lie down in the clear cool water of the stream, among the reflections of the stars. That would be good enough, peaceful and safe, lovely and silent.

The silence was suddenly broken by a rustling of leaves across the creek. She believed she saw something moving among the trees. Then the noise stopped and there was nothing to see.

She looked away, she stepped back from the water, all the while telling herself it could not be Emmett Holt, it was nothing, a raccoon, a prowling cat, or just a trick of the moonlight. In any case, it was on the other side of the stream. She stayed on her side, stepping from one large rock to another, each one cool and slick beneath her feet. A breeze, smelling of tree bark, gusted up, pressed against her body so that she felt a tingling all over. She pressed her palm against her womb, but felt no motion yet.

She came to a smooth and flat boulder and sat down upon it, stretching her legs before her.

And then out of the breeze came the sound again, this time followed by a voice.

I reckon you think highly of yourself, girl, the voice said.

Dudley Crider came straight at her out of the darkness.

Hannah Ruth, he said, sidling up next to her, his hand closing over hers. It's me. Your Dudley boy.

I know who you are, she said.

And, she thought, I'm beyond you now, Dudley Crider. Whatever use you might put me to has nothing to do with me. You can't hurt me anymore.

He took her in his arms and the warmth and hardness of his body against hers was like the caress of memory, of loss. She saw again the room in Knoxville above the viaduct, with its slanting bed, its sloping, worn-linoleum floor, the room she had come alive in, as she was alive now to his touch. It meant nothing, she told herself.

Afterwards, he went away, almost politely, saying he would see her tomorrow. She dressed quickly and returned to her attic room, but could not stay there. It was as if Dudley's presence had canceled out whatever calm she could claim. She went out. She walked the dark streets of Bristol down to her mother's house, looking for Dudley in every shadow. But she didn't see him, and when she crawled into bed next to Mama and Singer Joe, neither one of them stirred.

She was sitting on the front porch early the next morning, remembering how he had come along, and here he came again, just as he had promised, tipping his soiled derby hat, grinning.

I'm a changed man, honey, he said, standing there on the front steps, the toe of his boot making little circles in the dirt.

He did not look so changed. He carried himself as tall as ever and in his brown eyes she saw the same steady brilliance that had drawn her to him. Mama stayed inside with Singer Joe, but Esther and Chloe came to the doorway and looked Dudley up and down. Hiram and Little Lewis had already left for school, and so should Esther and Chloe, but they weren't ever in any hurry. Dudley looked at them a little too long, Hannah Ruth thought, and they didn't mind the attention.

She told him about the birth of their son.

I reckon I already seen him, he said.

Where? Where would you have seen him?

I run into him just yesterday. He was with your mama, sucking at her. I tell you, he give me a looking at! I believe he knew who I was.

You didn't tell me that last night.

I reckon I forgot.

He's blind, she told him. Our baby boy is blind.

You don't say, he said, looking at Esther. I didn't know that. Well, he's a fine strapping boy. I reckon he takes after his daddy. What do you think, girls.

Chloe, ungainly at fourteen, pretty without knowing it, said she saw no resemblance. Esther—who, though just a year older than Chloe, looked twenty—said she saw a kinship, all right, a definite resemblance, in the eyes.

Dudley grinned broadly and winked at her, and Esther smiled prettily, fluttering her eyelids.

Hadn't you girls better be getting to school, Hannah Ruth said, but they ignored her.

He's a right handsome baby, in his way, Dudley said. Maybe he sees inside.

Inside?

Looks back into himself, you know, because he can't see nothing outside.

Lot of good that will do him.

I'd like to see inside me, Esther said.

Maybe you will someday, Dudley said.

Or maybe somebody else will, Esther said.

Read you like a book, huh, Chloe said.

Hush, sister, Esther said. You might as well be blind, for all you see.

Hannah Ruth grabbed Dudley by the hand and pulled him past Esther and Chloe. Inside, she took Singer Joe away from her mama and stuck him in Dudley's arms. The boy was so still, alert, that you'd swear he saw something, and she wondered if Dudley was right and Singer Joe's vision went back inside him.

It's all right, honey, she told the baby. It's your daddy come to see you.

Come back from the land of the dead, Dudley said.

The boy began to cry then, kicking and squirming, and Dudley put him down quick.

Look at him go, he said, as Singer Joe crawled across the room to Mama. Vision or not, he knew where she was.

Ain't he walking yet? Dudley asked.

He's taking a few steps, Mama said. When he wants to.

She gave Dudley a dark look then and said:

You've got some explaining to do, young man.

I reckon, he said.

You better reckon.

Hush, Mama. It's my business.

Look to it, then.

There's no explaining nothing, Mama.

Don't that boy talk none yet? Dudley asked.

When he wants to, Mama said.

Mama stood stiff like a guard alongside the kitchen door, never taking her eyes off Dudley, holding Singer Joe close to her and stroking his head.

Let me see that boy again, Dudley said.

He approached Mama and Singer Joe, cooing at him, and took to kissing the back of his head, nuzzling him, until finally Mama handed him over. Dudley lifted him up into the air and turned him this way and that. Daddy's boy, he said. A man some day.

Singer Joe bore it, Hannah Ruth would say, like a little man. He showed no emotion. He reserved his opinion. When thrown into the air by his father, he held his little legs stiff, his fists clenched.

Lord a mercy, Mama said.

But Dudley caught him, and Singer Joe made a noise that might have been taken for a laugh.

That was when she heard music coming straight from Dudley, poor Dudley, her sorrowful, sly betrayer of a husband, his arms now wrapped around the boy that he would no doubt abandon again in the wink of an eye. It was a sad, sad song, as sad as any she'd heard.

Then Singer Joe began to scream.

Here, he said, handing him to Hannah Ruth, but she couldn't comfort him, and so passed him back to her mama.

He stopped crying then, grasping at her breast. Mama gave him what he wanted.

Ain't he a hungry boy, Dudley said.

You think you can be a father to him, she asked him.

Yes, he said. Oh, yes. I mean to be a good father.

And he looked so solemn, his eyes dark and deep, she almost believed him.

All the same, he was gone the next day without a word.

It's good that he's gone, Amelia said while Hannah Ruth brushed out her hair. You're not the same woman you were when you married him.

Sunlight streamed in through the broad window. Amelia smelled like lilacs.

I have a child, Hannah Ruth said. I'll have another.

Yes. That's certainly something. That's a great fact. But that's not what I mean. Don't you feel it, how different you are?

I feel the same, changed or not.

This was not the whole story, she knew, but how could she begin to sort out the strands of it. She could only sing, as Amelia would say, and let the music tell it. But there was no music in her just now.

And you love him, Amelia said.

No. I think . . . maybe I don't love anybody.

Well. That's good, isn't it. You can do something, be something, with your art.

What art.

Your music. Your singing. Through it, you love. I know you do. I hear. It's not love.

She turned away from Amelia. Oh, it would be easy to trust her to know, to make up her mind for her, determine the course of her life! Why didn't she call her feelings for Amelia love? She supposed she loved Amelia, and she knew Amelia loved her. But where could such loving take you? The child in her womb—Emmett's, not Amelia's—surely was no child of love.

Still, she stayed with Amelia most of the nights of that fall, and when she woke, the morning sun streaming through the broad, oak-framed window, it was a blessing to draw her body close to Amelia's and say to herself, This is not love. Forget about love. She would have to go away soon. Amelia had made arrangements for her to go to an aunt in Knoxville. Amelia would visit frequently. When the baby was born in the spring, she would return. Then Amelia would let it be known that she was adopting an orphan child. But what about Singer Joe? What about the boy Dudley had given her?

Oh, the boy would be all right, her mother told her in a voice rich with sacrifice. I reckon he will be in good hands. It's some was meant to be mothers, others not. I don't know why in God's name you have got yourself another child growing in you, though.

Maybe I'll be a better mother for this one, Hannah Ruth said, almost believing it.

She grew lazy, stopped singing. Ever hungry, she slipped into the kitchen and spirited cornbread, side meat, salet greens to her room. Some days she didn't leave her room at all, lying in her bed, crumbling cornbread into buttermilk, making it so thick she had to eat it with a spoon.

One night in November, Emmett came to the attic room, stood there, stooped over, trembling, his thick yellow hair matted, his blue eyes reflecting back the light from her lamp. She thought he must know of the life he had started in her, such a look as he gave her, as if he could see whatever he wanted to see.

What do you want from me, he said.

It was what he'd asked her before, she remembered, when he'd pulled her into his room. He didn't frighten her, though. This poor trembling creature could not hurt her.

I don't want anything from you, she said. Please don't come here again.

I won't, he said. You have my word as a gentleman. I won't trouble you again.

His eyes drew her into their swirl of blueness. Who was she, his eyes asked. Who are we. She had no answer. He was beyond her.

Thank you, she said.

He bowed slightly, then turned, his shoulders shaking, and was gone.

9

Amelia's Aunt Judith was tall and lanky, with deep-set black eyes and long, knobby fingers. Her hair was iron-gray, her face drawn and wrinkled, but her eyes sparkled like a bride's and her bearing conveyed vigor. She was, Hannah Ruth understood, Amelia's mother's older sister, a widow whose young husband had been killed at Shiloh before he could make her a mother. A lady Aunt Judith most definitely was, down to the erect shoulders, the long, graceful neck, and the tightly corseted waist.

Men have made a mess of the world, Aunt Judith said, reading the war news in the *Knoxville Sentinel,* the endless reports of advances, retreats, the mud and death in France. Hannah Ruth thought of her brother Alvin then, tried to imagine him in one of those muddy trenches, the dampness in his boots, the chill, the foul smell, the waiting and the fear. Lord help him.

In the mornings, far from the terrible German army, in the high-ceilinged parlor with its long, lavishly curtained window and hardwood floor that smelled of wax, Aunt Judith sometimes played the piano for Hannah Ruth.

I had promise, she said, letting her fingertips touch the keys. They told me I had promise. Promise means nothing.

She played stormy chords followed by slow, dreamy melodies in which you could picture gentlemen and ladies dancing in grand ballrooms.

Sing for me, she said, and Hannah Ruth sang.

I've heard worse, she said.

I have promise?

Aunt Judith looked at her intently.

More than promise, she said.

Some evenings they had supper in the dining room of the new Hotel Farragut, beneath crystal chandeliers, and then went to a motion picture at the Strand Theatre, where in a vast darkness they laughed and laughed at a baggy-trousered tramp with a cane.

Amelia came to town several times, riding the Southern from Bristol. Aunt Judith did not entirely approve of Amelia's travels on behalf of her father's business, not so much because it was unladylike (though of course it was) as because it seemed a waste of her true talent, which was music. A lady could sing, certainly, ladies had always sung, and she might also play a musical instrument—a violin, say, or the piano or flute or even the clarinet—if she deported herself properly. To demonstrate her point, she took Amelia and Hannah Ruth to the Hotel Atkins dining room, where a young lady named Mrs. Walburn played portions of famous violin concertos while people ate roast beef and potatoes.

Young Mrs. Walburn, wearing a loose-fitting chiffon gown with long flowing scarves, her violin held under her arm, seemed to float into the dining room. She had beautiful yellow hair, held in place by ivory combs. People put down their forks and knives and clapped vigorously.

She's from Ohio, Aunt Judith said. She studied at the conservatory in Cincinnati.

Listening, watching Mrs. Walburn bring the bow rapidly across the strings of the shiny violin, Hannah Ruth seemed to see herself as the lady Aunt Judith tried to make her into. She hadn't a thing to do with anyone else, was a world entire, a spirit constantly soaring, and it was very fine. When Mrs. Walburn rose to acknowledge the applause, Hannah Ruth saw something else, though. She saw that beneath the loose-fitting chiffon another body had begun its life, the swelling well underway. Yet Mrs. Walburn played as if for no other life than her own.

There is a *lady*, Aunt Judith said as they sat before their empty plates and Mrs. Walburn withdrew after playing "Humoresque," her third encore.

Oh, Auntie, Amelia said. She isn't any lady. Otherwise the music would be insipid.

Nonsense.

Well, "Humoresque" was a lady's choice, to be sure.

There was the Brahms, however, Aunt Judith said.

Brahms, Amelia conceded, is not for ladies.

Ice cream was served, and Hannah Ruth was thinking, unaccountably, of the brush arbor revivals her mother used to take her to, the great tent rising from the tree-circled field, the sweat-glazed brows of the men and the veins throbbing in their hands, the women's palm-leaf fans going back and forth, the smell of dust and sweat and something sweet almost to the point of rottenness, a tall thin man in a black frock coat waving his fist in the air. The soul, he shouted. Look to the soul, for the body returneth you to dust, to worms, you can count on that, my friends.

One afternoon in late March or early April, Hannah Ruth's time surely no more than a couple of weeks away, Aunt Judith spoke of Emmett.

I know, Aunt Judith said, I'm not supposed to mention him, and I know why, of course, and you can stop me if my talking of him troubles you.

The drapes in the parlor had been pulled back, and brilliant light shone through the window panes. On either side of the fiercely ticking mantel clock stood ceramic shepherd boys, the height of a hand, their gilded locks and crook-necked staffs gleaming. On the adjacent wall hung an oak-framed portrait of a young man in a gray uniform, a pretty soldier with wavy black hair parted in the middle and full pink lips, but trouble in his dark eyes.

Hannah Ruth was in fact curious about Emmett, and Aunt Judith, her long fingers working at an intricate piece of tatting, continued.

He stayed with me for a time, you know—almost a year. He was seven years old, the sweetest little boy. And I was lonely, no children of my own. Imagine my sister—my baby sister—I was eighteen when she was born, old enough to be her mother—sending me her Emmett, saying she thought I might do something for him. I saw right away how it was, him standing there looking at me with those blue eyes brimful of tears that he wouldn't for a minute let loose, and his long yellow hair still in curls. It was a passionate nature—too passionate.

I did what I could. His people had acknowledged his talent, and that is what I was charged to attend to. I did the best I could. He played the piano, don't you know.

I took him to Ike Melton—Professor Isaiah Melton, I should say, only I've known him since I was a little girl; I believe he might have loved me a little once, before the war, but he was shy and then of course Mr. Tipton came along, not a grain of shyness in *his* heart.

Ike could do nothing for Emmett. Sent him back to me after three months. And yet I'd heard the boy play beautifully. I knew he had music in him.

I indulged him. It was as if he was the child Colonel Tipton would have given me—and, Lord help me, the child was a daughter. Oh, yes, I looked into those blue eyes and I saw a girl, a sweet pure girl instead of the mischievous boy that had been sent to me. For a time, the fancy held, but in the end he turned on me, too, just as with Ike Melton and, I can only suppose, my sister.

Dear Hannah Ruth, there are some that cannot abide the world as it is and want to make it into something it is not and cannot ever be.

Maybe, Hannah Ruth said, he'll find what he was meant for.

I'm afraid not. The boy who came to me has lost himself, and I'm afraid for him. Music might have saved him, though I suppose it damns as freely as it blesses.

Aunt Judith laid the tatting aside and wiped softly at her eyes with a lace-edged handkerchief.

I scarcely know him, Hannah Ruth said, suddenly seeing in her mind the trembling figure who had asked her what she wanted from him. At that same moment the baby, Emmett's child, gave her a kick that took her breath away.

10

Unlike Singer Joe, Alexander Jeremiah Holt struggled against birth, tearing her badly. Once born, however, he was sweet and delicate, with wispy reddish hair. He sucked and rooted at her, a boy like the other but with sight and all other senses intact, as far as could be told. She put him down and he cried as if still hungry, and then the wet nurse, a tall woman with bloodshot eyes and pale thin lips, took him away.

A beautiful child, Aunt Judith said.

He has your eyes, Amelia said, and your hair.

But Hannah Ruth saw no resemblance to anyone but Emmett.

She began to feel like a captive in this spacious house, and one day toward the end of May, she and Amelia and the thickly swaddled baby, six weeks old, boarded the train to Bristol. The very next day she took him to show to Mama, who seemed by turns sullen, resentful, weepy-eyed, affectionate.

He sees, Mama said.

Yes, she said. I believe he does.

Will you leave him with me?

She would not. It was enough for Mama to care for Singer Joe.

What he'll have, she said, will be my doing, Mama.

Don't think for a minute Singer Joe's not your doing, too, Mama said.

While Mama held the child, Hannah Ruth felt her head suddenly flame up with sound, sweet, sorrowful, wordless music, and she took her baby boy from Mama, drew him to her breast, stroking his head, singing as best she could the music she heard. Mightn't it after all have come from him?

He's been here, Mama said, your Dudley Crider.

Did you tell him—about the baby?

I didn't tell him a thing.

Is he coming back?

He didn't say.

Emmett was gone from the Holt house. She was relieved, though also, to her surprise, disappointed that he should not have cared to see his son.

The baby was kept in a room as big as her mother's house, a bright, airy room that had been Amelia and Emmett's nursery. Wrapped in a pale blue comforter in his white crib, his thin fingers curled into tiny fists, he looked as if he could not live, and each day she held him he seemed lighter. But he was not. He grew plump and strong. She could hear his booming cry from any place in the house, and she went running to him, but, by the time she reached him, he was calm again in the long arms of the wet nurse, Miss Alva.

Other times, Amelia rocked him, cooing and calling him her love-bud, her lamb, her little flower.

Hannah Ruth began to think again of Dudley. She would see him as if from the hotel window in Knoxville, striding along the viaduct, the burlap bag over his shoulder, or else from the dark woods, coming to her while she stood naked in the moonlight. At her mother's house, she sat again on the porch steps in the morning sunshine just as on that day she'd first seen him. And so he returned to her in her mind again and again before the day he actually appeared, not in the morning but in the gathering darkness at the end of a hot August day, walking up the lane as though he'd never been gone, swinging his arms and kicking up the dust with his long stride, and she knew instantly that if he claimed her again, she would go.

He sat down beside her, took hold of her hand, and then Little Lewis came running up, breathless, his shoeshine kit hanging from a much-worn strap at his shoulder.

Howdy, young fellow, Dudley said.

Hey, Little Lewis said, as if Dudley sat there every day of the week.

And then, to her: Look here what I got. A letter from Our Alvin, you bet.

Lewis, still called Little Lewis even though he was ten years old and not so very little, waved the letter at Hannah Ruth and rushed past her and Dudley, up the steps and into the house, slamming the door behind him.

I believe he favors his big sister, Dudley said.

Which one, she said.

The pretty one, he said, squeezing her hand.

Where do you go, she said, when you go away from me.

No place, he said. Places is all one and the same.

That doesn't tell me a lot, mister.

It's the truth, though.

Why do you go, then, can you tell me that.

That's even harder to answer, honey.

Try.

He released her hand, scratched his head, rubbed his chin.

I get in a bad way, he said, his voice so low she almost couldn't hear him. Ain't nothing to do with you, I swear.

What is it to do with, then?

Sweat was coming to his forehead.

I'm not a good man, he said. Baby, I'm bad. Nobody's bad like me. I tell you, honey, I done some things I'm not proud of. Bad things.

Like what.

I just can't say. It's not something I can explain to you. I can't even think about it right now. I'm sorry, honey. Truly I am.

She wanted to say that, whatever it was, it couldn't have been as bad as he made it out to be. Didn't she know him, hadn't she loved him? At the same time, she knew she wasn't any angel of mercy and that whatever it was in him that was calling to her she wanted for its own sake and not just for the sake of his salvation.

She took hold of his hand.

Anyway, she said, we've got each other.

The baby, the seeing one, her little Alex, she'd not tell him about. Alex would remain her secret son and no man his father.

Interlude:

Alex

How was one to know who his parents were? He could not have said. Beyond the facts—the dates of birth, of marriage, of death, beyond the accounts given by the principal parties themselves, which surely were by definition suspect—there was no telling.

You had to listen for what wasn't said, in some cases even for what couldn't be said, the unsayable that lurks in silence, clear only as dreams are clear.

Hush. Listen.

He remembered: the clarinet, finding it one day beneath the bed and taking it out, the smell of it, the very scent, surely, of her spit, long dried, on the mouthpiece and reed, how he had ever so tentatively taken that mouthpiece to his lips. How old would he have been. Five? Eight? He had been careful, his instincts telling him he was in dangerous territory. Sweet danger!

I am an ear. Fill me up, Sound.

Hard, the mouthpiece, and dry. Hard and cold. How could music have begun here?

It had, though. He knew she had made music from it, surely knew it even before she told him so, from the touch of her fingers, the feel of her lips when she kissed him goodnight. He longed to play his mother's secret clarinet. No matter. He could not. He had no music in him, could only take the mouthpiece to his lips and, licking the reed, listen for what might have been.

He remembered: the photographs and newspaper clippings in a cardboard box beneath the bed, her bed, next to the clarinet case. In the photographs the woman's mouth formed an *O*, she was singing, the fiddler, ridiculously thin, standing behind her, grinning. Pink Miracle and Argenteen Dupree. The Songbird of Old Tennessee. The picture was the same, and the article varied little. Only the dateline changed, now from Arkansas, now Tennessee, now Oklahoma, Texas, Louisiana, New Mexico, Mississippi, Alabama, Georgia, North Carolina. Where did she get these clippings, his mysterious mother? And who were they, Pink Miracle and Argenteen Dupree?

He remembered: the end of summer, the heat bearing down, time to be sent off to school, boarded in a place where the snow came early and stayed long. In that cold place it dawned on him that he was separate, not only from others, but in some profound way from himself, and this was a good thing to know. Shivering, he sat at his small desk, the book open before him, a book on geography, naturally, the maps seeming to slide from page to page while the wind howled and shook the windows in their frames. His roommate, a boy from Pennsylvania, tall and thin, gap-toothed and hook-nosed, sat across the room, humming some impossibly inane ditty that could be heard whenever the wind died down.

On one of those August departures—would he have been eleven, twelve years old?—his bags packed, his thoughts already on the classrooms ahead, the stuffy lessons, the other boys with their inscrutable histories, she sat him down across from her in the stuffy parlor, she on the fainting couch, he in the chair that still smelled of his grandfather's cigars. An electric fan, squat, ugly, loud, hunched upon the windowsill, stirring up the warm air, pushing it across the room. Her skirt, a drab brown color, nonetheless had a kind of sheen to it, as if shot through with gold, and he remembered thinking, though not for the first time, My mother is a handsome woman.

Handsome she may have been, but she was not, she gave him to understand on this occasion, his true mother. It was time he knew that.

And you, then—

I'm your aunt. I've fancied myself as good as your mother.

Oh, yes, he said. Yes, Mother.

And your father . . .

His father, he might as well know, was not the man she'd told him about, the man whose life had seemed so complete, stabbed through with a bayonet in the Argonne Woods, an invention (she confessed it with such pride that he believed it better than truth), not this gallant hero, this creature she had so carefully constructed, placed piece by piece—heart to hand, as it were—into the chambers of his mind, but a distinctly unheroic character whose existence he had scarcely been aware of: her lost brother Emmett.

She spoke calmly, as always, and he did not remember feeling shocked or in any way upset by the revelation. It was not important, this business of one's parents, whose lives, already impossibly remote, would keep receding, become rapidly imperceptible.

She didn't mention that he, Alex, might have a brother. She didn't speak of the identity of the faces in the newspaper photographs that she kept in a cardboard box beneath her bed.

Part Two:

Pink

11

ome from the war, Our Alvin lifted Hannah Ruth off her feet, swung her around in the yard until she was dizzy and almost fell down with her into the scrubby evergreen.

Sister, he kept saying, as if he had forgotten her name. Sister, sister, sister.

She almost didn't see the other fellow at first. Standing a few feet behind Alvin, he was actually a little taller and older than Our Alvin, but even though he, too, wore a uniform, he didn't look heroic. He leaned to one side, as if he had one leg shorter than the other, and he carried a duffel bag slung over his shoulder and a black fiddle case held shut with rope.

They all went inside. The fellow dropped his duffel bag to the floor but not the fiddle case. He was shivering and skinny and his greatcoat looked big on him, weighing him down. Alvin put his arm around him and said:

This here is my buddy Pink Miracle that saved my life.

How do, Pink said, looking at Hannah Ruth, grinning, still shivering, and she saw that one of his front teeth had been chipped, broken almost in half, straight across. He shook hands solemnly with Little Lewis and Hiram, nodded and tipped his cap to Chloe, Esther, and Lewetta, and then looked at Hannah Ruth again and winked. He extended his hand to Dudley, who was seated next to her on the little sofa, but Dudley looked away and didn't get up.

The hand didn't have all its fingers. Hannah Ruth looked away, embarrassed for him. A broken tooth and lost fingers!

Pink and I was gassed, Alvin said. I reckon we won't never be the same again.

Who'd've thought, Pink said, waving the maimed hand in the air, that a big old ugly fellow like Alvin Bayless would have a mess of sisters so pretty. Hey, Alvin, I believe they're prettier than Frenchies.

He kept looking straight at Hannah Ruth, smiling, broken-tooth and all.

I never noticed, Alvin said.

Why it's plain as the nose on your face. And your mama, too. I see where the beauty comes from.

Hush, now, Mama said, grinning, sitting there on the rocker with Singer Joe on her lap.

Alvin laughed loudly and sat down on the floor, letting Pink take the remaining chair.

How'd you save his life, mister, Little Lewis asked Pink.

Aw, it wasn't nothing to brag about, son.

Hell it wasn't, Alvin said. Listen here, folks. This old boy carried me across enemy lines, shells exploding all around. Carried me on his back two, three mile, all the way back to the trenches. I thought it was Jesus.

Was you shot? Little Lewis asked Alvin.

I reckon. Bullet went in right above my heart.

Hiram looked interested.

Did it hurt, he asked.

Hurt? Why, no, I reckon not much. Like somebody punched me a good one when I wadn't looking. Then I was in dreamland, boy.

Somebody else would've come along, Pink said. If it wasn't me, would've been somebody else.

Was you shot too? Little Lewis asked.

You bet, Pink said.

And he pointed to the broken tooth and then held up his right hand, showing the two stubs.

You got shot in the mouth? Little Lewis said.

Gosh, Hiram said.

Pink laughed.

Naw, he said. I was just fooling about the mouth. Knuckle sandwich did that, before the war. These fingers, now, I still can't say exactly how it happened. I was on patrol and felt a little itch and looked down and they was gone. They might've exploded on their own, for all I know.

Where'd they go? Little Lewis asked.

Fell in the mud, I reckon.

Couldn't you find them?

Didn't care to look.

Alvin laughed loudly again, and Hannah Ruth thought there was something she had never before heard in her brother's laugh, something not funny. She did not want to look at him or hear such a laugh. When he stopped, he said: .

Say, once I saw something shiny in the mud. Picked it up and it was a toe. Some fellow's big toe, the toenail shining like a dime. Imagine that.

A Hun's toe? Hiram asked.

Might've been. Couldn't rightly tell.

Esther went pale and excused herself, tugging Chloe and Lewetta along with her, back into the kitchen. Hannah Ruth wasn't upset. What was it, after all, to talk of toes lost, of teeth and fingers gone. She had a boy with eyes that couldn't see, didn't she. She reached for Dudley's hand. It felt cold.

I reckon you're Our Hannah's fellow, Alvin said to Dudley.

Husband, Dudley said. Ball and chain.

Ha, ha. You said a mouthful, fella.

She supposed he might be beginning to feel a little like a husband. He had been around now, though with a few lapses, for over three months. He wouldn't stay at her mama's house, and so they had found a dingy room at the Telford House Hotel on State Street. Although he promised to pay for the room, and actually had held a few piddling jobs for a day or two at a time, the money came mainly from what she had saved up from her Holt money.

She had kept her resolve not to tell him about the birth of Alex. It was not his concern. But she slipped over to see the baby whenever she could, and she missed her little room in the attic with its view of the long yard and the row of trees.

Hey, Alvin, Little Lewis said. Say somethin French.

Parly-voo Fransy, mon poteet, mon share, mon mare, mon pear.

That ain't French, Hiram said.

Alvin gave Hiram a light slap on the back.

And how about this little feller! he said, and then got down on his knees and crawled across the floor to Mama's rocker and started oohing and aahing and tickling Singer Joe, who began to whimper, then wail in earnest.

Hey, ain't I your uncle, boy? Don't you remember me? I'm Uncle Alvin, home from the war.

Singer Joe carried on so that Mama took him off to the bedroom. She'd nurse him, Hannah Ruth knew, though he was going on three years old.

Alvin seated himself heavily in the rocker. Whew, he said, wiping his forehead. That crawling tuckered me out. What's in that box, mister, Little Lewis asked Pink Miracle.

Just a fiddle, Pink said.

From France? Hiram asked.

Naw. It's a Stradavary, made by hand in Chattanooga. My old uncle Laclede give it to me a long time ago.

Pink carried it across the sea, Alvin said, and played it for the Frenchies.

Let's hear it, Dudley said. Let's hear some hot shit from that fiddle.

Dudley looked menacing and ugly like a dog tensed to jump. And for what reason? None that Hannah Ruth could see. Pink Miracle had done nothing to him. She pulled her hand free from Dudley's.

You play that son, Dudley said.

Pink Miracle looked puzzled for a second, but then that sweet gap-tooth smile broke all over his face, and he set down the case and opened it up.

And that's when she knew he was somebody she might love. It could have been nothing more than the sight of the fiddle, shiny in its black case, or the way he picked it up from its bed of green felt, tucking it gently and neatly beneath his chin, or how he took out the bow, tightening it just so, stroking its long white length with a little piece of rosin, all the while holding the fiddle firm with just the pressure of his chin. It could have been the way he gripped the bow so gracefully with only the two remaining fingers and thumb.

Then he began to play the fiddle and what she heard shocked and lulled her, all at once.

What it was, was her own voice.

12

On July of 1908, when he was twenty-one years old, Pink Miracle set out for East Tennessee in search of his Uncle Laclede. The year before, Oklahoma Territory had been joined to Indian Territory and made into the state of Oklahoma. Pink, having run away from his sodhouse home in Oklahoma Territory at the age of thirteen and, after long spells in Texas, Louisiana, and Arkansas, ending up on Beale Street in Memphis, had not once gone back, nor cared to, but when he saw on the front page of the *Memphis Commercial Appeal* a cartoon drawing of an Indian maiden marrying a white man, he found it of such interest that he purchased the paper.

Look here, he said to Sonny Boy Jimson, the old bluesman who had become his friend and teacher. Look here, Sonny Boy, what do you make of this picture?

Sonny Boy took off his dark glasses. They were sitting at the bar in Pee Wee's, in dim light.

I don't think much, he said, squinting, putting the glasses back on.

It's where I came from, Pink said. Oklahoma.

Oklahoma. I thought you from the Delta.

This was a high compliment and in fact a misconception Pink had slyly encouraged. A white man wasn't readily welcomed on Beale Street.

I used to think you was blind, too, he told Sonny Boy.

Never been blind a day of my life.

I ain't never been from the Delta.

Play blues on that fiddle like you from the Delta. Sound rat black when you stroke them strings.

You look like a blind man, wearing them dark glasses all the time.

Can't stand the light. Too much light in the world for a old man.

Well, Pink said, I wish I might have come from the Delta instead of from Oklahoma.

Black man from the Delta wish he white, use that Golden Peacock skin bleach by the tubful, slick-straightening his kink hair with a hot comb and grease. White man ain't gone be black, nor black man white. Mostly, the black they wantin to be white. Shee-it. Jesus, He white. And God, His Daddy, why ain't He gone be white, too? So most folks, they want to be like they father in heaven. Me, why, all I wish is for some pretty girls singing and dancing for me, black as night, a-waving and a-calling to me. Come on here, now, Sonny Boy, they calling. Play us something sweet on that guitar.

The Indian maiden in the cartoon wore a dress with beads and long fringe. She had a feather in her hair and on her headband was inscribed "I. T." for Indian Territory. She wore beaded moccasins. The man next to her wore a broad-brimmed cowboy hat and a dark coat with tails. He had on cowboy boots and his hatband had the letters "O. T." for Oklahoma Territory written on it. The minister wore thick-lensed glasses and had a broad toothy smile like the president's. The caption read, I pronounce you Oklahoma.

It was surely not enough in itself to make him consider returning to the state of his birth. He had never seen an Indian maiden in such fringe and with a feather in her hair. In fact, he had never seen an Indian maiden to his knowledge until he had left his father's soddy and was drifting down in eastern Oklahoma, the old Choctaw Nation. The Indian maidens all dressed pretty much like the women in O. T., home-spun and plain in Mother Hubbards and poke bonnets with nary a feather, though occasionally a ribbon or two, and old high-top button shoes, right-down dusty.

As for cowboys, he would guess he'd seen plenty of them, all right, for the Strip was cattle country when it opened and, going by his daddy's experience at farming, should have been left to the cattlemen. Pink had seen cowboys in the store down at Freedom and heard their talk about the long drives up the Chisholm Trail. They were rough-looking fellows to a man that you could not imagine donning a tailcoat or even a frayed Jim-swinger such as the Baptist preacher, Reverend Smallwood, wore when preaching. Their colorless hats looked like a horse had stepped all over them.

Well, the place kept on going, it appeared, in his absence, and changed. Why, his daddy might be driving cattle now, swinging a lasso, married to an Indian maiden, for all he knew.

He wished his daddy well. Maybe if things had gone better, Daddy would be a better person, the soddy long gone or else Daddy long gone from it. If Mama still lived, surely Pink would want to go back and would have been back many times. But he couldn't muster up any affection for that man who had worked him like a mule and tried to keep his fiddle from him, calling it the devil's box. If Daddy had prospered, likely he became more and more righteous. Nor did the thought of his brothers Junior and Ollard or his sisters Josephine and Ellen stir up longing or affection in his heart. They never did do their share. Likely they had families of their own, eking out a living on a hardscrabble quarter-section that some earlier fool settler had already worked to death.

That Oklahoma there, Sonny Boy said. They pretty girls in that place, Pink?

Naw. Not to my recollection. It's just old cattle country, mainly.

You can't trust a cow, my opinion. I knew a fellow, killed by a cow. On purpose, they say. Outta meanness. Leaned on him, mashed him into the barn door.

I'm not aiming to go back there just yet.

What is it you aiming to do then, showing me that picture.

It's just a picture. It's not Oklahoma.

That Teddy Roosevelt there, dress up like a preacher, ain't it, marrying them two folks. I think he ack lack a preacher. More preacher than president, my opinion. Lotta words, lotta struttin. What is he, reckon, preacher or president? Was a soldier-boy, once 'pon a time, climbing old San Juan Hill and a-shooting Spaniards right and left. What you reckon he is, preacher or soldier or president? What he always grinning about? Lotta teeth. You think he know something we don't know? I think he just wishing hisself along, making hisself up as he goes, no different than you and me, boy, forgetting where he come from and going where he is headed.

Pink allowed as to how that might be so.

The question is this, Sonny Boy said. Where you headed, Oklahoma-boy?

Nowhere, Pink said. Right here where I am is where I want to be.

This wasn't true, though. He did like Memphis—hadn't he stayed here almost seven years now? The woman he loved best, name of Dinah, had played out, but while she lasted she was what he needed. He still saw her now and then on Beale, though she had moved away from the neighborhood. Some said she was holed up in a shack over in the Greasy Plank, near where W. C. Handy lived. Some said she was actually living with W. C. Handy, his white concubine. Last time Pink had seen her was a year ago in Hammitt Ashford's saloon, across the street and down the block from Pee Wee's. She came up behind him, touching his bowing arm while he was playing, and he didn't mind missing the beat, caught it soon enough, nobody the wiser except for Sonny Boy, playing by his side. They had been playing "Stagolee."

Memphis, in the persons of Dinah and Sonny Boy and Mariah England and Hammitt Ashford and Sweet Cindy Lewis and Fireball Jimmy Franklin and Little Willie Jackson and Joey "the Duke" Dumas and plenty of other old-timers, some of them on Beale since the typhoid epidemic of 1878, living to tell about it, this was the Memphis that, after he proved himself worthy, had taken him in. He no longer had to go down to the docks and wait to be picked for backbreaking work in the cotton fields. He didn't have to report to no mill at the break of day, answer to a hard-hearted boss, and work his ass off until dusk. Instead, he could play his fiddle in Beale Street dives such as Pee Wee's or Ashford's or the Panama or even the Palace (not just on amateur nights either) and be treated like a king. Even better, feel like a king, because of the music, the musicians playing with him, almost all of them black, sons of slaves, blues in their blood, leading him, a white boy from Oklahoma, into the music, making him play his way into and then out of feelings he didn't ever know he had. Rotgut flowed, cocaine was plentiful and cheap, and the saloons fed you, even if they didn't pay much more than it cost to rent a room. Just a few months ago, he believed he might could live this way forever.

It was close, but it wasn't the place. That cowboy in the cartoon might have been the image of his daddy. It wasn't enough to send him packing back to Oklahoma, no, but it shook him up, and then the music lost something, as if the thought of Daddy had been enough to jinx his bow arm, hex his fiddle.

You ain't who you think you are, boy, was what he heard his fiddle telling him.

Well, who am I, then? he asked as he drew the bow across the strings. Tell me who I am.

Sweet Cindy Lewis sang, her voice as full of longing and sadness as his mama's ever had been. The duke's trombone wailed and moaned through its mute, as angry as it was sad. And his fiddle, all it could do was scoff at him, taunt him.

It's all right, honey, Sweet Cindy said.

You gone come back, the duke said.

But where was he going? The new year came and went, winter passed, trees leafed out, and still his fiddle rebuked him.

Then, in the summer of that year, 1908, he saw, while walking past the Gayoso Hotel, a man in a broad-brim white cowboy hat step out of a hansom cab. The man paused at the curb, reaching in his pocket, and looked Pink in the eye. He looked enough like the man from the cartoon to give Pink the shivers, and it all came back, the death of his mama, his visit to her grave just before he lit out, the warm Oklahoma sun shining down, her telling him from the tomb he had to get right with himself. He stopped dead still, right there at the entrance to the Gayoso Hotel, a black man in a gold-buttoned uniform looking him up and down, the man in the white cowboy hat stepping briskly past him, the hansom cab clattering away, the big dappled mare dropping a steaming column of shit onto the cobblestone street. What he felt was cold, dead, and the last thing he remembered before falling was his mama's voice, distant but now clear, shrill: Laclede, the voice said. Laclede Miracle.

He woke in his own room. Sonny Boy sat beside the bed, shoulders slumped, head bowed, eyes closed. Pink watched him—it seemed for a long time, the light, dim though it was, shifting, now reflecting from Sonny Boy's cheekbones, now from his long sloping nose. Sonny Boy wasn't a big man, but when he played, he made Pink think of a machine, efficient and powerful. Sitting in this small room, he looked like the old man he was, fading fast, his flesh losing out, skin drawing into his bones. Sonny Boy's breath came in great sucking gasps, followed by such long silences before the next that Pink kept imagining there would be no other.

He felt wide-awake himself. The force of his dead mother's voice had felled him, he was certain, and the words he had heard her pronounce before he lost consciousness echoed now throughout his entire being: *Laclede Miracle, Laclede Miracle.*

Go out to East Tennessee, she was telling him, where it all began.

Cosby, Tennessee, where he understood Uncle Laclede to live, was a good two days' journey from Knoxville on winding mountain roads. He hitched rides on rickety, wobbly wagons drawn by mules that looked like they might give out at any moment. The mountains kept lifting up higher and higher, blue and pointy in the distance, so beautiful and wild and terrible they might have been of another world. The roads grew narrower and narrower, ever rocky and dusty and deep-rutted, lined by thorny and twisted shrubs as tall as Oklahoma trees. Where it was not a green tangle of leaves and vines it was rocky cliffs, boulders, fast-flowing rivers, winding creeks. Not much in the way of crops, true. You saw little patches back behind some of the cabins, but they had to run up the hillsides, mostly steep ascents and rocky. It was wild things that wanted to grow here, grow with a dizzy beauty that made your heart beat faster just to look upon it. You could never take it all in.

He tried to imagine his daddy leaving this place, the long western trip that ended in Oklahoma, the reverse of his own journey. Well, he figured, that flattened land might have looked good if all you wanted was crops, money. Coal mines he'd heard spoken of with some enthusiasm as he made his way across the ridges of the Cumberlands, but they were mainly to the north, up in the Kentucky and Virginia and West Virginia mountains.

Cosby was a general store, a schoolhouse, a graveyard, and a few ramshackle houses spaced far apart. In the general store, Pink learned that Laclede Miracle lived beyond the graveyard, up high, back deeper, past where the logging roads ended, up on Snake Den Mountain, near the bald. The man at the general store, a plump fellow with a mustache so thick it covered up his lips, said a man might walk the distance if he had the fortitude and shoe leather for a rocky path, but he'd be a sight better off on horseback. He then offered to sell Pink a horse, but the price was high and the horse, with its buckteeth, sharp jawbone, and long ears, looked as ancient and temperamental as the mules that had hauled him this far. Calculating that he had a good six hours of daylight left of this fine cloudless midsummer day, he reckoned he'd climb the mountain afoot, and after the man pointed him toward the creek, where the trail began, he set out at a brisk pace, his fiddle case swinging from one arm, his satchel from the other.

Up he went, soon out of breath, working up a sweat, much set upon by all manner of swarming, whining, swooping insects. The trail kept disappearing, leading him into thickets of the twisted and thorny shrubs. He was frequently thirsty, grateful when the creek reappeared and he could dip his hands into the clear, swift-flowing stream and drink to his heart's content, then splash the cool water over his head and soak his swollen feet.

He was about to keel over, his legs weak and shaky, back giving out, bitten all over by big black flies, spooked by snakes, and it was getting dark, the air starting to cool, when at last he saw, set deep in a hollow in a narrow clearing alongside a silvery creek, the shady outline of a log house crisscrossed all over with vines.

Uncle Laclede, he called out, walking quickly up to its low-slung front porch. When he stepped up onto that porch, a man in a white nightshirt came out from the dark doorway, followed by a woman dressed in the same fashion.

What is your business, the man said. His voice was gravelly, low. He was a small man, smaller than in Pink's memory, his shoulders sloped, his back humped, his head tiny, with a neck scrawny and stringy as an old rooster's. He appeared to have about three teeth. The resemblance to his father was not obvious, and at first Pink thought he might after all have the wrong man. But the man answered to Laclede Miracle, and when he trained his eyes on Pink it felt as though his daddy had caught him at last.

You're my daddy's brother, he said. I'm Blue's boy Pink.

Blue? Uncle Laclede said.

Bluford Miracle, Pink said. From Freedom, Oklahoma.

Oklahoma?

Pink backed off out of the shadows so that the man could see him better and almost fell off the porch.

Watch your step, the woman said, her voice as gravelly as the man's. She was a good head taller than Uncle Laclede, about Pink's height, maybe even a little taller, which would make her almost six foot. Her gray hair billowed out all over her head, wavy and thick, falling below her waist.

State your business, sir, the man said again.

Family business. I reckon you're my uncle. You play the fiddle, don't you.

I heard tell of it.

You give me this fiddle, Pink said, holding up the black case.

Uncle Laclede backed away, as if Pink was trying to hand him a rat-tlesnake. The woman, her thick hair swinging, walked quickly around Uncle Laclede and put herself between him and Pink as if to prevent a fight. She had broad, sharp-boned shoulders, and her long hands extended from the sleeves of the nightshirt. Her face was thin and sharp-edged and shiny like his mama's, and when, after a slight pause to look him up and down, she was upon him, hugging him tight, saying, I know who you are, son, I know you, sure, I know you, boy—he felt like he had come home.

He don't recollect much at all no more, Ida Miracle told Pink. They's good days and bad, of course. Mostly bad, though, seems like. Times he looks at me like I'm a rank stranger. Lord knows, I'm a stranger to myself some days. We all have a cross to bear. God don't pile on no more than a body can stand to carry. Mercy.

The cabin had a big room with a loft, and a lean-to added on to the back for the kitchen with a woodstove, a safe, and shelves for canned goods. Uncle Laclede and Aunt Ida slept in the loft, Pink on a pallet in the corner of the big room downstairs. The floor was splintery and soft in places, with considerable gaps between some of the boards for the convenience of spiders and other critters. In the mornings Uncle Laclede went off into the woods, carrying a dinner pail and a shotgun, and came back for supper, which he consumed rapidly in spite of his few teeth. Not long after, he and Aunt Ida climbed up to the loft and went to bed.

After the first few days, seeing that Uncle Laclede didn't know him, Pink thought he might as well leave, but Ida told him he might should wait a spell.

Uncle Laclede's fiddle was hung up on the wall by its neck from a leather thong looped over a nail. He used to play that thing all the time, Ida said. Every time it was a square dance in this country, they'd call on Laclede Miracle to play for it, and he never said no. I know he enjoyed it, I just know he did.

Ida was so friendly, hugging Pink and patting him and feeding him, that he wondered if her mind, like Uncle Laclede's, had gone a little astray and she might be confusing him with someone else. But soon enough he saw that it was just her nature to be that way. She knew him, all right, had once, long ago, been out to Oklahoma Territory with Laclede. She remembered Pink's mama well, could see her plain as day standing over the stove in that dark soddy. You was knee-high to a grasshopper, she told Pink, and there was a baby crawling on the floor, a little girl, I recollect, and two little boys chasing around, and your mama big with another tyke. Your daddy tried to talk Laclede into coming out there. There was going to be more of them land openings, he said, and he wanted Laclede to go in with him, but Laclede said he couldn't live in such a flattened-out place as that Oklahoma. This would have been in '94, I believe.

That would make me seven years old, Pink said. And Josephine was borned in '94.

Yes, we was sent word of the birth after we come back. A right pretty woman, your mama, and strong, so I thought. And gone now—how long did you say?

Eight years next month.

We was never told. Not one word did we hear about your mama's passing.

August the tenth, aught-zero, a god-awful hot day.

We haven't heard ary a word from your papa for the longest time.

Likely he's at the same place I left him in.

I admired your mama.

Yes, ma'am.

Your papa worked hard. I reckon he was too busy to write letters. It was your mama sent us word of the babies. And then we heard nothing.

Folks have to get on.

Yes, they surely do. I'll tell you, though, a family's not much count if it's no forgiveness. It's mighty mean for a fellow that's put out and has to go it alone.

I never wanted no one to go along with me. I didn't want no forgiving.

Land, we never had childern live long enough to need forgiving. Two dead in the breach, another in the crib. It was a judgment, Laclede said. A mercy, I sometimes think. Laclede thought the world of your daddy. Bluford, he said to me, Bluford, says he, is the only one of my brothers and sisters worth a tinker's damn. And he was the one left this country altogether. Never looked back, I guess.

I never knew any other of Daddy's kin.

It's a hardness between them.

They talked like that while Uncle Laclede was away off in the woods somewhere—making moonshine, Pink suspected—and it was passing strange at first for Pink, but he came to like this woman and how she would talk of many things it had never occurred to him to think about. He began to believe that his thinking, up until this point, had not amounted to much. In the evenings, he looked at Uncle Laclede, sitting across from him at the supper table, saying nothing, looking at nothing except what lay before him—beans and cornbread and salet greens— and he thought about his daddy, saw him as if in the dark cool of the soddy. What did his daddy know, out in that flat country, what did his daddy think when he walked out into his parched fields, breathing dust. He did not imagine that Blue Miracle would forget him the way Uncle Laclede had forgotten almost everything. If Daddy forgot, it would be his intention to forget. It would be to say that this son of mine who ran off in the dead of night is dead in my heart.

He has been dead in my heart, too, Pink thought. But can I make him alive there? Is that what I ought to be trying to do?

A week passed and still Uncle Laclede looked at Pink as if he was a stranger who ought long ago to have gone away. Pink decided that he *should* go away. What had he expected from this visit? Folly, pure folly.

His mama's words had been nothing, some other sound from the street, a squeaking wagon wheel, the whinny of a horse.

I'll go back to Knoxville, he announced at the supper table. People in Knoxville are friendly.

It was then that Uncle Laclede suddenly had something to say.

God help a man with friends such as them, he said.

Why, Laclede, honey, Aunt Ida said.

Before Pink could consider what to say, Uncle Laclede looked him in the eye and said:

You're Blue's boy, ain't you.

Ida grinned and handed Pink a chunk of cornbread, hot from the skillet.

Yes, sir, Pink said.

Tell him I remember, Laclede said.

Yes, sir. Remember what, sir.

Son, that Stradavary I give you was made by Samuel Dewberry of Chattanooga in eighteen hunnert and sixty-seven. He was Ma's cousin, was Samuel Dewberry. Son of old Uncle Zeke Dewberry that was Grandma Dewberry's baby brother, killed at Lookout Mountain. I was a lad back then. Lord, a lad. Ma took me with her to Chattanooga. I aver I never saw a place like that. I couldn't stop looking at all the people. But most of all, do you know what I remember? I remember Samuel Dewberry's hands. He had such long old fingers, longest I ever did see, the veins thick and purple and twisted every which way. Right scary they was. I remember them well to this day. Yes, sir, I surely do. Them old hands.

He stopped, shivered. Aunt Ida passed the cornbread. Uncle Laclede looked at it, and he had tears in his eyes, but he broke off a small portion of the cornbread and set it carefully on his plate.

I was just a lad, he said, sniffing.

He picked up a dainty piece of cornbread, put it in his mouth, and swallowed it almost without chewing.

But you learned to play that fiddle of Samuel Dewberry's, honey, Aunt Ida said. You know you did.

Yes, I did. Snuck off Saturday nights to the dances at McKinney's barn and watched them fiddlers. That's how I learned myself the fiddle, by watching them old fiddlers. Ain't a soul showed me a damn thing. I listened and watched, and then I done it.

Ida stood behind Laclede, her hand on his shoulder. She leaned down and softly said to him:

Don't you imagine you could still play, honey?

I mought could play, yes.

Well, then—

I reckon they're all dead, all them old fiddlers.

You ain't, though.

No, I ain't.

This young feller come a long ways to hear you play the fiddle.

I know who he is.

Of course you do.

I would hear him play, would he favor me with a tune.

Pink, not wasting a minute, took out the Stradavary and played "Soldier's Joy." He played it with energy and care, he believed, the way he remembered learning it from his uncle, leaving out the slides and twists he'd picked up on Beale Street. But when he was finished, Uncle Laclede's eyes were dry and he said, In a hunnert more years, you mought get the hang of that tune, boy.

Yes, sir, he said. I mean to work at it.

Fotch me that fiddle, son.

Pink handed him the fiddle, and Uncle Laclede played something Pink had never heard before. His tone might have been a little scratchy, his hold on the bow surely weaker than in former years, but the tune had a slippery, eerie sweetness to it, moving in strange ways, one part giving way to the other before you knew it, with sudden shifts of chord, and the strings resounding like so many tongues.

What was that called, Pink asked.

That was "Soldier's Joy," Uncle Laclede said.

Lord have mercy. I'd have never known it.

That's right. A hunnert years from now, maybe you'll know it.

I've heard dozens of fiddlers play that tune, and not one played it that way.

Learned it from old man Linton Givens from over to Sugar Cove.

I thought I learned it from the way you played it.

Old man Givens was eighty years old if he was a day. His daddy fought at King's Mountain. Said he had it from his daddy. They was heroes in them days. Yes, sir.

Pink would have to listen again, work it out one phrase at a time. Better, he would play it along with Uncle Laclede, get the feel of the rugged bowing and listen for the cunning notes that had come from old man Givens. But Uncle Laclede would play no more that evening.

It's time a man got some rest, he said, pushing his plate away.

Lying awake on his pallet that night, Pink kept trying to hear the tune again in his mind the way Uncle Laclede played it. How could he ever remember it, such twists and turns? Did he ever play it that way, then forget, or else change it without knowing?

And then he was seeing clearly. He wasn't meant to go back, nor make things again the way they were. It was the twisting and turning, not back and forth. He was here, as far back as he could go, in the country that his daddy and his daddy's people had come from. From here on was anybody's guess. Out in the night, crickets filled the silence with their crazy winged songs.

13

The morning after Alvin's return, Hannah Ruth saw her sister Esther back behind the lilac bush, kissing Dudley. The bare lilac bush didn't hide a thing.

It was Sunday, but nobody had gone to church. She had come over meaning to see Alvin again—and Pink Miracle. Last night back at the Telford House Hotel, the voice from Pink's fiddle still humming inside her, she wouldn't have minded a little attention from Dudley, but he was still sullen. She thought awhile of Amelia's sweet touch and then wondered how Pink's hand with its missing fingers might feel, pressing her just so. Right nice, she imagined.

She woke at daybreak, hearing the fiddle again and feeling the desire. Dudley wouldn't wake up. At last she fairly dragged him out of bed.

He disappeared as soon as they got to Mama's house, leaving her in the front room with Singer Joe on her lap. Pink and Alvin had been out all night, Mama said, and hadn't come back yet.

Hannah Ruth, why don't you let Singer Joe nurse you. He's wore me out. Maybe you got milk left from that other.

She bared her breast to him, though she was pretty sure she was dry. Alex had come to prefer Alva, his wet nurse. Singer Joe, sitting stiffly in her lap, maybe got a trickle out of her, maybe not, poor boy, took what he could get, too big anyway for suckling, even Mama said so, baring her breast. Chloe sat across the room, darning, Hiram was in the corner, reading a fat book about Napoleon. Little Lewis, industrious even on

Sundays, was gone off to the train depot with his shoeshine kit, and Lewetta was in the kitchen scrubbing pans. And Esther—where was handsome Esther, comely Esther, bold Esther, too pretty for her own good? Where was Dudley, where was her brown-eyed Dudley boy?

Singer Joe's sucking stopped, as if he had choked or tasted something bitter. Mama took him, and the child nuzzled against Mama's breast as if to sleep.

Maybe Dudley had run off again. If he did, she would go back to her attic room, to Amelia. Of course when she slipped away to see Alex, Amelia was almost always there too. After Dudley's return, she had treated Hannah Ruth a little coldly at first, but soon enough, the two of them taking turns holding and rocking the baby, singing to him, she became friendly again.

One day, in Amelia's room, as Amelia touched the clarinet to her lips, Hannah Ruth heard the piano downstairs. Amelia seemed at first not to hear it, licking the clarinet's reed, but the piano grew louder and then, laying the clarinet across her lap, she looked at Hannah Ruth.

He'll wake the baby, she said.

But the baby was shut up in its room, Alva poised nearby. The piano grew louder, the music quick and rhythmic, not the music she would have expected from Emmett, nothing melancholy or plaintive about it. Dance music such as she'd heard coming from the doors of saloons in Knoxville. Ragtime. She liked it. She had wished Dudley might take her to one of those places, but he did not.

Hold this for me, Amelia said, handing her the clarinet.

A minute or two later, the music stopped.

Amelia returned. Her cheeks looked red, and she fairly snatched the clarinet from Hannah Ruth's lap.

Sing, please, she said.

Another time, she met Emmett in the hallway. He held his head down, didn't even look at her. She didn't hear him playing the piano again.

Dudley, on the other hand, would come to her with such huffing and puffing and pulling and tugging that you would have thought his life depended on it. Sometimes, he seemed an altogether different man from the Dudley of before, or not even one man but several, one of whom bore a resemblance to the old Dudley and struggled to rise up above the others, usually without success. She began to think if he could be more than one man that maybe the man she needed would turn up one of these days among his repertoire.

But now, on this day after Alvin's return from France, there he was, smooching with Esther at the lilac bush. In the kitchen Lewetta smiled prettily, her hands in the washtub. Hannah Ruth walked into the front room where her mother still held Singer Joe at her breast and sat down opposite them. She guessed she sat down. Had she been standing, walking? And then she thought: which Dudley was this one outside with Esther, was he one of her lovers, the one she was hoping for, misdirected, aimed away from her?

The back door slammed, followed by a high-pitched laugh that quickly stopped. Dudley sauntered up to the door, his hands in his pockets. Esther was nowhere to be seen.

How's my baby boy, Dudley said, smiling, leaning against the door frame.

Nobody answered. The back door slammed again, she heard voices in the kitchen, and then Esther, her little hips swaying just so, walked briskly into the room.

Right cold out there, I imagine, Chloe said from her chair, her knitting needles going like crazy, clickety-clack.

It's been colder, Esther said.

You was out there without a coat?

Wasn't out there long.

I believe, Dudley said, she's hot-blooded, ain't she.

Esther, her cheeks reddening, folded her arms across her chest and took a deep breath.

My blood's my business, she said, almost whispering it.

It certainly is, sister, Chloe said. You'd best look after it.

There was a stomping noise from out on the porch. The door opened and Alvin walked in, his military overcoat belted tightly around him, his eyes red and puffy.

Look what the cat drug in, Mama said. You ain't been to church, I reckon.

Aw, Mama, Alvin said.

Out all night. I declare.

Lordy, Mama. We was celebrating the armistice.

The armistice. Three weeks ago they signed it.

We wasn't back yet.

Lord help.

Where's your friend, Esther said.

Downtown somewheres, I reckon. I don't know. Why? You interested in him, sister?

I ain't interested in no one, brother.

Alvin laughed again in that unpleasant way, the laugh, Hannah Ruth supposed, he'd picked up over there. She admired her sister's scorn, though. It was smart of her to be interested in no one. Keep to yourself, girl.

You all have you a big time last night? Chloe asked.

Big time? Laws, honey. We had us a time, all right, we done celebrated. I wouldn't exactly call it a *big* time, though.

Oh, I know. You seen Pay-ree. What's little Bristol, Tennessee, to gay ole Pay-ree, France.

If it's whoring and boozing you want, Mama said, East Tennessee's as good a place as any.

Oh, Mama, Chloe said, giggling behind her knitting needles.

Aw, Bristol's all right, Alvin said. Whewee, it's warm in here.

Take off your coat, Mama said.

It ain't a bit hot, Chloe said.

Alvin hung his overcoat on the peg beside the door and sat in a chair pushed back against the wall, stretching his long feet.

Whatcha making, Sis, he said to Chloe. A muffler for your big brother, home from the war?

Esther laughed. Chloe said: It's a cap for Singer Joe.

There came another fit of stomping from the porch, followed by a loud knocking at the door. It was Alvin's savior, Pink Miracle. He still carried the fiddle case with the rope tied around it, and his other hand, with its missing fingers, just barely stuck out from his army coat.

How do, folks, he said, and started coughing, a high-pitched little raspy cough at first, but deepening, and then he was bending over so far, still coughing, that you thought he might fall down. Alvin went to him, led him to the chair he himself had been sitting in, and Hannah Ruth thought that here was something else her brother caught overseas: an impulse to sympathy.

Pink was sick, anybody could see it. Alvin didn't look so good himself. While he patted Pink on the back, with his other hand he was wiping sweat from his own forehead.

Are you okay, buddy, Alvin said.

Fine, Pink said. Fine.

And he leaned forward from the chair and fell in a heap onto the floor.

It was Alvin that was sicker, though. The chills set in, and he lay dead in the bedroom for five days, the smell beginning to affect them all, waiting for his turn to be buried. He had to be put in a new section clear on the other side of the graveyard because Mama, lacking money, had never thought to purchase a plot next to Little Sister.

Pink, who after the burial was moved from the pallet in the front room and into Alvin's bed, coughed violently, slept, woke coughing, tried to get up, fell back, couldn't sleep, slept, woke moaning. Hiram fell ill while reading about Napoleon, laying his head down on top of the book, and Mama turned her attention to him, leaving Singer Joe to Hannah Ruth. If a titty was handy, he'd suck it, dry or not. After all he ate plenty else and stayed plump and healthy. Alex didn't catch the flu either.

People fell sick right and left—the paper was full of accounts—but babies and older people seemed immune, as if the flu wanted to take only the strongest.

Dudley's meanness would keep the flu away from him, Hannah Ruth felt certain, but a few days after Alvin's burial Dudley began to shake and rasp and spit and sweat. She went back and forth from their hotel room and her mama's house, sometimes five times in a day, a good mile each way and hilly. Mama couldn't take care of everybody. Esther sat like a princess, reading a magazine, and then all of a sudden leaned forward, stood with a deep sigh, a little cough, walked slowly into the bedroom where Alvin had died and where the feverish, sweat-slick bodies of Hiram and Pink lay in the bed, and curled up against them. She did not die prettily nor gracefully. Her face twisted up, she coughed, heaved, moaned, tossed wildly in the bed for two days, cursing Hannah Ruth, who cooled Esther's forehead with dampened washrags, who held her hand, who spooned oatmeal and warm milk into her mouth, who said, There, there, sweetheart, honey, darling sister.

Esther spit the warm milk into Hannah Ruth's face and flung the washrag to the floor.

Damn you to hell, Hannah Ruth. God damn you, sister.

They were her last words. As with Alvin, it was five days before the gravediggers could get to her. Dudley got up from his sickbed, still coughing and short of breath, unsteady on his feet, and stood alongside Hannah Ruth at the graveside. He held onto her hand and kept turning his head to one side, hawking up phlegm. He was there, Hannah Ruth knew, to offer his farewell to Esther, that was all. Pink Miracle was there too, coughing into his bandanna, shaking, standing on the other side of Hannah Ruth, between her and her mother, pale and forlorn.

It was bitter cold, the wind strong and howling, but the ground could still be broken and the hole looked deep, its walls smooth, the red-streaked dirt piled in a neat mound alongside. The preacher, Mama's brother Nimrod from up on Roan Mountain, a tall and skinny man with long strands of white hair streaming from beneath his high-crowned felt hat, stood slanted against the wind. Crows flew across the overcast sky, shrieking.

Bless the dirt, Preacher Nimrod Fugate said, bless the dirt, our first and last friend. Dear Jesus, welcome this poor sinner and wash her in the blood of the lamb.

On and on he went with his harsh, flat voice, like a man uttering a threat. Hannah Ruth would as soon listen to the crows. Never had the world seemed so full of ungodly sound, all a grating and scraping, thumping and tearing, a rush of hisses, taps, clicks, and squeaks. Was this the hell her sister had wished on her?

She wanted to shake Dudley, sick though he was, and tell him look what his lust for her sister had come to.

But her anger passed, and she could only think how alive she felt and how she wanted to go far away from this place.

14

A fiddle case was generally made of thin pressed deal painted with a hard black enamel. It was frequently coffin-shaped, either tapering in a smooth line from neck to belly, bowed up slightly to a little ridge on top or, like the Stradavary's case, just flat. After his buddy Alvin was buried, the blackness of the case got to Pink. He told Hannah Ruth to push it under the bed. He couldn't stand looking at it.

In France, when Alvin had mentioned Hannah Ruth you would hear puzzlement in his voice. He didn't know what to make of this sister of his who made up songs at the drop of a hat, songs about dishwater, sweet corn, birds and frogs, clouds and sunshine, trees, old shoes, noses, teeth, anything at all. She might be a little slow, Alvin suggested, but to Pink she sounded pretty good, she interested him more than Esther, whom Alvin wanted to fix him up with when they got back to Tennessee.

That this Hannah Ruth was already married seemed unfortunate, but mainly just inconvenient. He had known more than one married woman in his time whose husband gave her grief or cruelty. Such a woman needed honest to God loving kindness, and couldn't it be his mission to provide it?

Alvin looked up to him, he knew—even before he saved Alvin's life. Older by almost eleven years, Pink had the feeling that Alvin thought of him as an older brother or even a father. Such admiration embarrassed him. He didn't seem worthy of the kind of worship Alvin seemed to need to bestow.

In Pink's opinion, if you had you a mother that was strong and good, you could do without a father. His mama kept something of herself, and that was important. When it came to guessing at the nature of that self, he supposed he'd always remain in ignorance. What came through, though, gave him a sense of his own strength and mystery.

You been to a lot of places, I reckon, Alvin said one dreary day in camp when they were dabbing at their gas masks with solvent-soaked sponges.

I been around some.

I never was no place but Bristol, Tennessee, Alvin said, except when I stepped across State Street and then I was in Bristol, Virginia. About the same, far as I could see.

I pawned a fiddle in Bristol, Pink said. Good one, too. Surely long gone by now.

I wisht I could play something. There was nary a fiddle around when I was a mite.

Pink had heard this kind of talk before. After dances and shows, in bars and backrooms, people came up and said they sure did wish they could play a fiddle like that. Just to play one simple tune! To a man, they reckoned it was too late to learn.

Fiddles, he told Alvin, are thick as fleas on a dog's back. Or you could get you a guitar easy as breathing.

I might could play a guitar.

Sure you could.

Can you play a guitar, Pink?

Not much, I reckon. A little.

Sheet. I bet. I bet you could learn me how to play some things on the guitar.

A few things, maybe.

My sister, sheet, she could play anything she wanted to if she set her mind to it. Lord, can that girl sing. But she don't sing no songs you ever heard of before. Makes them all up as she goes. Don't that beat all.

Passing strange, all right.

Seems like it's nothing much at all I can do, unless I work at it.

It'll come to you one of these days, what you need to do.

Might get myself killed before that happens. I think I'll likely die before I know what I can do.

Pink didn't have anything to say about that. Of course, Alvin might get killed. So might the rest of them. They were in a war, after all, doing their damnedest to kill and others doing the same unto them. Everybody had a coffin waiting at the end of the line. It didn't bear dwelling on. Still, the next patrol they went out on was when Alvin was shot and Pink lost two of his fingers. With blood pouring out of the stumps on his hand and Alvin riding on his back, Pink thought more than once that he might fall himself, die in the mud with his dead buddy keeping him down before anybody might come along and lift Alvin off. Death seemed to him his natural state then, the place he'd been restless to get to, believing he was getting away from Oklahoma and his father's soddy. Why, what was a soddy but a replica of the grave, a little space of air with dirt all around. Good preparation, growing up in a soddy, starting out at the end, far as you could see.

But death hadn't caught up with him. He had carried Alvin back to the lines and Alvin had lived only to fall again, not by virtue of a German bullet but the Spanish flu, and now Pink thought that after all he knew little of death, only his two fingers dead to him, the skin smooth over the little stubs, and all the rest of him alive in Tennessee. Here in Tennessee was this sister of Alvin's, this Hannah Ruth the singer, her every motion announcing more life than she knew what to do with.

When she stared at his fiddle case, he was keenly aware of its resemblance to a coffin. I'm not one of the dead, he wanted to tell her when he played the fiddle, and still she gazed wistfully at the case and then looked up at him with sad eyes, as if certain he was next in line for the graveyard.

And so one day that winter of 1918–19 while she was away, when he was almost over the flu, sleeping now on a pallet in the front room alongside her little brothers, he went down to State Street and purchased a can of white paint and a brush. He was in a hurry and didn't trouble to remove the black paint, just scruffed it up a little with sandpaper and slapped the new paint right over it. The first coat came out more gray than white, but the second coat gave him hope that it would last awhile. In this way he came to have a white fiddle case.

15

Esther in her grave, Dudley slunk back to bed, coughing and shaking. Hannah Ruth, in spite of her resolve to leave, took pity and stayed put, his nursemaid.

Rent on the Telford House room came due and she didn't have it. When she thought Dudley had at last fallen asleep, she slipped out of bed and checked his billfold, left on the dresser. Empty. She laid it down, turned, and saw him looking straight at her.

It's some ain't rich, he said. It's some ain't living in no mansion on the hill.

This is a hotel, she said. We owe for this room.

He laughed, unpleasantly, and then coughed, his face turning red.

I know where I'm at, he said.

Well, that's good.

And I know where you go off to when you go off. You need money, you ask them Holts for it.

I won't do it.

You ask them.

I'm telling you, no.

He took to coughing again and didn't say anything more.

It was stubbornness that kept her from asking Amelia for money. She knew it well enough. But she was no longer kitchen girl nor handmaiden and she wasn't going to ask.

The next morning the hotel manager, a tall stoop-shouldered fellow named Briggs, appeared at the door. They must depart the premises, he said, rubbing his pale white hands. Word of a bad case of influenza would quickly spread. He was afraid it already had. It was bad for business.

I'm not a heartless man, he said. An IOU would be acceptable under the circumstances.

At the word "IOU," Dudley raised up his head. Briggs left then.

I reckon we'll go to Mama's, Dudley said, his voice hoarse but sharp. I reckon Mama'll take us in.

She packed his bag. That was the easy part. Getting him out of the hotel was another story. They were on the third floor, and he studied each step, placing his foot just so, then resting up for the next. Halfway down the first flight, she calculated it had taken a quarter of an hour, him gripping the stair-rail with one hand and with the other hanging onto her arm, squeezing so hard it hurt.

In the lobby, she got him into one of the upholstered chairs, then went back upstairs for their bags. When she came down with them, he was gone.

She set the bags down and rushed to the door, looked both ways and didn't see him, and then something light and fluttery like a bird alighted on her shoulder, Briggs's hand.

Madam, please, if you will follow me.

She followed him back of the desk and through a doorway covered by dark stale-smelling curtains. Dudley lay on a narrow cot with a brown wool blanket pulled up to his chin, his long feet in their black boots sticking out from the end of the blanket. His eyes were opened wide, but he didn't seem to see her. Had he died, she wondered, was this the end of her drifting Dudley boy, the last sly turn of his meanness? The thought sent a quick shiver through her, very like delight though surely it was fear, as when he drew his long body up against hers in the dead of night and he smelled like some gone-to-seed flower, his hands moving quick all up and down her.

As soon as you left, Briggs said, Mr. Crider tried to stand up, and before I could assist, he collapsed. I was able to help him into this room. Madam, I ain't without charity.

We'll be going shortly, she said.

The room was small, windowless, lit by an oil lamp placed on an upturned crate. Dudley tossed aside the blanket and began to lift himself from the cot. Briggs, trying to help, took hold of Dudley's arm.

Easy, now, he said. Easy does it.

Dudley pushed him away and, though shaky, managed to stand. She took his hand—its coldness shocked her—and got him back into the lobby.

My goods, Dudley said, as she eased him back into the chair he'd escaped from minutes before.

Honey, she said, keep your britches on.

He started coughing, a raspy dry heaving cough. Briggs, who had followed them, beat a quick retreat to his desk.

Dudley's breath came heavily back to him and then he was up again and she tried to grab hold of him, but he pushed her away, moving with amazing speed. She ran after him, out into the cold December morning sunshine, the gusting wind.

Where's the depot, he said, almost falling into her arms.

He knew where the depot was as surely as she did, but she figured his mind was addled by the flu and so humored him, telling him it was just around the corner. It was in fact a good six blocks, all uphill, but she got him there. Never mind the suitcases and his "goods" in the footlocker. She would get him to his mama's house.

Set back in an unnatural clearing among fallen or skeletal houses, puny beneath a sky blocked by hills on either side, Dudley's homeplace looked as if it might collapse in a strong wind. Everywhere the arched and thin limbs of greenbrier, long as horsewhips, had their way, piercing through ancient walls, rotted floors. Doors hung open, porches sagged. It was a sorrowful place.

Dudley knocked on the door. Imagine that, knocking on the door of your mother's house! He had to knock twice, loudly. A big man with a thick mustache came to the door.

Is that you, Dud, the man said. The mustache was so thick it didn't even look like he'd said anything.

Let me in, O. T., before I fall down, Dudley said.

Most certainly. How do, little lady. Come right in.

Dudley walked in front of her, why not, a miracle he'd walked this far and was still standing. Let him get somewhere, then maybe he'd feel

better, as though there was some place to get to. The man with the mustache took hold of her arm at the door. His grip was firm and he smelled
like wet newspapers.

Dudley made a beeline for a rocking chair that sat between a
straight-back chair and a cot with a ratty wool blanket folded at one
end. Across from the rocking chair and cot was a sofa with legs missing
on one end. The big man led her to it, and she sat down, warily, on the
low end. Next to it stood a dresser with a gilt-edged Bible on top, resting upon a piece of yellowish tatting. The room was warm and at the
same time drafty and she didn't feel like taking her coat off. She smelled
something cooking—greens—and realized she was hungry.

Dudley started coughing, but the man didn't pay him any mind, kept
looking at her as though she was something good to eat.

A drink of water might help, she told him.

The man actually bowed at her before he walked away, the second
man in her life that had ever done this, the first being Emmett Holt.

Is that your brother, she whispered to Dudley.

He nodded forlornly, still coughing, and in a minute the brother
came back, holding out a tin cup to her.

For him, she said, not me. For Dudley.

To be sure.

Dudley gulped the water down, took a deep breath, dropped the cup
to the floor. His brother leaned down swiftly and picked it up.

Now, Dud, he said, shaking the cup. Ain't you going to introduce me
to the little lady.

Dudley gave a weak gesture toward her and said, My wife.

A pleasure to make your acquaintance, honey! Allow me to take your
coat.

She shook her head, shuddering, still cold. Dudley asked where his
mama was, but the man didn't seem to hear. Looking her up and down,
he told her he was generally called Reverend or Preacher, but since she
was family she could call him O. T., long as she didn't ask what O. T.
stood for.

Stands for Olden Times, Dudley said, ha, ha.

The laugh got him to coughing again.

Dud took a bad cold, did he? O. T. said to her. These chilly winds
don't do a soul no good, come whooshing down the holler like a house

afire. Like the song says, I'm goin where those chilly winds don't blow. Where might that be, though.

I'm dying, Dudley said.

You do look a mite puny.

He winked at her then.

He's got the Spanish flu, she said to O. T. My brother and sister died of it.

The Spanish flu. Naw.

She nodded yes. She didn't want to talk to him. Where was Dudley's mama? He should get some food in him, it must have been dinnertime. Then he should lie down and rest. She meant to leave him on the mend, not six feet under.

I want to see my mama one more time, Dudley said, his voice little more than a whisper.

Well, I swan. I guess you do, boy, I guess you do. She'll be here directly, I reckon. She never drifts far.

He walked to the door, turned to face them again, but then looked downward, sighed, shrugged his shoulders. Was he going to pray? Looked like it. Before he could start, though, a tall figure appeared at the doorway from the back part of the house, another brother, she thought from the overalls and heavy boots, but then she saw the thick hair braided and coiled, the big womanly eyes. The woman's mouth hung open, making a dark circle. She didn't have any teeth.

Merry Christmas, Mama, Dudley said.

Christmas, the woman said. It ain't Christmas yet, is it, son?

No, ma'am, O. T. said. A week from tomorrow.

Mama, Dudley said. Mama, I'm sick.

Mama looked at Dudley then, and you'd've thought she saw the devil. Maybe Dudley was bad, she thought he was likely bad in ways she couldn't even imagine, but just then she couldn't see any evil in him. He tugged at his coat as if it was a blanket.

What have you come here for, his mama said.

Don't have no other place to go to, Dudley said.

His mama stepped over to the rocker and laid her hand on his shoulder, leaned down, cupped his chin in her hand, and raised his head so that she could look at him. He looked back at her, and you might have thought they were mirror images of one another. But she said, You look like your no-count daddy. He always come back, too, until they smashed his head in with a tree trunk.

Dudley's eyes, half-shut up to now, opened wide, and he muttered something under his breath.

I give you teeth, she thought he said.

His mama spit on the floor.

Food I can't eat ain't worth the trouble, she said.

I give you a good set of teeth, Dudley said, clearly now. Then she heard a moaning that she took for the wind at first, but it was O. T., starting to sing: *Going where the climate suits my clothes. Going where those chilly winds don't blow.*

Be still, son, his mama said, and O. T. stopped singing.

Dudley's mama let go of Dudley's head and stood up straight.

This boy is sick, she said to Hannah Ruth.

Yes, ma'am.

And you've brought him that is your husband here for me to take care of.

He wanted to come here.

She spit again.

The wicked, she said, boasteth of their heart's desire. You, O. T. Fetch me a kivver. Then get this girl something to eat. Looks like she mought blow away.

O. T. stepped briskly out of the room. Dudley's mama passed her palm across Dudley's forehead.

He's got the fever, she said. He's burning up.

It's the Spanish flu, Hannah Ruth said again.

Spaniards killed my uncle, Dudley's mama said. They was in Cuba where they didn't belong. Sons of Sodom and Gomorrah.

Dudley was in Knoxville, mainly, I think, or Bristol.

Contaminated, all our cities, them of the mountains and of the plains. Where is the city set upon a hill? Nowhere, child.

O. T. returned with a threadbare quilt, which his mama wrapped Dudley up in.

I'm hot, Mama, Dudley said.

It's poison in your body, son. Let go of it.

All right, Mama.

Let me touch him, Mama, O. T. said.

Not yet, son.

I have the power of healing, he explained to Hannah Ruth.

Keep your hands off of me, Dudley said, leaning forward, throwing aside the quilt. He almost fell and grabbed his mother's arms.

Behold the prodigal son, O. T. said, looking upward as if to address the ceiling. Mama let Dudley hug her for a minute, then asked O. T. to help her move him.

Hannah Ruth picked up the quilt and followed them through the kitchen and into a cold, dimly lit room with a bed in it, which they eased Dudley into without troubling to undress him. He lay curled on his side, eyes closed and teeth chattering. His mama sat down beside the bed in a straight-back chair and bowed her head. O. T. sat at the foot of the bed, also bowing his head. While they prayed, Hannah Ruth spread the quilt over Dudley and felt his forehead. It was cold.

Is there another cover, she asked his mama.

Get him the pallet, she said to O. T.

What're you going to sleep on, Mama, O. T. said.

Floor.

Aw, Mama, you can have my bed, you want it.

You give her your bed.

Oh, no, Hannah Ruth said. I'm not staying here tonight.

Where have you got to go to, girl?

Home, she said. There's people sick everywhere. There's my baby—

Baby, Dudley's mama said, I heard about that baby.

That's the blind one, ain't it, O. T. said.

You mought fetch that child here to me, Dudley's mama said.

I'll lay hands on it, O. T. said, and that child will see.

I never saw my only grandbaby. It would surely pleasure me to see it sometime. He ain't sick, is he.

He's blind, Mama, O. T. said.

He's not been sick a day of his life, Hannah Ruth said.

Kin to his grandmama. Crinch blood.

It's some Cherokee blood, O. T. said.

Bring that blind boy to me, she said. I'll teach him what knowing is.

Hannah Ruth believed she could get home before dark if she left now, and she drew herself up quick, took a deep breath and started to say farewell, but O. T. began to sing again, and it was so pretty it stopped her dead in her tracks: *Down in the human heart, crushed by the tempter, feelings lie buried that grace can restore.* His mama told him to shut his mouth for God's sake and go get that pallet for his brother.

There wasn't much celebrating that Christmas of 1918. Hannah Ruth bought apples and candy canes for the boys, hankies for the girls, and a bonnet gaily decorated with red ribbons for her mother. She gave Pink an apple, too, handed it to him in his sickbed. He tried to take a bite of it and choked, started coughing again.

Of the sick ones yet living in her mama's house, it was only Hiram and Pink Miracle. Hiram improved quicker and was up and about early in the new year. I will never be sick again, he foolishly announced. By the time Pink Miracle could stay on his feet without weakening fast, the January thaw came along with brilliant sun and calm breezes, making you think spring was upon you, when all the time it was February fixing to happen.

Don't you be in no hurry to leave, Mama said to Pink. You saved my boy's life. I ain't forgetting that. You stay until your strength's come back.

There never did seem a time to mourn for Alvin or Esther. Mama seldom spoke of them, and when she did she referred to them as though they were still alive. Once she called out Esther's name, meaning to say Chloe. Chloe didn't even correct her.

Hannah Ruth went up on the hill again, working in one kitchen and then another, paying off what she owed to Mr. Briggs of the Telford House Hotel a little at a time and putting back some for the time when she could leave. After work, on the way home, she might call on Amelia and the baby Alex. At home she tended to Pink Miracle. It didn't seem she had to be in a hurry about leaving as long as Pink was still there and in some need of her.

16

Nights was quiet as a tomb, Dudley would swear, but for the sound of his mother's breathing. That first night she lay beside the bed, on the floor, but the next night they put him on the floor, wrapped in a ratty pallet.

He couldn't hardly tell the difference. He shivered, then broke into a sweat. He might have been awake and he might have been sleeping. Mama fed him soup so hot it burned the roof of his mouth.

Then, all of a sudden, he felt strong again, strong enough to get up and move about the house.

How long, he asked O. T., have I been here.

A spell. Two weeks, maybe three, four.

I lost track.

It's only earthly time, brother.

O. T. was sitting across from him at the table. It was a gray day, still February from the sound of the wind. Mama was away. She never said where she went. O. T. told him about the infant child that had turned up in a Bristol, V-A, household. Repeated to him what people said about that child's being fathered by Emmett Holt, heir to all the Holt fortune.

Ain't no business of mine, he told O. T.

Well, that may be. It ain't my business to tell you what your business ought to be. It's some that say, is all, the mother of that heir is somebody you know.

Somebody I know.

Yes, sir. Somebody you know pretty well.

Quit beating around the bushes.

Ain't your wife acquaintanced with the Holts?

It might could be.

Well, you know how people talk. There's rumors.

Ain't none of my business, Dudley said again.

Once O. T. left, though, Dudley did some thinking. It was possible, he concluded, that Hannah Ruth could have borned a child after he went away the second time, same as with Singer Joe. He remembered how he'd come back and seen that baby sucking at its grandmama's nipple, its long feet sticking out of the blanket, and not figured out until later the ugly child was his son.

And he remembered following Hannah Ruth up the hill. Frisky, wasn't she, a-swinging her ass and wearing a fine white dress like a lady. Sashayed into that big house like she belonged there.

That night he had gone after her again, this time slipping around back of the house, following the line of the fence down the long, sloping yard, the moon so bright you could see your shadow. From the creek, the lights in the windows looked like little bitty stars, way back up across a stretch of clean darkness, darkness groomed and shaped, and back of him the dark of the woods, trees tall and bent. He had thought to wait in those trees until the lights went out, and then maybe look for a window left open, a door unbolted. Once inside, he wasn't sure what he'd do. He'd have to see. Maybe he would find Hannah Ruth and carry her away.

It was a warm night, though October, dry pine needles beneath his feet, soft enough to lay down in. He was of no mind to lay down, though. He needed to be alert.

And along she came, naked as a jaybird. Walked right out of the clean darkness and set herself down on a big rock, the moon beaming down on her. He knew this was what he was supposed to be alert for and he wouldn't need to go into the house at all.

Now, gathering his strength at his mama's table, he thought it likely he had bigged her that night at the creekbank, giving her the infant O. T. said was to inherit the Holt fortune. She would've had plenty of time to have a baby while he was gone.

Thinking these thoughts, he set out for Bristol. It was cold. He still felt a little puny, but he could walk, he wasn't dead yet. Soon the sun was shining and the wind wasn't much, the air warming. On the Elizabethton Pike he caught a ride with a peddler in a mule-driven cart and was in Bristol by dinnertime. He considered getting his footlocker from the hotel, but the fellow might try to collect for the room. He rested on a bench and then started up the hill on the Virginia side.

Climbing the hill was the worst part. The door wasn't even locked. He opened it and walked in.

It was a quiet house, clean-smelling and warm, likely a fire burning in every room. He found a soft chair in the front room and sat in it, resting his feet on a velvet-covered stool.

He was dozing when he heard the baby cry from somewhere upstairs. It wasn't a loud, wailing sort of cry and it didn't last long. He heard footsteps. The floor in the room above him creaked and the wind howled. The howling sounded human, like a woman hurt. He got up quietly and stepped toward the hallway. A clock chimed—the mantel clock behind him—three chimes. When it stopped, he heard the howl again, for sure coming from a room upstairs.

Pausing at the landing to catch his breath, he smelled bread baking, maybe a cake. Could've used a bite to eat. Maybe he ought to be looking for the kitchen, talk somebody out of a piece of bread, a cup of coffee. Naw, keep going. Keep to your word.

What word.

Why, to find out what was what. To see that baby. To introduce yourself. Beyond that, just wait and see.

He hadn't bargained for what he saw coming down at him from the stairs, though. It looked like a ghost, stepping down toward him so slow it appeared almost to be floating. It had one hand raised up in the air like a wing. The other hand held a pistol, aimed right at Dudley's head.

Might as well be now as any other time, he thought. He couldn't hardly run, anyway, puny as he was.

Shoot me, he said. Go on. Blow my head off. I don't care a bit.

The hant smiled.

I don't belong here, Dudley said, but I don't belong nowhere else neither.

The hant laughed.

All right then.

He turned to go. The hant was saying something, but Dudley couldn't understand for the laughing. He believed the hant might be saying to wait a minute. Wait a minute? Why, certainly. He was in no hurry to get back to his mama's house. He had all the time in the world. He explained to the hant how he, Dudley, was surely the daddy of the infant in this house and therefore with certain rights.

Certain rights, the hant said. Yes, to be sure. Have at them, my friend.

The hant, with pistol lowered, showed him the door to Amelia's room. By then Dudley had figured out that this was no hant at all, but the woman's brother that he had heard talk about from time to time. A crazy fellow, it was said.

The howling was her blowing into a black tube. She was sitting up in a big bed that had a kind of tent over it, the covers drawn up to her waist, the baby in a cradle alongside the bed. She didn't see him at first, but the baby took note. It began to wail and whoop. The woman looked up then.

Howdy, Dudley said.

She looked at him briefly, then set the tube down. The baby kept howling.

That one's a bawler, he told her.

A lanky lady wearing a white apron came in, snatched up the whooping baby, and it quietened. The tall lady carried the baby briskly away.

I know you, Amelia said.

And for sure she looked at him as if she had seen him before, almost as if she had been expecting him.

Well, he said. I don't recall we've ever met.

I know you, she said again. I believe I know you as much as I want to. What do you want from me.

He looked around. The clock on the mantel had gold hands and numbers. He didn't have much of a fondness for clocks, though. Now, that big bed with the roof over it, he admired it, but a fellow couldn't hardly carry it off by himself.

What's that thing you was blowing into.

It's a clarinet.

Damn loud, ain't it. Louder than a mouth harp.

It belonged to my father.

Ain't that sweet.

Get out of here.

She stood up from the bed, holding the clarinet like some kind of club she might hit him with.

Lady, he said as he backed away, it's not a damn thing I want from you.

17

Even in the best of times, when his sister Amelia's will did not conform to his own, Emmett Holt resisted. But on this bleak February day he sensed the urgency in her voice, understood it had something to do with the strange visitor he'd met on the stairs and ushered into her room, and God knew he had time on his hands. At least the errand would put him in the Stutz Bearcat with the kitchen girl, a kind of reprieve.

So he put on his cap, placed pistol and knife, his little secrets, in his coat pocket, wrapped a woolen scarf around his neck, and climbed swiftly into the driver's seat of the big car bestowed upon him by his dear daddy, whose disappointment in his son led him to such guilty acts of generosity.

His mother was less generous—or less susceptible to the little spurts of guilt that would make her generous toward the son who had caused her such grief. It was all his fault, she would say—indeed, had said it, and more than once. He must take hold of his life. Be proud. Be bold. Be manly. If she had been born male and with such advantages as he had, why, she would have made something of her life.

She was born female, though, wasn't she. A nice kettle of fish, eh. A different story.

And why, she would ask him, didn't he marry and settle down? Twenty-seven years old. Would he be a bachelor all his life?

He gunned the Bearcat. This was his marriage—to speedy departures, quick escapes.

Well, but he loved his dear mother and he loved the Bearcat and, as he drove out into the winding, hilly roads that led away from Bristol, postponing for a time his mission on Mary Street, savoring the smooth deep thumping of the big engine, the vibration of the steering wheel, the cold air swooshing around him, he thought he might be a little in love with the kitchen girl as well. How would Mama like that, a kitchen girl for her son's bride.

He had no business fancying himself capable of love for another human being. He regretted his dealings with the girl, so of a piece with former transgressions. That Amelia loved her was abundantly clear, and he knew himself well enough to know that, even if he resisted her will, he was prone to imitating her. All too prone.

Well, now she had a project that would engage her, this orphan child she'd taken in. Who would have thought—Amelia fancying herself a mother. Even more far-fetched: that he become a father.

Not that anyone had asked him to. It was assumed by all concerned that he would have nothing of fatherhood. A fitting assumption. You could not prove, surely, that the child was his, at any rate. The kitchen girl—Hannah Ruth—had a husband somewhere, didn't she.

Really, he was weary of it all, bone weary, blood weary. It was an old story, the story of his life, the sense of being born into some other body, some other world. A mistake, in short, a ludicrous mistake.

The roads were mud-slickened—wasn't it February, after all—and the bare branches of the trees looked like whips held above him. The sky, perilously close, crouched just the other side of the trees.

Let it descend. Wrap him up into these hills.

For a time, he had been happy with himself without knowing who he was. Just when it was no longer enough, he could not say with any certainty, no more than he could put his finger on the time he stopped being the sweet and vulnerable-looking boy in the photographs yellowing in his mother's scrapbook. He knew facets of himself, of course, knew himself possessed of mystery—owned by it, he almost would say—and this had seemed knowledge enough to keep him going tolerably well.

Now he wondered, crossing State Street into the Tennessee side of Bristol, had he been born female, would that have made a difference? It would, of course. But enough of a difference? Likely not. It was nice to think so, though, pleasant to imagine that other life, the silk under-muslins smooth against his skin, as when years ago, alone in the house, he went to his sister's wardrobe and was no longer Emmett but Emily, standing before the mirror in her shiny pearl-button shoes, her satin skirt figured in velvet, her basque with the puffed sleeves and braided cuffs, his waist as narrow as a girl's, surely, laced up tightly in her corset with its whalebone stays.

And then there had been the time, a delicious if slightly delirious time, when he'd slipped away from St. Stephen's in a stolen cadet's uniform, ridden the train from Mobile to Nashville, and paid Amelia a visit at Miss Gordon's School for young ladies. Fourteen years old, he would have been, my God, a century ago it seemed, the week before Christmas, a blustery gray day, the girls all preparing to depart, packing their trunks, chattering about this or that upcoming ball, what they'd wear, bless their hearts, how they'd contrive to be noteworthy, seen by this boy or that, and, oh, the tedium of one's own poor family! Amelia's room-mate, on the other hand, was not going anywhere. She was, he quickly ascertained by her flashing dark eyes, a kindred soul, and when she explained that she would have to stay at the school over Christmas because her mother was dead and her father traveling in Europe, he decided he would keep her company.

Her complicity had shocked even him. Amelia left on the omnibus for the depot with all the other girls, and he stayed behind as her room-mate's secret visitor, hiding in the room while she did what she had to do with the few teachers who also remained at the school. Once the early December darkness fell, the two of them did as they pleased, and what pleased him was to fancy himself a girl at this school—a girl not like the others, of course, but one like this roommate of Amelia's, Susannah her name, a rebellious, somewhat bellicose girl, a soldier in skirts. Amused when he'd first suggested this little game, she cottoned to it soon enough, taking pleasure in dressing him in her dark silks—mourning garb for her mother, who had been a famous opera singer—and coloring his cheeks.

Lord, you look prettier than your sister!

Then, to his disgust, he had suddenly fallen ill and the game was up. It was two days before he had sufficient strength to rise from his sister's bed and return home, still weak, his throat raw, explaining that he had stayed at St. Stephen's in order to see his friend Owen through a bout of the catarrh and in that way had caught the illness himself. Amelia knew better, of course, but did not betray him. It occurred to him later that his father would have known better, too, no doubt suspecting schoolboy shenanigans in the gaming rooms of Mobile, pranks involving shady cardsharks and harlots, which had been the indiscretions of his own youth and therefore could easily be forgiven.

At the graveyard he brought the Bearcat to a stop. It was not out of the way, on the hillside no more than half a mile from the address he'd been given on Mary Street. People visited graveyards all the time. But he had it all to himself on this day now that the flu epidemic had subsided. The knife—only a jackknife, but with a three-inch blade, sharp as a razor—felt warm in his pocket. He left it there, and, still sitting in the Bearcat, removed the pistol, grasping its handle, admiring the bluish sheen of the barrel, taking aim at a nearby stone, one Elijah Leander Wade, Beloved Father, Devoted Husband. Born 1841, Died 1910 in His Savior's Arms.

Hello, Elijah.

The sound echoed, but the stone held firm, yielding no more than a sliver. He meant no disrespect. What difference could it make to the dead?

He jumped down from the automobile and, after considerable wandering during which he stepped, whenever convenient, on more than one mound, he found the headstone of his grandfather, whom he had never known, Mama's beloved daddy, memorable through the tintype framed and set upon the mantelpiece in the parlor beside a miniature shepherd molded in plaster, glazed in glossy blues and reds, with a gilded staff. A merchant in Abingdon, dealer in dry goods, so Mama had said with precious little pride in her voice.

Also engraved upon the stone was the name of his grandmother, whom he did remember, though only slightly, a frail woman with no teeth but huge ears beneath her upswept silver hair.

What did they know?

It was not recorded.

Again the sound echoed. This time a piece of the stone flew forth, but so small that he couldn't find it in the brittle grass.

The pistol no doubt lacked force, a vest-pocket Colt .25 automatic, purchased on a whim some years ago at a pawnshop in Knoxville. You never knew when such a gun might come in handy. Once he had fancied himself officer material, strutting alongside the creekbank in back of his father's house with a wooden sword tucked under his belt, imagining himself with a Winchester rifle on his shoulder, but that was long ago, and even then he had preferred his sister's crinolines and capes to epaulettes and sabers.

He was sent to St. Stephen's in Mobile, a military academy, and then, of course, to VMI, where he had lasted two months before being turned out. Not for insubordination, no. He was a good soldier, his brass always polished, and on the drill field he marched with precision, zeal. In the classroom it was another story. How could you take those lecturing fools seriously? It was enough to drive a fellow to drink. And it did.

He shivered, remembering his homecoming that time. Amelia had been away, of course, at her women's college up North, so that he'd had to bear his father's gloom and his mother's anger without his sister's sympathy. He might have gone to her instead of slinking back to the family mausoleum, as he then styled his father's house, but something in him wanted the predictable humiliation, the shame, as if to announce, once and for all, the failure of his life.

He let his foot descend heavily upon the ground above the tomb of one Jeremiah Lucius Cunningham,

1839–1863
CSA 61st Infantry Regiment—Co. E
Killed at Big Black

Yon marble minstrel's voiceless stone
In deathless song shall tell,
When many a vanquished age has flown,
The story how ye fell.

He listened carefully, heard neither song nor story, only the sound of the Colt echoing for a third time, the bullet breaking loose a fist-sized chunk from the corner of the marker but leaving the words intact.

No one heard. Someone might have come after him, alarmed by the sound of the pistol shot. No one listened. He imagined the sound reaching the rooftops of the little houses in the distance, a woman at her kitchen sink pausing, cocking her head. He saw her with an ivory comb in her hair, her cheeks flushed, a child to tend to, an onion to be chopped, a husband to amuse. A woman's work is never done.

Ah, well, he had his own work to do. It was time he accomplished something.

18

Hannah Ruth woke on that February morning with the feeling she was back in Knoxville in the little hotel room, and she would any minute hear the downstairs door slam and then Dudley's footsteps on the stairs. It frightened her. But then she saw the familiar chest of drawers, her shirtwaist hanging from its peg in the wall, the window opening not onto the viaduct but the lilac bush, barren now, where Dudley had stolen a kiss from Esther. The space in the bed usually taken up by Mama and Singer Joe was cold. They must have been up for some time. She couldn't imagine why she'd slept so long. Why, it must be time for her brothers and sisters to be off for school. No, it was Saturday. She smelled coffee and heard talk coming from the front room and the squeaking of floorboards.

She dressed hurriedly and went into the front room, where Pink sat with the fiddle case on his lap. Little Lewis stood next to him, watching the case as if something wonderful might jump out of it. Hiram and Lewetta and Chloe were chattering in the kitchen. Mama and Singer Joe, she guessed, were in there with them.

You all right? she said to Pink. He still looked pale and unnaturally thin.

I mean to live, he said.

Well, that's a good thing.

He's going to play the fiddle, Little Lewis said. Ain't you going to play it, mister.

Don't you be bothering him to play, Hannah Ruth said.

He ain't so sick anymore that he can't play the fiddle, Little Lewis said.

I want to hear you play, Pink, Hiram shouted from the kitchen. Although recovered in every other way, Hiram was still coughing from time to time, and he started up then.

Mama came in from the kitchen, balancing that big boy Singer Joe on her hip while carrying a cup of coffee in her other hand.

Fiddle, fiddle, Singer Joe was saying.

Get you some grits, Mama said to Hannah Ruth, if them girls hasn't polished them off.

I will directly, she said.

Mama sat in the rocker with Singer Joe on her knee. He held himself erect, listening, his eyes aimed downwards, his hands making small circles in the air. He looked, Hannah Ruth thought, as ornery and arrogant as his daddy and with his daddy's scowl, even though he had never seen hide nor hair of his daddy, of course. His nose was long and sharp like her mama's. She didn't see herself anywhere in him.

Best not to burden yourself, Mama said to Pink.

I'm right determined to play, he said. He took the fiddle from the case, held it up like a prize, and then let Little Lewis take out the bow, which he swung around like a sword, jabbing at Singer Joe, almost poking him in the ear. Mama swatted Little Lewis a good one for that, and he handed Pink the bow, rubbing his head.

Hiram grinned, pleased that Little Lewis had been slapped.

Pink, with the fiddle resting in his lap, rosined up his bow, stroking it vigorously.

Magic dust, he said, grinning, showing his broken-off front tooth.

Aw, it ain't, Hiram said.

Sure is. Without it, the bow would just slip and slide across the strings something awful. Old fiddle'd squeal like you was hurting it. Yeow.

Aw, that ain't so.

Yes, sir, it is.

Sit down, honey, Mama said to Hannah Ruth. Did you sleep any?

Lord, yes, she said.

You was a-tossing and a-turning all night.

Chloe and Lewetta, drying their hands with dishrags, stepped into the room.

You get your beauty sleep? Lewetta asked.

Don't look like it, Chloe said.

Chloe, almost sixteen, had grown up taller and darker and leaner than her sisters, and men would stare as she passed by. Maybe she had already had a version of Dudley or two chasing after her. If so, she kept it a secret. She moved slyly in her long body, as if a little surprised or embarrassed by its beauty and spaciousness and secrecy but pleased by it, for all that, and pleased to keep its secrets to herself. She was in for it, all right.

Pink took the fiddle to his shoulder, getting it just so, then touched the bow to the strings. One note gave way to another, then another, and then kept on coming, fast, Pink's heel beginning to tap in time on the floor, where Little Lewis sat with his legs folded in front of him and rocked his head back and forth. Oh, it wasn't the music of sickness. Hannah Ruth felt she understood the fiddle's language just as clearly as when she'd first heard it, before Pink and Alvin had fallen ill. It was as if she might find the words within herself to answer if she only knew how to call them up.

When he stopped all you could hear was the sucking and wheezing of Singer Joe at Mama's breast. Hiram, standing at the doorway, stood still and straight, both hands to his sides. Little Lewis asked what that tune was called.

That was "Soldier's Joy," Pink said, his face no longer pale, almost florid, flushed.

Ain't no joy in being a soldier, is it, Mama said.

No, ma'am, not much.

Pink addressed Mama but looked at Hannah Ruth.

I'm going to be a soldier someday, Hiram said.

Soldiering ruint Our Alvin, I kindly believe, Mama said.

Pink began to play again, this time a slow tune, a waltz. Hannah Ruth watched his long slender fingers touching the strings and found admirable the delicate grip of his three-fingered right hand on the end of the bow. She believed he could have done without another finger and still moved the bow in long graceful strokes. He kept his eyes closed at first, and when they opened they aimed at one place and then another, as if to get his bearings and keep from floating away. Still, when his eyes alighted on her, they hesitated long enough for her to take in his meaning. For sure, he was playing for her.

There was a sound like singing. When she realized it was coming from her, she felt her cheeks flush. She kept on, though. It wasn't words, not even words from faraway countries such as Amelia tried to teach her, but what the words might come from. The sound of the fiddle quickened, the varnished top flashing like a signal, saying yes, yes, I know exactly what you mean. Another sound started up then, not the same as what she was singing, but with her somehow, wordless like her voice. A shiver ran up her spine. When the fiddle stopped playing, the air was still thick with music. Didn't anyone else hear that other sound?

They did, and now she understood. The music was coming from her boy, Singer Joe. Everybody was looking at him, listening. He sat up straight on Mama's lap, his hands clasped and held before him, his mouth hardly opened at all, his song little more than a moan now, high-pitched and wavery but lovely and strong and pure. He sang as if there wasn't nobody else in the world but him listening. It scared her.

Declare, Mama said, her breast still bared, extending plump and brazen from her loosened shift.

Lewetta at the door, leaning against the jamb, said it was right amazing. Hush, Little Lewis said to Singer Joe. But Singer Joe didn't hush until Mama stroked his yellow hair. Then he cocked his head to one side, as if listening. Mama cleared her throat. Little Lewis asked Pink what was the name of that song anyway.

Which one? Pink asked, grinning, looking at Hannah Ruth. Seemed like we had more than one going at once.

The one *you* was playing, Little Lewis said.

Why, that was just something I heard over there. Don't recollect ever hearing the name of it.

A Hun song?

Naw, it was somebody else. Somebody I heard somewheres.

A soldier?

It wasn't no soldier, I reckon. It was a lady.

Declare, said Mama. A French lady?

Yes, ma'am. Heard it coming from inside a house as I was passing by. Stopped me in my tracks. Wasn't no marching by then, you know. A dusty road through a little old town. I stood there and listened though I couldn't understand a word of it, and I vowed to remember it and learn it as soon as I come back to my fiddle.

And you did, too, Little Lewis said.

Well, I got some of it—the spirit of it, maybe.

You understood, all right, Hannah Ruth thought. You understood well enough that French lady's song, its grieving and its longing.

I wish I could go to France, Lewetta said.

I'd settle for Knoxville, Chloe said. They understand you there.

I'm going to be a soldier, Hiram said, and shoot me a Hun.

At that moment there came a banging noise, surely loud as cannon fire. Singer Joe jerked his head to one side and covered his ears.

Honey, it's just a automobile, Mama said to Singer Joe.

The noise grew louder until it stopped right outside. Hiram swung open the door to look.

On the porch, leaning first one way and then another, huffing and puffing, his blue eyes glimmering behind big goggles—Hannah Ruth knew him all right—stood Amelia's brother, Emmett Holt, behind him the automobile they'd heard, sleek and long, its motor still running. He wore a navy blue cap like a little boy's, tight-fitting yellow kid gloves, and a checkered duster so long that it hid his feet.

I beg your pardon, ladies and gentlemen, he said, leaning on the door frame, lifting the goggles off his eyes. I've come for the kitchen girl.

All right, she thought, though his words angered her. She knew it was Amelia that would have sent him for her and Amelia would not put her in harm's way. Anyway, she was not afraid of him. She put on her coat and followed him outside. A gust of wind caught the hem of the checkered duster he was wearing, lifted it up for an instant, and she saw his feet, as small as a lady's in shiny black boots.

He drove fast, a little recklessly, in the fancy automobile, and it excited her some; she liked getting somewhere fast. The cold wind stung her cheeks and made her feel awake and she liked it when the wheels hit a muddy patch and the automobile swerved and slid on the sharp curves. She had ridden in automobiles before—some of Mama's gentlemen friends took her and her brothers and sisters for rides in their flivvers—but never had she ridden in such a low-slung, fast-moving motorcar as this one. He said nothing to her, could not, after all, have been heard above the sound of the motor and the wind.

At the curb in front of the Holt house, he helped her from the automobile, escorted her up the sidewalk, offering his arm, which she took, and opened the broad dark door of the house for her. The baby was crying upstairs.

Nothing wrong with that one's lungs, he said. And then: I guess you know the way.

But before she could reach the stairs, Amelia's mother stepped into the foyer from the parlor. She looked haggard, her face almost as white as her dress.

So you've come, she said.

Delivered safe and sound by the dutiful son, Emmett said.

Mrs. Holt stepped past Emmett as if she didn't see him. He cleared his throat, crossed in front of Hannah Ruth, and, without taking off his long duster, went up the stairs, slowly, silently in his little boots, as if on tiptoe.

I believe you've lost some, Mrs. Holt said.

Lost some?

To the influenza.

Oh. Yes. A brother and a sister. Is Alex—

He's fine. Don't trouble yourself about him. A baby must cry. He's being cared for. See for yourself, of course, if you must.

I'll look in on Amelia first.

One moment, please, if I might.

Mrs. Holt took hold of Hannah Ruth's arm and led her into the parlor.

Please sit down, she said. Let me take your coat. Have you had any breakfast, child?

Yes, she said, though she had not eaten. She was not hungry. She let Mrs. Holt take the coat and guide her into the big chair Mr. Holt usually favored, a thickly padded chair smelling of old cigars. Mrs. Holt placed the coat over the straight chair and then seated herself, grimly, on the fainting couch, her shoulders erect, her head tilted upwards and turned at a slight angle. Hannah Ruth, sinking into the smelly chair, thought she saw a glimmering of Amelia in Mrs. Holt's military bearing.

My daughter has always thought highly of you, Mrs. Crider.

Thank you, ma'am.

You must know, however, that my daughter's friendship with you does not please me.

I'm sorry.

It's too late to be sorry, I'm afraid. She has your child, doesn't she. Truthfully, I could accommodate myself to that. I'm not an unreasonable person. I do not—contrary, I'm sure, to what my daughter has led you to believe—place special value on old-fashioned notions of marriage and the family. A man is of no great significance without considerable income. A woman's fear of loneliness drives her to marriage, that and a lack of means.

Hannah Ruth nodded her head and shifted in the chair. She did not know what to make of Mrs. Holt. Amelia had spoken of her as if she were little more than a ghost, frighteningly oppressive at one time but now harmless, almost companionable. Hannah Ruth's own impression had been that Mrs. Holt lived in some other world and was as inaccessible as a statue. You did not expect it to speak to you, much less have views on marriage.

My daughter, Mrs. Holt continued, has at least proven that she can do very well without a man. In this, she has pleased me. It is surely better for women to look to one another for the fulfillment of their needs, or else look to no one at all. Only a woman can know another woman's heart. I know this. My disapproval of you is not based on any scruples regarding the love of one woman for another. Do you understand me in this, dear?

Hannah Ruth nodded her head. She did understand.

You are not without intelligence, Mrs. Holt said. When you first appeared at the door, pale and needy, virtually a beggar, I saw your promise and wanted to help you with all my heart. But I hoped you would not have to stay in this house long. Your needs, the want of your soul, I felt sure, would not be met here.

Mrs. Holt lifted her arm, glanced about the room, and the gesture amused Hannah Ruth, struck her as funny—so histrionic, Amelia would say—and it was as if Amelia sat by her side and made her laugh, poking fun at her mama, her ridiculous somber mama, talking about the soul, which surely she knew nothing about.

I've heard you sing, Mrs. Holt said. There was no mistaking your voice. I see how it was that my daughter came to love you. I understand her better than she knows. I was the one who saw that she begin instruction in music, though I'd hoped she would play the piano. She chose the clarinet—her father's clarinet—to spite me. I don't know what happened to change her, take her beyond me. She is my daughter. It might be better if you could think of her as dead. Can you? It would help if you could.

She didn't wait for Hannah Ruth to answer.

Listen, she said, I'll pay you to go away from here. How much do you require?

I'm going away. I've already decided that. I'll pay my own way.

I'll help you get a long way from here. Your child will be cared for. Only say how much you require.

I'm going now.

But she went only to Amelia's room. The heavy drapes were pulled shut, keeping out the morning light. Amelia lay on her side in the big bed, facing away from the door. Not until Hannah Ruth reached the bedside did she sense Emmett's presence. He sat just inside the room beside the door, as if to guard it, but he was clearly asleep, his shoulders slumped, his head hung low, his legs extended before him, his small feet in those glossy boots propped on a plump footstool. He wore a collarless broadcloth shirt with yellowish stains on it.

It occurred to her that Mrs. Holt had stationed him there, a kind of spy. She sat down in a chair next to the crib, which was empty, Alex being kept mainly in his own room now. Amelia stirred but did not wake up.

It's true enough, she thought, that I must go away from here and it is better for Alex to stay than to go with me. Singer Joe, too, will do fine with Mama. Maybe I'm not like other women, lacking in the instinct to be a mother.

What she wanted for Singer Joe was that he not give up, that he find what he can do, never mind his blindness, and keep on doing it. He might sing. She hoped he might, as he'd done to the sound of Pink Miracle's fiddle that morning.

She began to sing, softly, for Amelia who lay weak in her bed, and for Alex, who no longer cried and might hear her from his nursery across the hall, even for poor dozing Emmett with his absurd pistol and shining boots. Sleep, she sang, sweet sleep, how fine to rest and dream the weary world away.

Amelia stirred, opened her eyes.

Is it you? she said, and then took to coughing, a hard dry cough, body-shaking.

There was a pitcher and cup on the nightstand, and Hannah Ruth, her hand shaking, poured water into the cup and held it to Amelia's lips. Amelia drank it all. So thirsty, she said.

I would have come sooner if I'd known, Hannah Ruth said.

It wouldn't have done any good. I was sleeping. No, not sleeping. I was out of this world, I swear.

You need rest.

Amelia closed her eyes again and lay so still, you couldn't even tell if she was breathing.

Sleep, sleep, Hannah Ruth sang. Sleep and dream. Going a long long ways, sleep and dream.

Where is there to go?

It was Emmett's voice. She turned. He was sitting up straight now, chin upraised, looking at her, his eyes opened wide, as if he saw something horrible. He held a pistol in one hand; in the other, a knife. There was blood on the knife and blood all over his lap. Then he quickly brought the pistol to his mouth and his eyes opened suddenly wider and when the explosion came it was very loud. Emmett's head jerked back and his legs kicked forward, stiff as boards, his ruined pelvis thrust upwards.

He didn't even fall out of the chair.

Amelia screamed, and there were footsteps, it seemed, from everywhere. Hannah Ruth didn't move. He was still staring at her. He wouldn't stop staring at her.

Interlude:

Alex

Alex said: Mother, who is my mother?
He might have been sixteen or seventeen by then, prepared to be shipped off to school in that cold northern state for another year. His aunt—the woman he still called Mother—was standing beside him while he packed his clothes. She smelled of flowers, always, flowers he couldn't name.

She had come to his room to tell him that his grandmother had died in San Francisco and she would have to go out there.

His question was inappropriate, he knew even as he asked it, inappropriate and thoughtless and rude, and in the silence that followed he was on the verge of apologizing. But to his astonishment she took hold of his arm and said, her voice calm, without any trace of anger or hurt, Come with me.

She led him to her room and sat him down at her writing table.

I'm sorry, he said, about your mother.

It's all right. You never knew her, did you.

No.

I didn't either. I'll grieve nonetheless. In due time, I'll grieve. As you surely grieve for the mother you never knew.

She went then to the big phonograph console, took a record from its cabinet and placed it on the turntable. She moved gracefully, he thought, as always. He resembled her, he liked to think, in the eyes, in a certain turn of his lips, but in her these features, in combination with others as astonishing, amounted to something, came together into a pleasing whole, whereas in him they went every which way. It must be a fine thing, he thought, to be possessed of such beauty.

She lowered the needle onto the revolving record. From the speaker came a jumble of clicks—she had played the record many times.

Here's your mother, she said, and in an instant the voice came forth. He recognized it immediately, though it had been some time since he had heard the recording. She used to play it often. He would hear it at any time of the day, beyond the closed door of her room as he passed in the hallway or, though less clearly, from his own room, from the parlor downstairs, even from outside on long summer evenings.

So it was as if he had in fact known her all along, her voice as fixed in his memory as he could have hoped. He had not hoped, of course, so that, listening now, he felt nothing much at all. He acknowledged that it was a fine voice, a strong voice, an unusual voice, but it did not seem to be speaking to him. Tell him that it would, in time, not only speak to him but also tell him the story of his life, and he wouldn't have believed you. He wanted it to be over.

When it was over, his aunt put the record away, carefully, and turned to face him. She seemed illuminated by the late afternoon light streaming in the window, her skin all aglow. He wondered at her long secrecy, her mystery. She had told him story after story of his father, the bold adventuresome Emmett who was her brother, but of his mother only that she had gone away.

She would say no more now. The voice was supposed to be enough, he understood.

We both have to finish packing, his aunt said, and he rose from her table and left her alone.

Part Three:

Dudley

19

The morning of the day Emmett Holt was buried, Little Lewis gave Hannah Ruth a card with a picture of a freckle-faced boy in a cap kissing a blushing girl. *Be Mine.* She had not remembered it was Valentine's Day, and the card brought tears to her eyes. Nobody else gave her a card. In the best of times Dudley would not think of such a thing, and surely Amelia would not on this day.

She had stayed with Amelia through the time that Emmett's body—cleaned up, surely, and kept company by Mrs. Holt—lay shut in its coffin downstairs. Amelia talked on and on about her childhood with Emmett. Who knew what had twisted his genius, turned him from that sweet, bright-eyed boy into such a man of sorrow.

For Amelia's sake, Hannah Ruth grieved for Emmett Holt, but she did not want to think about him. Still, the image of his body jerking, his bleeding private parts thrust suddenly forward, the knife in one hand and the pistol in the other, remained vivid in her mind.

The service, held in the Presbyterian church, conducted by a tall white-haired minister in black robes, seemed to go on forever, with little said about Emmett and considerable about eternal life for the chosen. That Emmett might not have been one of the chosen seemed likely to Hannah Ruth, but she did not begrudge the family consoling thoughts. Escorted up the aisle to the front pew by Amos Holt, Amelia's mother walked haltingly, her shoulders stooped, head bowed, a dazed look in her eyes. The black bombazine of mourning, so in contrast to her usual white dress, made her look almost like a different person. All during the sermon, Amelia sobbed, her face drawn and pale, her cheeks unnaturally flushed.

As the last mourners filed past the casket and it came time for the family to say farewell to the body inside the closed coffin, Hannah Ruth saw again the knife, the bloodied loins, the blood spattering from his head, onto the wall, and the way he had kept staring at her.

Amelia, kneeling at the flower-covered casket, trembled and looked as though she might faint. But she straightened herself with dignity and walked on. Mrs. Holt was shaking, too, but when she stood from kneeling she lifted her hand and suddenly, with great energy, began sweeping and tossing the flowers off the coffin. They flew all about while she called out, My son, my beloved boy—and when all the flowers lay scattered across the shiny, hardwood floor, she stretched her arms around the coffin lid and kissed its varnished surface.

Mr. Holt, who had hung back behind her, his head bowed, tugged her away.

At the graveyard, the wind had calmed, its chilly bite gone. The sky was deep blue. You could almost have done without a coat, yet the women and men alike were bundled up in heavy wool, necks wrapped with thick black scarves. Amelia took hold of Hannah Ruth's hand, squeezed it hard, held onto it all through the farewell prayer and the first shovelful of dirt.

While Hannah Ruth was at the funeral, Pink listened to her blind son sing softly to himself and was suddenly remembering Sonny Boy Jimson back in Memphis. Sonny Boy, like most on Beale Street, had resented him at first. He was white and this was colored town. Whites Keep Out was the message, clear and loud, in their faces, and one night, early on, he received the message from their fists. But he had gone back, his face swollen and bruised, and taken out his fiddle and played. After that, it was better. They let him alone, and then Sonny Boy, best of the lot, a guitar player, took him to one side and said, You gone be around awhile, I spect.

I mean to, Pink said.

Well, white boy, you gone play blues, you got to know something about the river.

It was midsummer and still dark when they walked out onto Beale Street, the air at its coolest before dawn. They walked through the quiet streets of downtown Memphis, past the dark show windows, the padlocked doors, down to the cotton exchange and then south along the railroad tracks, stopping only at Sonny Boy's shotgun house to get poles, line, worms. By the time they reached the banks of the river, the sky was a pale gray, giving way to pink back of the humped bluffs. The dark seemed to be slipping down into the river just ahead of the light, entering the water through a thin layer of silvery mist. Then the mist was gone and the river took to shimmering, little pools of light from over the bluff flickering atop the deep brown darkness, all the way across to Arkansas, a dark sliver between the sky and the river you could hardly see for all the water, and you almost couldn't see the water moving at all, but hear it lapping softly against the shore and smell the good strong dark slipperiness of it washing over and smoothing out and shining up the dirt and rocks. Across the river, way beyond Arkansas, lay Oklahoma. He seemed to see the soddy, a hump on the hard windswept ground, the long fields beyond, stretching on to a treeless horizon, his father's tall frame outlined against a huge fiery sky.

Sonny Boy handed him one of the fishing rods. He had never gone fishing as a boy. There wasn't time for such foolishness, was Daddy's opinion. Sometimes Pink and Ollard and Junior had slipped away of a summer afternoon and swum in the Cimarron, but this was rare. It was hard to put anything over on Daddy.

You can ride this Mississippi River, Sonny Boy said as he began to work a worm onto his hook, ride it all the way up from New Orleen. Keep going nawth. Sane Louee. Upriver, damn thang branch ever which way. Chicago. Louee-ville, Cincinnati. Big places. That be the direction. Nawth. Where the music going, you see. Smart fellows going there, upriver. Yeah. Play they music upriver.

Here, get you a worm.

Pink dug a worm from the can, meaning to imitate Sonny Boy's method of applying it to the hook, but the worm wriggled free and he lost it in the grass.

Get another, Sonny Boy said.

Sonny Boy threw his line into the water. Plop.

Now, he said, we gone see what come of it all. Maybe something.

Maybe nothing. We gone wait and see. That is what fishing teach you. Maybe something, maybe nothing. Wait and see. Wait and see. Most times, nothing. That be the blues, you see. Lot of waiting for nothing. Most times. Ever so often, though, why, you see, something happen, what you been waiting for, you bet.

That was a long time ago with Sonny Boy Jimson on the Mississippi River, before the war. A fiddle, Pink was thinking now, as he listened to Singer Joe singing and waited for Hannah Ruth's return, a fiddle took you far as you might go, only you had to listen to it and be guided by what you heard. Hannah Ruth's singing was something he wanted to get into his bow arm, and the Mississippi River, glimmering in the early morning light, and Beale Street and Uncle Laclede up on his mountain-top where the frogs sang from the trees and the soddy in Oklahoma plop down on the flat treeless plains, and how it all connected up to the barbed wire and the mud and the flares of the Meuse-Argonne, the faces of the German boys when they asked you for a cigarette and when they stood up from their trenches with bayonets poised.

His hand in bandages, he had felt the blown-off fingers tingling, itching for touch, and he thought: music is like this, it is a feeling for what is lost, gone for good. It is the presence of what you're missing.

The first time he heard a Victrola, it was somebody singing in a foreign tongue. Where was the singer, he wondered. Not in that little cylinder. Nowhere, that's where. Pretty fair singing, for all that.

It was the body, he thought now, listening to Singer Joe's mournful sweet voice. Everything came down to what you could do with your fingers, your arms, your tongue, lips. You might hear the world roaring in your head, and if your fingers were stiff, your bow arm weak, your tongue sluggish, you couldn't say what you'd heard. He hoped the two fingers he'd left in France sang mightily as they rotted, but doubted it. They lacked the body.

When he asked Hannah Ruth where her music came from, she said she guessed she had it before she was born, and he saw that she, too, was here and not here, as mysterious in her beautiful body as the music she and her blind son made.

• • •

That night, waking from dreams that frightened her, dreams in which she walked in a field of corpses, of bullet-cleft heads and bleeding penises, severed hands and feet such as Pink Miracle had described as being strewn about on the battlefields of France, Hannah Ruth heard Pink's fiddle and said to herself, So he is still here. The thought calmed her. It gave her pleasure.

As the days grew warmer, thoughts of Dudley came to her, uninvited, uncalled for, like Dudley himself. She would see him wrapped up in his mother's mangy quilt, shivering, and she would feel sorry for him. But she did not want to go to him.

The Holt household seemed somber in those weeks after Emmett's death. When Mrs. Holt appeared, she came quick as a ghost, then vanished. Mr. Holt's presence was felt in the smell of his cigars or in the rustling of papers and a low-pitched cough from a distant room. Although the blood had been washed off the floor, the absence of Emmett lingered like a bad smell.

Amelia, sitting at the little writing desk by the window, staring outside, sometimes said nothing to her, taking hold of Hannah Ruth's hand, squeezing it as if to the beat of some unspeakable thought or feeling.

Alva, the wet nurse, would bring in Alex, and the baby seemed to know her, smiling when she sang to him.

One bright afternoon early in the spring, the sun bursting through the big windows of the room, Amelia pressed Hannah Ruth's hand to her lips and said, There was a reason, you know.

What?

A reason I sent for you on that day.

Hannah Ruth didn't understand. Which day?

The day, Amelia said, the day . . .

She took a deep breath. She looked healthier now than a few weeks ago, more color in her cheeks. Her hair, coiled atop her head, had body and sheen.

That day, she said, and she looked toward the window, as if the day was out there hiding in the distant mountains that you could just see through the barren limbs of the trees, as dark as shadows.

You mean, she said, the day Emmett died.

Amelia cupped her head in her hands, then looked up, anger flashing from her eyes.

Yes, she said. On that same day, your husband came here. That's why I sent for you.

Dudley? Dudley came here?

Yes, yes. Your Dudley Crider.

Hannah Ruth shuddered. She could envision Dudley making his way through the woods, up over the ridges, down the muddy roads, the branches of the bare trees arching overhead. He might have been on his way to claim her again, thinking he'd find her here, as he'd done that time down by the creek, coming to her out of the dark of the trees.

I had been ill, Amelia said, but was feeling better, and when your Dudley came into the room, I was playing the clarinet—for Alex. Dudley was out of breath and white as a sheet. I thought he walked with a limp. Alex began to cry, as he usually does when I stop playing, and Alva came and took him away.

Amelia withdrew her hand from Hannah Ruth's.

He stood there stiffly, she continued, for all the world like a gentleman caller waiting to be told he might sit down if he wished. A handsome man, Hannah Ruth. You never said he was so handsome. Those eyes! But he meant me no good, I knew.

He wouldn't hurt you, Hannah Ruth said, and then immediately she wondered if she had cause to believe that. She pictured him standing there, leaning toward Amelia, his brown eyes glittery, standing there as if he belonged in this room and it belonged to him.

No, Amelia said. He didn't hurt me. He said he wanted nothing from me, and he laughed. I hated him, standing there so polite and handsome and menacing. And I thought: This is the man she married. And he became, in that moment, the embodiment of you, of all that you keep to yourself, withhold from me. I told him to get out. I told him to leave.

Did he leave then?

No, not at first. He said something about Alex, what a handsome child he was, and I told him if he didn't go away, I'd send for Sheriff Bateman. He left then, but he took his time, sauntering out of the room. When he opened the door—Jesus, there was Emmett, looking for all the world as if he was waiting for Dudley. But he didn't follow Dudley. Emmett stood there, leaning against the door frame. That was when I asked him if he would mind going to you, bringing you here to me.

You might have asked somebody else.

I know. I don't know why I thought—he was standing there, though, and there was something beseeching about his manner, as if to say what use am I. And I had a use for him just then. I felt ill again, as weak as ever, and couldn't go myself. When I think, an hour later . . .

You were in bed when I got here.

Yes, and Emmett—

Sat right over there.

I didn't realize—

I didn't either, at first. He was always quiet.

Yes. Oh, Hannah Ruth, I'm sorry you knew him the way you did.

It's all right. He was your brother. I came to think of him that way and not dwell on the rest.

You're very charitable, Hannah Ruth. I tell you, though, I have no such forgiveness for your Dudley. If I thought for one moment he might harm Alex—

Has he . . . come back?

No. But listen, dear, you have to rid yourself of that man. If you don't, he'll fester and kill you. I feel this in my bones.

I was going to leave, she said. I meant to leave, after I took him to his mama's house.

She said nothing about Pink Miracle.

You must go, Amelia said. Go where he can't find you.

And leave you?

Leave me, yes. You must.

It's what your mother wanted me to do.

My mother?

That same day, before I came up to your room, she told me she'd pay me to go away.

Pay you!

She thought I was bad for you, or else you were bad for me. I wasn't sure which.

I've disappointed her. But she's right. You must leave.

You might come with me.

You don't want that. It hurts me to hear you say it.

What do you want. What can I do.

Take care of yourself. It's all I've ever wanted.

Take care of herself. All right. She would take care of herself then.

She reached for Amelia, took hold of her hand, but she was thinking how fine it would be to leave with Pink Miracle, holding onto his sweet maimed hand.

If your Dudley Crider comes here again, Amelia said, whispering, her voice so soft, so tender, you might have thought she was declaring her eternal love, If he comes here again, she said, I'll kill him. I'll kill him with my bare hands.

20

Iseen that child, Dudley said to O. T. on the morning after coming back from his meeting with Amelia Holt. He was stronger by the day, but he should not have been rambling around the country, and he had paid for it afterwards, scarcely able to move off his pallet, sore all over.

I seen that child with my own eyes, he said, and I seen myself in that child's face. I tell you, brother, I am the daddy of that baby boy.

If it's yours, O. T. said, then why does Amelia Holt have it, answer me that.

I seen with my own eyes.

You see what you want to see. Everbody knows Emmett Holt was the daddy and that is why Amelia Holt took it to raise.

I seen him, too. I seen that Emmett Holt.

Emmett Holt? When?

Yesterday. When I seen the child.

You must've been one of the last that seen him. Emmett Holt blowed his brains out yesterday. I just come from town. Everbody says he put a pistol to his head and blowed his brains out. Some say that ain't all he did. Some say he cut his pecker off.

I saw him, I reckon, before he done that.

And he told you he wasn't the daddy?

Why, no. He took me right to that room with the infant and Amelia

Holt in it. Said a daddy ought to look to his son. Say, when was the youngun borned? Can you tell me that?

I ain't privy to that information. It's most a year old, I believe.

I come back one time, why, little over a year ago, and we kindly had a frolic. I surely bigged her then. Did she give the boy a name?

Somebody did, I reckon. Alexander is what they say it's called.

Alexander. What kind of a name is Alexander. She might have named this one after me.

Might have named him Jesus Christ for all the relation it has to you, brother.

O. T. got up then, pushing the chair to one side with his foot.

Alexander is a heathen name, he said.

Where you going, O. T.

Take care of business.

Say.

What.

Help me to the privy before you go. I'm feeling puny.

Surely.

Much obliged.

The body is a burden, son. Praise God, it don't last forever.

Pink Miracle's quickening strength could be heard whenever he drew the bow across his fiddle. He still might stop midtune, taken by a sudden fit of coughing, but it happened less often. I ought to be leaving, he would say, I'll go back to Memphis, see what's happening these days on Beale Street, but when he looked to Hannah Ruth, as if to ask her was it all right, she couldn't say a word, and he said, I reckon I'll stay another day or two.

Sometimes his presence dizzied her so that she had to go outside and walk. Sometimes she walked all the way to the Holt mansion without knowing where she was going.

The baby grew plump and stout. It laughed at the slightest provocation. Amelia made a good mother, staying at home instead of chasing off on her father's business. She was grieving, too, of course, for her lost brother, but Alex was pulling her up from her grief.

Hannah Ruth worked for the houses on the hill, but the money no longer seemed important, and so she did less and less of it. Once she walked out of a kitchen, having looked at the hardened fat in a skillet too long. Left without collecting her pay. Lazy, she told herself. I'm lazy. And so she did little to earn the money that would allow her to leave.

Dudley did not come again to bother Amelia. Nor did he visit Hannah Ruth. She knew he was healthy again, though. Mama had word of him through a friend that went to O. T.'s church out on the Elizabethton Pike. He had been seen up on the roof of that church, Mama reported, hammering at something or other.

O. T.'s church, once a country store, still smelled of feed and harnesses. The steeple, installed by the pastor before O. T., looked like a privy with holes in the sides. It appeared to lean southwards. There had once been a bell, O. T. said, but vandals stole it, and now it was just pigeons up there.

O. T. was as bad as Mama at finding chores for him to do, but at least it wasn't chopping greenbrier. The grand project O. T. had in mind for him was to right the steeple, rid it of pigeons and pigeon droppings, mend its roof, and put a cross on top.

I ain't a-climbing up there, Dudley said. I ain't overly fond of pigeons.

But he climbed up onto the roof of that building—a tin roof blotched and streaked with rust—and by shouting and waving his hands (almost falling off) he chased away the pigeons. It give him some satisfaction to hear their clucks of alarm followed by the rapid thunder of their wings and see the dumb birds flutter off into the trees. He wasn't about to fool with the mess they'd made, though. You'd have to scrub it off with a wire brush, and then they'd come right back and foul it up all over again.

As he began to shim up that privy called by O. T. a steeple, which was taller than it looked from the ground, about ten, twelve foot, thoughts of Hannah Ruth sometimes came to him, roosting in his head like one of those damn pigeons that kept coming back. He wondered if he might take her along with him when it was time for him to leave. Would she go? She was still his lawful wedded wife, last he heard, but she had more spunk and grit than necessary for the job. Her skin was mighty soft. At the same time, hammering shims beneath the base of the privy, he was starting to remember the wide dark streets of Knoxville, the big houses and their downspouts that he might climb, the unlocked windows, the woman-smelling rooms.

Once, thinking such thoughts, he almost fell off the roof. Hanging onto the ridge, he lay there a minute or two. That tin roof, warmed by the sun, felt right hot against his skin.

Hannah Ruth, he thought while hanging there, might cramp his style.

Maybe he'd be better off alone. In the next instant, though, pulling himself back up, getting his balance, straddling the ridge and inching towards the privy-steeple, he was thinking of that blind baby boy, and the other one with Amelia Holt. I am their daddy, he told himself. What business does a daddy have, climbing up downspouts, tiptoeing through the dark hallways of other people's houses, letting himself into the rooms of ladies. I will raise my boys up, and they will be ever grateful. I will not be the way my daddy was to me.

We sure do thank you, Daddy, his boys would say.

We don't need no mother when we got a daddy like you.

He would take them to a far-off country such as Texas. Maybe O. T. was right, and Jesus would help out.

He righted that privy, and in the next couple of days he put two coats of white paint on it and nailed up a cross. It was something to do, but gave him no satisfaction.

That was the spring of Chloe's running off with a boy from the knobs, a banjo player that had come around because he had heard of Pink Miracle's fiddling. Six and a half feet tall and no more than a hundred thirty pounds, he showed up late one afternoon, carrying his banjo in a flour poke, the neck sticking out at the top. It was midnight before he left, and he couldn't have said more than three words all that time, but, Lord, could he frail that banjo. Lewetta attended mercilessly to him, bringing him dipper after dipper of water, but he had eyes only for Chloe, who hung back, most demur in the straight-back chair, her cheeks flushed, her hands working at her needles, her foot tapping.

It had been a fine session. Hannah Ruth could not have gone to bed to save her life, though everybody else had. Pink Miracle seemed to aim his music straight at her heart.

After that, the tall, skinny banjo player—his name was Egbert Cook—showed up often. Sometimes Pink was there and sometimes not. Pink had taken to wandering off in the afternoons, sometimes staying gone until dusk, and these times, remembering Dudley's wanderings, his nighttime drifting, she felt a coldness come over her. He isn't Dudley, though, she told herself. He's not the least bit like Dudley Crider. Still, she wished he'd stay put.

Even when Pink was gone, Egbert Cook would take out his banjo and play for Chloe. He played fiddle tunes on that banjo, thumb and fingers all going at once. Every now and then he broke out with some sad ballad about a dying lover or a train wreck, while Chloe stitched up a storm, making such a mess of the yarn that you knew she'd have to do it all over later.

When he sang, Mama sometimes joined in, then Lewetta, and Hannah Ruth herself, though it embarrassed her, hearing her own voice so loud above the others. She tried to tone it down. Egbert looked at her like he'd seen a ghost, then back down at his long, skinny fingers, scrunched into a claw-shape, rapping at the banjo strings. His hands were white and smooth. Chloe, who had a pleasant voice, feigned bashfulness and never sang a note.

When Pink was on hand, his fiddle joining itself to Hannah Ruth's voice, sending chills up and down her spine, it was as though there wasn't another soul in the room but the two of them. She sang even when there were no words to the tune, and when Singer Joe joined in, his voice nestling up against hers and snuggling close to the sound of Pink's fiddle, it was pure pleasure.

One pretty night in April, not long after Alex's first birthday, the sky all gaudy with stars, tree frogs loud, Pink began to talk about France. He told how funny the Frenchies talked, more like singing than talking, and how old the towns looked, their narrow cobblestone streets, their houses made of clay, with little bitty windows and shutters most often closed, their rooms dark as closets, a dry smell like straw and dust, the floors soft beneath your step, squeaking, always squeaking.

Suddenly there was a squeaking noise, and everybody jumped. It was only Egbert Cook, though, tricking them by scratching on his banjo strings.

Mama laughed. Chloe smiled ever so slightly and looked away.

Singer Joe, sitting upright in Mama's lap, began to moan, leaning his head to one side. She put him down on the floor and he raised himself up, stood there for a second, arms stiff at his sides, and then marched straight across the room to Hiram and grabbed hold of Hiram's leg. Hannah Ruth believed he could tell who you were by the sound of your breath. It had taken him a while to figure it out, but once he had it, he was sharp.

I'm a-going there someday, Hiram said, taking hold of Singer Joe's hands. I am, now. I'm going to France someday. Singer Joe and me's going to France, ain't we, little buddy.

A Fran, Singer Joe said.

War's over, Little Lewis said.

It might be another war. I kindly think there'll be one when I get old enough to join up.

Lord, Pink said, don't wish for that.

I'd fight for that Napoleon Bonaparte, Hiram said, and he lifted Singer Joe up into his arms, a pretty sight to behold, her fourteen-year-old brother and her blind almost-three-year-old son. Hiram had a determination in his eyes that made him look like a man, and she shuddered, imagining him in a uniform like Alvin, trained and ordered to kill.

Singer Joe squirmed to be let down. He would go all around the room, Hannah Ruth knew, touching knees and hands until he had touched everybody.

Yes, sir, Hiram said, Singer Joe and me's going to France someday. You wait and see, now.

Would you go back there, she heard herself asking Pink.

I ain't sure I ever left it, Pink said.

Is that what I hear in your fiddle playing, Lewetta said. Is that French music?

What is it you hear? Pink asked.

Why, I don't rightly know, Lewetta said. I thought it might be French I heard.

Pink cleared his throat. Some of the color went out of his face.

Likely it's some French in it somewheres, he said.

21

Dudley was replacing the rotting porch steps of the church when he felt a hand on his shoulder.

It was Uncle Fremont.

What you been up to, boy, Uncle Fremont said, his breath announcing that he was liquored up good. He appeared to have put on some weight in his gut since Dudley had seen him last, which was a long time ago, maybe ten years, twelve. It was a wonder that Uncle Fremont even recognized him.

You're the spittin image of your old daddy, Uncle Fremont said.

Ha, ha.

God's truth. Hear him in your voice too. Jesus God.

Dudley pulled loose, but Uncle Fremont grabbed hold of his arm.

Listen here, Uncle Fremont said. I seen your daddy, seen him clear as day.

Hell you say.

Uncle Fremont broke out into a broad toothless grin.

Big as that tree, he said. Fat as that bush yonder. Devil been feeding him good, I reckon.

Well, where was he, then.

Uncle Fremont grinned again, let loose of his arm, and stood there swaying.

I ain't telling, Uncle Fremont said. Made me swear on a Bible not to tell. I'm a man keeps his word.

Uncle Fremont walked away and later that same day Dudley started getting the sweats and chills again.

I can't work no more, he told O. T., who now was trying to get him to help out around the chili parlor in Elizabethton where O. T. worked as a partner with Cousin Franklin. Disowned by his father (Uncle Fremont) for his unruly ways, Franklin had since been reborn in the waters of the Watauga after O. T. laid hands on him and cured him of his dose. Now it was Uncle Fremont's soul that O. T. worried about, he told Dudley. Fornication and whiskey, don't you know. Him that had once danced to God's tune danced to the devil's box now.

I seen Uncle Fremont, Dudley told O. T.

God loves you, brother.

Dudley felt like answering: Why'd God send Uncle Fremont after me, then? But he said he appreciated the thought.

He took to rising early and walking in the woods so that O. T. wouldn't drag him to work. One day, on a deer path near the top of a bald, he sat down to rest on a flat-topped rock. The rock was warm from the sun, and a mild breeze blew steady in his face. He was beginning to doze when suddenly from the other side of the bald came a thrashing noise and, remembering what Uncle Fremont said about seeing his daddy, he jumped up and lit out for the trees. After some rough going in laurel slicks, he came to another path. Out of breath and sweating, both arms laced with bright red welts, he stopped for a minute to consider. The woods all around were still now except when the wind gusted up and shook the leaves. Surely, nobody was coming after him. Uncle Fremont was a crazy man, and Daddy was dead.

But the thrashing noise started up again, and it was nothing but to head straight down the mountainside, damn the briers and the brambles and the thistles and the grapevines and the hidden roots and unforeseen rocks big and small, tall and short, sharp-edged and hunched, tripping him up as he ran, the fallen trees like fences to hurdle, the many ditches for twisting his ankles in. Once past the laurel slicks it was easier going, a gentler slope through bigger trees, tulip poplars and oaks, the ground leafy and soft. He heard deer snorting, caught a glimpse of them, white tails flashing, just as they bounded back up the mountain, a doe and two fawns.

At a creek he stopped, worn out. The water flowed pretty and sweet, clear and fast, over the white rocks. In the distance a crow squawked and then, closer, something rustled in the underbrush, a chipmunk or towhee. He sat on a flat rock in the shade along the creek and took off his shoes and dipped his sore feet into the cool water. The holler looked familiar, but they all did. On the other side of the creek where the ground flattened out stood tall trees, maples a hundred years old by the height and breadth of them, beeches, sweet gums, white oaks, and in their midst a little clearing that would have made a good spot for a cabin.

Lord, it *was* a cabin there. Set back in the deep shade, it was easy to miss, just a slightly flatter kind of shade until you looked closer and saw the sharp outlines of the logs and the white rocks the house sat upon. It hit him then just where he was. This log house was where his first love, Cousin Rosalee Rankin, had lived. Up there on the other side of the holler, where the next mountainside began to rise up, would be the grove of tulip poplars where he and Rosalee, naked as jaybirds, had mingled and twined in the noonday sun.

Vines grew all upside the house, hogweed circled and swooped about the porch. The house looked about to fall and the outhouse was half sucked into the ground. He approached the front steps carefully, pulled open the door, and breathed in the stinking dust.

Whatever become of her, he wondered, standing in the middle of the front room, the floor soft as mud.

He remembered a picture of her dear departed mama hanging on the wall and wondered where it might be, then remembered he had lifted it from its nail himself, the first memento of a lady he ever took. Likely it was still in his trunk in that Bristol hotel.

He kicked at something in the floor, a piece of wood, maybe, but it didn't budge and in fact hurt his toe. It was a big rock. How did that get in here. Maybe there had been a flood. Sure, that was it. That was what the smell came from. Heavy rains. Old mud. Water washed some rocks up here from the creek. The fire next time, as Mama would say.

God never give me the time of day, he told himself. I don't believe in nothing.

This here was the kitchen, there the fireplace, its grate empty, the mantel coated with dust.

Everybody's got to die, he thought, as he stepped through the moldy curtain that stretched across the door of the room Rosalee slept in with her sisters. It was dark in the room. It smelled bad. He stepped on something that looked like a human hand.

When he saw something in the bed grinning at him, his first thought was it was Daddy. But it was Uncle Fremont. His mouth was open and his eyes about half-shut. A fly crawled on his nose. Whether Uncle Fremont was dead or just dead drunk, Dudley didn't care to investigate. His rifle lay alongside him in the bed, cradled in his arm.

Outside, he could not run as briskly as he would have liked. He ached all over. Climbing the ridge, he was panting and sweating before he knew it and soon had to stop and rest and take a leak. Next thing he knew, he was lying on the ground, his pecker still dangling from his britches, and something was on top of him, hitting at him.

Get up, he heard somebody say.

Lord, he heard somebody else say.

Is that you, Dudley Crider, the first voice said.

I don't know no Dudley Crider, he said.

One of them laughed. Then they had hold of his arms and were pulling him up.

It's Dudley, all right, one of them said.

He don't know us, the other one said.

I don't know no one, he said. He could hardly stand.

Again they laughed.

Tuck yourself in, boy.

He did. Then he knew. Shitfire, it was his daddy's other two brothers, Uncle U. S. and Uncle Crockett.

Lord a-mighty, we thought for sure we had us a revenue. That's the truth, now.

I'm your flesh and blood, he told them.

22

Chloe ran off with Egbert Cook on a warm night late in May. Earlier in the evening Hannah Ruth listened while Pink and Egbert played some music. Then Pink began to talk about Oklahoma. He was glad to be out of that place, he said.

Still, Egbert said, I reckon you want to be going back there someday. A fellow gets homesick.

Pink didn't comment.

I'd like to go to Oklahoma someday, Hiram said, as if it were as far-off and strange as France. Ain't Geronimo in Oklahoma?

Yep, Pink said. Saw him in a parade once. Fourth of July. Old fellow, hunched over, face full of wrinkles, selling pictures of himself for a nickel. Give him another nickel, he'd write his name on it for you.

Write it in Indian?

Son, I never asked.

I'll bet it was Indian.

Singer Joe, making his rounds of the room, had reached Lewetta. He was singing so quiet and pretty you almost didn't notice it. Lewetta was fond of Singer Joe and kissed him on the cheek, but he didn't smile.

It's a boom out there in Oklahoma, Egbert said, twirling his banjo around and looking into its head as if he'd lost something there. In Oklahoma, them Injuns sit right on top of black gold, don't know what to do with all that money. I believe I could show them plenty of uses for it if I went out there.

Pink laughed.

Go to Texas while you're at it, Mama said grimly.

You mean like Daddy did, Lewetta said.

I ain't studying your daddy, Mama said.

I wish Daddy was a Injun, Little Lewis said.

What was he, anyway, Mama? Hiram asked.

Why, he was your daddy.

What kind of blood, I mean.

Foolish blood. You better hope you didn't get much of it.

English stock, Hannah Ruth remembered him telling her once. English and Scots-Irish. Ancestors came to these mountains before the Revolution and stayed and stayed because the mountains reminded them of the ones they'd had across the ocean. They felt at home and wanted more elbow room and so took to driving the Indians out.

I scarcely recollect him, Little Lewis said.

You was just a baby, Mama said. He took a notion to depart not long after you was borned. I was nursing you just like this one here.

I recollect him some, Hiram said. He was awful big, wasn't he.

Not so big, Mama said.

I believe he'll come back someday, Little Lewis said.

He ain't coming back, Mama said.

Do you know any Injun music, Little Lewis asked Pink.

Pink said he played a tune called "The Lost Indian," but didn't think an Indian made it up.

"The Lost Indian," Hiram said. How's that go.

Pink played it, and from the fiddle came the sound of the Indian whooping and hollering. It made Hannah Ruth's blood jump and stopped Singer Joe dead still in the middle of the room. When the tune was over, Singer Joe headed right to Mama, climbed onto her lap, and started snatching at the buttons on her dress.

Micky, micky, he said, his word for milk.

Keep your britches on, Mama said to him, sticking her nipple out for him, which he lost no time in sucking.

In bed that night in the room Daddy had meant for himself, Hannah Ruth felt a cool breeze with the faint smell of honeysuckle in it. Mama lay alongside her, breathing deeply, and Singer Joe slept in the trundle bed. Some nights he climbed into the big bed and snuggled up between her and Mama, but tonight he'd gone right to sleep.

She fancied that this was how the spirits of the dead made their way back, on breezes such as this one, in the dark of night. Maybe the tree frogs were really hants singing. They surely meant no harm, these hants, even Emmett Holt, should he be among those who visited her, and Esther, who would have had time by now to repent of her last curse. That curse had resounded in Hannah Ruth's head often at times such as this, as she lay waiting for sleep. *Go to hell.* The last thing she said to anybody, and she'd said it to her own sister. But death would surely take the spite out of you.

Little Sister, because she had lived such a short time and had less distance to travel, would be among the first of the spirits to arrive, getting here before sleep itself, while the old ancestors—Mama's mama Hannah Fugate whose red hair Hannah Ruth had inherited, and Mama's little brother Aaron, and all the others lined up back of them, going clear back to the ones freshly come from across the ocean—wouldn't arrive until deep in the night. They were the ones, she imagined, who led you from dream to dream into the stories of their lives whether you wanted to or not.

She heard a whispering sound, the rustling of leaves outside the window, and then something like a human sound, a muffled laugh, someone saying hush, hush, now. She thought of Esther again, pretty Esther with a handsome beau, maybe Dudley, maybe the hant of Esther had wooed Dudley away from his mama's house and would carry him to the land of the dead. A spirit had the power to change itself into any shape it wanted. Oh, you're imagining things, Hannah Ruth, she told herself, but she rose and looked out the window.

It was nobody but herself, she thought at first, herself escaping, running across the dewy grass, her dream of flight made plain as day in that dark night. But the woman outside, she saw soon enough, was Chloe, dear sister Chloe, suitcase in one hand, the other clutching the hand of that banjo-playing man Egbert Cook. It was Hannah Ruth's suitcase, too, the one Mama had given her when she went to Knoxville with Dudley Crider.

The next morning Mama said it was one less mouth to feed.

23

Dudley dreamed of devils with hands sprouting from their heads. Waking in a sweat, aching, he tossed and turned. The bed felt as though it had rocks in it.

Well, it did. He was outside on the hard ground, among numerous rocks.

He smelled smoke and heard a hissing, rasping noise. The smoke had a raw stench to it—must have been from his uncles' still. The sun shone in his eyes and Uncle U. S. was leaning over him.

He's awake, Crockett! Uncle U. S. said, his voice as close to shouting as it could get and still be a whisper. Uncle U. S. looked shorter than Dudley remembered, his shoulders hunched. He was clean-shaven and toothless and smelled sour.

We was worried about you, son.

Uncle Crockett came up beside Uncle U. S. He had a broad-brim gray hat on, and, unlike Uncle U. S., he appeared not to have shaved in about a week.

Dudley tried to sit up, but his back felt like somebody had stabbed him.

Easy, Uncle Crockett said.

We'll take care of you, son.

They brought him coffee, propping him up and pouring it down him. It tasted of mud and rotgut. He spit it out, told them just bring him the rotgut and hold the coffee. They laughed. You sound like your daddy, Uncle U. S. said.

I sure do miss old Milly, Uncle Crockett said.

Uncle U. S. laughed and laughed. You'd've thought this was about the funniest thing he'd ever heard.

Well, I do, Uncle Crockett said. Reckon you miss most anybody if they stay gone long enough.

Ain't he a card, Uncle U. S. said to Dudley, handing him the tin cup. This was fine rotgut and it set a fire in his belly.

Uncle U. S. held up what appeared to be a lady's hand mirror and looked into it. It had a silver frame and handle graven with flowers.

Reckon I'd best shave, he said, though he didn't look like he needed a shave.

Goin to a wedding? Uncle Crockett said.

I don't reckon.

He flicked open a long-handled razor and scraped it dry across his cheek. The mirror flashed sunlight in Dudley's eyes and he looked away, thinking it passing strange for Uncle U. S. to have such a pretty mirror, let alone bring it along with him out here in the woods. When he looked again, Uncle U. S. had laid the razor on a rock. A bright line of red curved across his cheek. God damn, he said, holding the mirror to his face.

Mought as well cut your throat while you're at it, Uncle Crockett said. And then, to Dudley: You see before your very eyes what love of the ladies will do to a man.

Love! Uncle U. S. said. He spit upon a blue bandanna and dabbed at his cheek with it. Don't talk to me about love, Uncle U. S. said.

You're going down to Elizabethton, is what I reckon, ain't you.

Who said anything about love.

Uncle Crockett laughed, slapping his knee.

He is a married man, you see, he said to Dudley.

So am I, Dudley said.

And I, Uncle Crockett said. And old enough to know better than go gallivantin down to Elizabethton.

A man ain't always satisfied, Uncle U. S. said. He put the pretty mirror and the razor in a leather pouch with a thong looping out from it.

I'm going now, he said.

And he walked briskly into the trees, the pouch hanging from his shoulder.

Dudley felt improved. Uncle Crockett kept passing the whiskey jar.

He laughed when Dudley told him about seeing Uncle Fremont in the abandoned house. Crazy as a loon, Uncle Crockett said. Poor old Fremont. Wanders all over. Lives in the woods, sleeps wherever he lies down. He don't hurt nobody. Carries that old Silver War rifle and says he's hunting for Milly. It's a bad batch of popskull done it to him. He's got to where he'll drink anything, don't you know.

Says he's looking for my daddy?

Says he's aiming to kill him, son. It was always bad blood between them two.

Daddy's dead. Ain't he?

Uncle Crockett laughed.

You might say so, he said. We buried him, anyway.

How's Uncle Fremont going to kill him, then?

Ought to be easier second time around, way I figure it.

They kept drinking. Tree frogs were loud from not so far off.

Once I had me a little son, Uncle Crockett said. Departed this life, age of three years. Run over by a train. You got a boy of your own, I heared tell.

Two of them, Dudley said.

You don't say. Two sons!

Dudley told him how he'd not been permitted to be a father to either of those boys. It seemed the truth and he felt the full force of the injustice of it.

Why that ain't right, Uncle Crockett said. A man oughtn't to stand still for such treatment without doing something.

After a few more swallows they vowed to go down into the world and right the wrongs done to Dudley. But Uncle Crockett found he couldn't stand without a good deal of trouble, and Dudley felt puny himself.

Waking later, though, he remembered the injustice and knew exactly what it was he had to do.

Hannah Ruth woke to the sound of Mama shouting from the kitchen:

He's gone, my baby's gone!

The first thought that came into Hannah Ruth's head was: Your baby? What do you mean *your* baby? The second thought was: This is Dudley's doing, Dudley's mischief.

She rose quickly, pulling on her smock as she headed into the kitchen. Mama sat at the table with her head laid down upon it, weeping, Hiram standing to one side of her, Little Lewis to the other, both of them patting her and stroking her hair. Lewetta sat next to her, holding onto her hand.

Gone in the dead of night, Mama said. My baby, oh, my sweet child.

What do you mean, gone?

It was a hant, Hiram said, come in the dead of night. I heard the planks a-creakin and saw a hant carrying Singer Joe out the door.

What'd it look like, Little Lewis said.

Like a man that was dead.

You saw, Mama said, a man come in and carry off Singer Joe and you didn't do a thing to stop him? Where is he? Where has he taken my baby boy?

I think I know, all right, Hannah Ruth said, for she had a clear image in her mind, as if just awakened from a dream, of Dudley slipping into the house. With the knowledge of his treachery came a sudden sense of power. This is how a mother is supposed to feel, she said to herself.

I'll go get him, she said.

You better go get Sheriff Shope. That's what you better do, child.

I want to take care of this business myself, she said.

All right, Mama said. Then I'm going, too.

Me, too, Lewetta said, echoed by Hiram and Little Lewis.

Hush up, Mama said. It's right for Hannah Ruth to go. It's her business, I reckon. The rest of you stay put.

A big clap of thunder broke.

Heaven help, Mama said. It's going to come up a storm and that child's out there somewhere in it.

Pink came in, breathing heavily, his face flushed. He carried a poke in one hand.

Why, good morning, he said. I got us some catfish. You all ain't et yet, have you?

Catfish, Mama said. A time like this.

Good anytime, Pink said, and he lifted from the poke three catfish hanging from a string, their heads big as a man's fists.

24.

Dudley set the boy down in front of his mama.

Praise Jesus, she said, and she lifted Singer Joe up off of the floor. He squirmed a little, his eyes shut tight, and she carried him to her chair, put him on her lap, and stroked his hair.

I'd a recognized him in a crowd, she said. Look at that curly yellow hair. That's my mama's hair.

He's blind, Dudley said.

Sweet Jesus.

How'd you get him, O. T. asked.

I went and got him. He's my boy. I'm his daddy.

He remembered the sense of rightness and the pleasure of slipping into that bedroom in the dead of night, seeing Hannah Ruth sleeping— she wore that old pink nightgown he'd given her, and he felt an urge to slip into bed alongside her, give her a good surprise. But seeing her mama there beside her, snoring to beat the band, and the boy in the trundle bed, he recalled his mission.

The boy woke up, but didn't make a sound. He surely knew it was his daddy come for him. Dudley carried him for a while, then put him down and let him walk. The boy never complained. He stayed quiet.

Now, though, on Mama's lap, he began to yowl.

Mama patted him on the back, which calmed him some. O. T. smiled and raised both hands into the air.

Praise Jesus, he said. Hold that little fellow still, Mama. I hear you, Jesus. I'm a-listening.

O. T.'s arms flapped up and down and then his big hands came down on Singer Joe's head, pressing.

Lord Godamercy, he said, come on down and do your work. Make us your vessels, Jesus honey.

Amen, Mama said, and she grabbed the boy's shoulders while O. T. kept bearing down on his head, calling out Jesus, Jesus, sweet Jesus, come here and open our eyes, his own eyes closed, shut tight, his jaw clenched, his big hands with their long fingers squeezing down upon the head of Singer Joe. And O. T. said:

Oh, yes, I feel the power now. Feel it, son. Feel the awful power coming down, a-running through you.

In truth, Dudley felt something himself, a shivery feeling, and wondered if Jesus was getting to him and his boy, two birds with one stone.

Singer Joe let out a yowl so loud it made Mama jump. Hush, you, she said, and she slapped that blind boy hard upside his head.

Say, now, Dudley said. Wait just a minute.

Mama took the boy from O. T. and shook him. Singer Joe hushed then. He hushed so much he appeared to have stopped breathing. Then he began to suck in the air. It looked as though he wanted to howl but couldn't. There was a red mark on his cheek where she had slapped him. Mama handed him back to O. T., and O. T. started talking crazy.

Dudley had a sour taste in his mouth. He cleared his throat. It was something he wanted to say. He didn't know what. A speck of heat jumped in the top of his head, then flicked on down, right quick, flaming up in his throat, exploding into his lungs, shooting back up and outward into his arms. He watched his arms jerk out, his fingers starting to wiggle.

I ain't myself, it occurred to him.

I ain't nobody else neither.

Who am I then?

You are a vessel, he heard someone say—but it wasn't anybody there saying it. A goddamn vessel of Jesus, the voice said, you sorry son of a bitch.

What he heard himself say was: Gimme back that boy.

He could not have said what he meant to do with Singer Joe if they handed him over to him, but it didn't matter because O. T. didn't step aside. He kept right on, and all three of them shaking, O. T. and Singer Joe and Mama, Mama beginning to babble as well, her eyes closed, her arms wrapped around Singer Joe's chest while O. T. kept on pressing down both hands on the boy's head.

Then that other voice rose above Mama's and O. T.'s, and it was his daddy's voice, he knew it now, and it was saying, Son, if you ain't right, get right.

What did Daddy know about getting right.

Depends on what you mean by right.

All right, then. Where are you, Daddy.

Here. Don't you see me?

I don't see nothing.

I'm here.

You ain't nowhere.

We're in the same place, boy, together, you and me.

You hurt me, Daddy.

That's what daddies do, you fool son.

All of a sudden it was quiet.

O. T. was looking at Dudley. So was Mama. Singer Joe sat still as a stone. He might have been looking at Dudley, too, if he could see.

Is the Lord speaking through you, Dudley? O. T. asked. Is it the Holy Spirit surging in you, brother? Hallelujah, Jesus be praised!

Dudley meant to say no, but his tongue quivered and his body jumped up, all electric with Jesus and Daddy gone back to wherever he came from. He felt compelled to sing, him that could hardly carry a tune in a bucket.

Dear Jesus, he said, I done forgot all the words. How do you expect me to sing.

Just sing, damn it, Jesus said. You think anybody gives a good god-damn about the words?

So he sang. He sang a lullaby for his blind boy.

Instead of going to sleep, the boy began to sing right along with Dudley. Why, they made music together. Something like music, anyway. A father and his son. Who was to say it wasn't happening, and that boy seeing him, too, yes, now he looked and saw. Dudley felt surefire seen where before he had been hidden.

Go to sleep, honeychild, they sang together, looking each other eye to eye.

And the Lord said again, Didn't I just tell you, it ain't about the words, you poor son.

Why, no, Jesus. I see that now.

It's about the singing.

I understand now, Jesus.

You don't understand a damn thing.

Well, I'm trying.

Keep trying. I'm a-telling you.

Jesus was almost as bad as his daddy. It seemed like no matter what he might do, it wouldn't be enough for Jesus. He quit singing. So did the boy.

But Singer Joe kept looking at him with his blank eyes.

I'm your daddy, Dudley said, or wanted to say.

The boy stared with his unseeing eyes, Mama hugged him, and then O. T. pressed his hands onto the boy's head again and raised them up, his fingers wiggling like worms.

And O. T. spit on the floor and said:

As long as I am in the world, I am the light of the world.

O. T. leaned down and rubbed his finger in his spit, took that spittened, dirt-smudged finger and stroked it across Singer Joe's eyes, saying:

Blessed are the pure in heart, for they shall see God.

Mama hugged the boy to her breast.

Poor child, she said. Now he can see.

Interlude:

Singer Joe

Early on, he learned lips, soft and slick, his mama's lips moving to his touch, the tongue tucked neatly back of the teeth like another finger, secret, safe, warm, easily aroused to motion. Was it ticklish? Auntie Lewetta's lips were drier but still soft, the teeth rougher, uneven. Best of all, Esther, with her lolling tongue, her lips that tightened around his finger, muffling the teeth, the sucking that made him laugh, made him want her to do it again and again, until she pulled his finger loose, squeezing it hard in her palm, saying, Now, that's enough, hear! I got better things to do than suck on your finger all day.

Noses came next, and easy, once you took the meaning of slope and curve and made sense of the quivers and wiggles. Hiram's nose had the liveliest array of bumps. Little Lewis's made out like a bandit with the air, huffing and wheezing and whistling.

Ears, hair, the way a neck went so suddenly down, becoming shoulder, collarbone, breast before you knew it. Eyes last of all, eyes most mysterious, don't touch, no, that hurts, honey, mustn't poke Mama in the eyes.

Eyes: soft, moist toothless mouths that will neither bite nor let you in. Helpless things, all a flutter, as if they might take flight. To see means to understand, to know. His life, he knew, was more than metaphor. He was seen; therefore he was. He did not see; therefore the world was not.

There was only himself, afloat in what he would not even know enough to call darkness until his hands told him so.

Bless these hands that bring me light.

With the light came singing. You made sense of air, of distance, of *themness,* and, even before your tongue found words, along came music, a humming in your soul. There was nothing wrong with his vocal cords.

He began pestering Auntie Lewetta for a guitar by the time he was six years old. A blind boy, you had to do something for him. He heard her say it, more than once.

Hell fire, Hiram said, let his mama do something.

She shut up then. There was no telling, of course, where his mama was back then.

But it was Hiram who found the money, bought the guitar, Hiram who listened, who said when nobody else was around, Son, you can play that thing. Hiram who sobbed when he, Singer Joe, sang.

And wasn't that a fine feeling, to know you had that, that your voice could do that to somebody.

I don't have no music in me, Hiram said, not a bit. It passed me on by. Hannah Ruth is the one, now. Why, your mama, Singer Joe, your mama was a musicianer!

Among other things, yes, she was a musicianer, Hiram. Who could doubt it. She passes in and out of time, is no place and everywhere. Reach for her, you get nothing. Sit still, set your tongue to humming, strum a few chords on the guitar, and there she is. It's as if there's no place else to be.

More. It was to see from inside the darkness and know what it meant and how it felt. It meant nothing. It felt fine. It was where your music came from.

Part Four:

Dudley and Son

25

Amelia had a child, and she loved that child.

Her Alex.

Hannah Ruth's Alex. Emmett's Alex. She said the words again and again. They made no difference. Alex was as good as her own son.

Oh, Emmett, Emmett. You should see me now, brother.

Lord, for that matter, you should see our mother. A letter came this week. Mother is in San Francisco, Emmett. Would you believe that? Our hidebound, white-clad, Bible-toting mama is in San Francisco, about as far from our father as she can get. She left him on the eve of their thirty-sixth wedding anniversary. Fifty-five years old. That took a certain nerve, wouldn't you say.

Of course your sudden, dramatic departure had something to do with it. I thought, for a time, she might find solace in her grandson Alex. Instead, she seemed to waste away, but when the warm days of April set in, I saw the color come back to her face, along with a kind of determination I'd never seen before.

And then she was gone. Not even a letter until this week, two months after her departure, though there have been reports along the way, from Aunt Judith in Knoxville, from Uncle Waldo in Memphis. Uncle Waldo tried, he wrote, to persuade her to return to her home, to her husband and hearth, as he put it. Aunt Judith claimed that Mother was a changed woman, full of energy and life, and could never go back. Fancy that—our mother!

Father is a shadow of his former self, but that is not such a bad thing, after all. He scarcely attends to business anymore. I did his work for a while. I could do it, you know. I have a knack for making the deal, the gentleman's agreement. I am still a tolerably pretty woman, don't you know, pretty enough to take those plump, red-faced bankers and brokers by surprise. But Father could never accommodate himself to the idea of his daughter's taking care of his business—of any business at all outside the hearth. It was not ladylike. He would have preferred a son for a partner, an heir. You, in short, dear Emmett.

I tried, brother, I studied being a lady, ever since my days at Miss Gordon's Academy. Eventually, it didn't matter what Father thought. When the business no longer mattered, why, then, I could do what I pleased with it. Nothing pleased him when Mother was here. Nothing pleases him now she's gone.

The family fortune has a life of its own. I have not squandered it and have possibly extended its life.

I like our sad deserted father. I think you might even like him a little. He has qualities, no doubt, that did not exist until our mother left. An irony you'd appreciate.

Is that what sorrow is for? To cleanse us of spiritual impurities?

The child is yours, Emmett. Anybody can look into his eyes and see it. Father, I'm sure, has seen it. He takes the child to his arms, tries to, tears welling up in his eyes, and Alex pulls away. Thirteen months old and he turns away. Even from me, he runs.

He will be provided for. Our father, in his youthful greed, saw to that. Had Father given vent to the tenderness arising now from his sorrow, it likely would have been otherwise for us. He's of no use now, Emmett. I love him, our now-useless old father, I cherish the sound of his footsteps on the stairs. Yes, I do.

I keep your ladylike pistol, brother, in my desk drawer. I take it out and wipe the dust from it with my lace-edged handkerchief. I spirit it off to the creekbank and take aim at crawdads. One day I shot at a squirrel, almost hit it. I keep its chamber loaded, brother, in your memory, and I have taken it to my mouth and tasted its barrel. If I did not have your son, I might consider a repeat performance of your little drama, Emmett. Not a day passes that I don't take out the pistol. I see you in myself. We go on, don't we, one way or another.

26

All the way to the creek, a good mile's walk through all manner of thorny underbrush and sudden rocks, O. T. called out the names of things for Singer Joe to see. When the boy took to whining, Dudley picked him up and carried him. Mama had stayed behind to pray.

The creek didn't run so deep this time of year, but O. T. found an eddy so clear you could see the rocks gleaming on the bottom and tadpoles scooting and skittering, and at this place he took Singer Joe from Dudley and dipped him into the water sideways, swished him around, saying:

Oh, my brethren, hearken to my words and look ye upon the signs and wonders.

While O. T. preached, the water swirled around Singer Joe and over him. Dudley, watching from the bank, hoped the boy wouldn't drown. He had become fond of the little fellow.

In the name of Jesus, Son of God, O. T. shouted at last, holding Singer Joe's head beneath the water, I pronounce this boy reborn!

Up from the muddy water, Singer Joe's face looked about the same as it did when he was blind, even with the creek water streaming down.

The way back was all uphill. The boy, heavy as sin, wouldn't walk to save his life, and O. T. wouldn't take a turn carrying him, saying it was a duty for the boy's father. When they saw Mama she was sitting in the rocker on the porch, drinking from a fruit jar. She put the jar down and jumped up when she saw them. The boy squirmed as though wanting loose, and so Dudley put him down. Before he could grab hold of Singer Joe's hand, the boy had lit out for the house. You'd have thought he saw it clear as day. He went straight for Mama, who was shouting at the top of her lungs: *Praise Jesus, praise Jesus!*

She pulled the boy to her and took off his wet clothes and washed him and dried him and laid him clean on a pallet. He went right to sleep, bless his heart, and Dudley, tired himself, stretched out next to him. When Dudley woke up, he smelled cornbread and Mama had Singer Joe on her lap at the table. O. T. was already seated. Dudley joined them. Singer Joe grabbed at everything, turnip greens and black-eyed peas and pickled beets and cornbread alike. Red juice from the beets trickled down his chin. When he stopped eating, he started moaning. It wasn't much louder than a hound's whine, but unsettling all the same.

Then the boy twisted around and begun to grope at Mama's chest.

Lordy, Lordy, she said, baring her breast. I don't reckon you'll find a drap of milk there, child.

That child went at it, anyway.

He's seeing real good now, O. T. said. I know he is.

You reckon? Dudley said.

O. T. grinned and said he believed both Dudley and his boy had seen the light this morning, but Dudley wasn't so sure.

Why, O. T. said, you was a caterwauling for the Lord, brother. You was taking a big through. Wasn't he, Mama.

Jesus might have come down, Mama said softly. She stroked the boy's forehead while he sucked at her dry tit.

Why, I felt the brush of His wings, O. T. said. The air got cold and still and I felt light as a feather.

He don't come light as no feather, Mama said.

Call on Him and He cometh, O. T. said.

He cometh, Mama said, whether you call on Him or not.

Dudley felt cleaned out, scrubbed raw inside. He couldn't state the nature of what had happened to him. A-singing. His voice a-singing. Tears coming to his eyes.

I'll take you to the creek, brother, O. T. said, putting down his saucer. I'll babtize you.

You ain't going to dunk me in no creek, Dudley said.

O. T. laughed.

Leave him be, Mama said, the boy dozing now against her chest.

Why, he's ripe for saving, Mama, O. T. said. The Lord done spoke through him.

Let somebody else dunk him.

Keep it in the family, way I see it.

It ain't family business.

Didn't I cure that boy, my blood kin, my own nephew? Wasn't it my hands laid upon him that give him back his eyes. And didn't I dunk him?

The Lord will destroy the house of the proud.

Mama, I am chastened.

You deserve to be chastened, for you speak with the mouth of a fool.

Aw, Mama.

I don't care to be babtized, Dudley said, but nobody seemed to hear him except Singer Joe, who opened his eyes and said, Bab-tie. He seemed to be looking across the way, out the window. Light rippled on the windowpanes.

A big clap of thunder broke.

Where you going now? O. T. asked. Dudley hadn't realized he had moved towards the door.

I got other business to attend to, he said, wondering what that business might be.

It's a storm a-coming for sure, O. T. said. No weather for a babtizing, anyways.

I'm taking him with me, he said. Gimme my boy.

Why, you can leave him here, Mama said. I reckon I can take care of a little tyke like this.

Mama, gimme my boy.

Mama handed over Singer Joe. The boy whimpered a little, but then was calm. He knows me, Dudley thought, hefting the boy onto his shoulders. He knows his daddy. He ain't as heavy as he was before.

The rain came down so hard you could scarcely see past the end of your arm, but Hannah Ruth was lost well before that. When Dudley had led her through these tangled paths to his mama's house last winter, the path had not been so narrowed by twisting vines and weeds. Now, in the driving rain, Pink pulled her off the path, onto a rock ledge where it was dry and with space to sit. The rain streamed around the rock like a curtain.

Think we're about there? Pink asked, shivering, his long legs drawn up in front of him, his arms wrapped around his knees.

I don't know, she said. We may be lost.

Oh, he said, grinning and running his hand through his wet hair. I figured as much a while back.

Thunder and lightning broke all around them. Branches fell. Gullies filled with rushing, riling water. She found herself wanting to tell him she was glad he had come with her, but you couldn't hear yourself talk above the rain and thunder.

She did not like the way being close to him was making her feel. He might have taken her in his arms and she wouldn't have complained. Wishing he might kiss her, she remembered Dudley, not the Dudley who stole her son from her in the night, but the Dudley who returned to her in that hotel room above the viaduct in Knoxville. Oh, she had loved him well enough then, well enough to conceive a child, the very child she now searched for. And she remembered Amelia, the first time Amelia had kissed her, so sweet, yes, but not the same as what she was feeling now for Pink Miracle under this rock ledge, her body wet and shaking.

I'm not a good person, she said to herself as she let him draw her close to him.

This way, she said to him, guiding his good hand to her breast.

The boy grew heavier fast and kept twitching. Dudley tried carrying him frontways, then shifted him onto his back, finally onto his shoulders. Nothing suited.

Well, walk then. See how you like it. Do you think I like carrying you? I been sick, you know.

For a while the little fellow would toddle along, hanging onto Dudley's hand.

It was thunder and lightning everywhere and now the rain was starting.

We are Criders and don't have no fear, he told the boy, and he imagined some of O. T., some of Uncle Crockett and Uncle U. S., some of

Daddy, some of himself, yes, and then all the Criders before them, granddaddies and grandmamas by the score, crowded up in Singer Joe's veins.

Then he reckoned he'd have to account for his mama's people. Crinch blood. Kin to some Indian princess, she said. Redbird. Redwing. Redeye. Mama didn't seem much like a princess. It was Bayless blood, too, and all them Fugates that was Hannah Ruth's mama's kinfolk, such as Nimrod Fugate the preacher and surely others back deep in the hollers and high up on the knobs, breeding and carrying on.

Surely a daddy counted for more than the rest, didn't he? But that brought him back to himself and his own daddy, and he quit that line of thinking.

He meant to take the short cut up over the mountain that would lead him near the still. He would leave the boy with Uncle Crockett, who would be as happy as if his own lost son come back to him. This notion occurred to him shortly after leaving his mama's house, as the boy began to get heavy.

In the meantime, he was soaked to the bone, the thunder getting closer and closer, and the boy clamoring to be carried again. He hefted him onto his back. Thunder clapped so close then that he expected a tree to shoot up in flames. None did, but at that moment he saw something that was just about as scarifying.

It was all grown over, a tangle of sawbrier and chokeweed and spidery blackberry, and there wasn't a marker, but he could see through the underbrush how the ground dipped downward ever so slight for about six foot.

It was his daddy's grave.

Come on, he told the boy, yanking on his hand. We got to get on.

And then he heard a voice echoing his.

Get on, it said. Get on.

It was the boy.

That's right, he said to the boy. We got to get on.

A clap of thunder sounded like it hit right in front of them, the flash following straightaway, and the boy squeezed Dudley's neck so tight he almost couldn't breathe.

Let up a little, son, he said, pulling Singer Joe's hands loose. I ain't going to let you get hurt.

He imagined himself fallen to the ground, struck by lightning, having thrown himself in front of the boy to protect him.

I'd do that, he told himself. Yes, I would. Protect my boy from the flame of lightning.

The boy began to kick him in the ribs.

Quit, now.

And the boy quit. Minded his daddy.

The sky was almost dark as night now, and it only some past midday. Thunder crashed and in the next instant the flashing light. The rain came faster, harder, and the wind whipped up, a roaring in the trees. The boy clung fast, choking him, and then Dudley felt his foot come down on nothing but pure air. They went down.

Late in the afternoon the storm clouds broke and for a while the sun shone through the leaves, glazing the brilliant green that everywhere poked up and sprawled and twisted and twined and bunched. The clapboard house in the midst of caved-in relics of houses appeared in such a heavy mist that it might have been afloat on a cloud.

Hannah Ruth's clothes had dried, but mud streaked on her skirt, caked on the soles of her boots, and her hair was tangled. Pink's shirt-sleeves were stained red by the mud. What they had been up to would be obvious, she thought, to a suspicious person such as Dudley's mother, who stood in the doorway, every bit as tall as Pink, her chin thrust forward.

And what might your business be, she asked.

I've come, she said, for my son.

Ain't nobody's son here, child.

He's gone. This morning he was gone.

They do go away.

Ma'am, Pink said, the child is only three years old.

What business is it of yours, sir, Dudley's mama said, squinting her eyes, training them on Pink.

I'm with her, he said, not flinching a bit.

Well, you're barking up the wrong tree.

Where's Dudley, Hannah Ruth asked.

Ain't no business of yours.

He's my husband.

I know who you are.

It went on like that for a good five or ten minutes, the sun making its way through the clouds, and then Dudley's mama said, as though she'd been waiting for the sun: The boy's healed, Jesus be praised. Him that was blind, now can see.

She smiled ever so slightly, scarcely disturbing a wrinkle, and then actually bowed slightly, moving to one side.

Worsh yourself off at the pump, she said.

Rinsing her face in the cool water, Hannah Ruth didn't doubt that Singer Joe had been made to see. At a brush arbor meeting when she was about seven years old, she saw a blind man throw away his dark glasses and cane and stride all around the tent, greeting friends and relations with hearty handshakes and hugs, tears glazing his eyes. The big, scary preacher gave her an evil stare. She knew even then that he probably looked at everybody that way, seeking sin, but at the time she had felt singled out, her sinfulness of special interest to him, arousing his righteous anger, yes, but something else, something, she would say now, like desire.

Yet he'd cured a blind man.

It was a little storm we had there, wadn't it, Dudley's mother said, standing at the door when they came back from the pump. I reckon you folks must've been caught in it.

She smiled her little smile again. She knows, Hannah Ruth thought. She knows exactly how we spent our time waiting out that big thunderstorm.

We was wetted down some, Pink said. Yes, ma'am, we surely was.

Plenty dry now, I take it?

Why, yes, Pink said, and his cheeks flamed up red.

And hungry? she asked. Would you take a bite of cornbread and greens?

I'd be much obliged, ma'am, Pink said.

They followed her into the kitchen.

Take a seat, she said.

She brought a skillet of cornbread and a pot of greens off the stove. The cornbread was thick and golden, and the greens smelled good and fresh.

Buttermilk? she asked.

If it ain't too much trouble, Pink said.

Dudley's mother stepped out onto the back porch and returned with a pitcher of buttermilk, which she set on the table. From the cabinet she drew down two tumblers, setting one before each of them and then getting spoons from a drawer. Pink, working fast, had the buttermilk poured, cornbread crumbled, and was spooning the mixture into his mouth by the time Hannah Ruth had finished breaking up her own portion of cornbread.

Wait just a minute, son, Dudley's mother said. Let us give thanks.

Pink stopped chewing and bowed his head. Dudley's mother, standing at the head of the table, leaned forward, her palms pressed against the tabletop, her head bowed, and said:

Lord God A-mighty, lead us not into temptation and deliver us from evil. In Jesus' name, Amen.

Amen, Pink said, resuming his chewing. Hannah Ruth was powerfully hungry herself and started in.

It was a satisfying meal, the greens tasty from soaking in fatback. Between the two of them, they finished off the entire pan of cornbread, eating some on the side with butter, crumbling the rest into the cool, tart buttermilk. Watching Pink saucer his coffee, she remembered their mission.

We'd be grateful, she said, for word of Singer Joe.

Singer Joe?

My son. Your grandson that Dudley brought here. You said he was healed.

O. T. babtized the child. I don't hold to no infant babtism, but it wadn't no stopping him. I reckon it don't hurt none. He's with his daddy now.

Oh, Hannah Ruth said. And where might that be?

Why, I reckon Dudley's took that boy back to his home. I wished he'd let the boy stay awhile, but he don't pay his old mama much mind. Never did, no, not a lick. Now, O. T., why, he takes care of his old mama. I'll say that for him. Don't have a grain of sense in his head, but he knows his duty to his mama. Yes, he does.

Listen here, she said at the door, you bring that boy here again sometime. It ain't right for a child to grow up without knowing his old granny.

The lanky, black-eyed woman standing over him like some angel of vengeance put Pink in mind of his daddy coming into the soddy after a day's plowing, knowing it was no hope.

Still, he was hungry and the cornbread was good.

He admired Hannah Ruth's determination. A mother she was, for sure. It warmed his heart, still plenty warm from when they'd stretched out beneath the rock ledge, soaked to the bone. He wouldn't've thought her a mother then. Wouldn't have thought, period. Didn't. That was the pleasure, not to think.

Holding her, he felt as though he was again slipping out of that soddy, fiddle in hand, while his daddy slept. Outside, it was the sky, big and starry, and the war had never been. A warmth came over him like nothing else.

A higher power, the woman said. She reckoned her son answered to a higher power.

The power was here, though, in his blood, beating its way away from home, carrying him where he needed to be.

27

Dudley felt the warmth of the boy's piss before he smelled it. Well, say. Didn't that beat all. A fellow that had fallen down a mountainside, been soaked by the rain, scratched up by rock and thorn, slathered with mud, pissed on by his own son.

The rain, anyway, had stopped. He could move his free arm and hand, and his feet turned tolerably. The other arm, trapped beneath him, hurt some, but likely was just scraped from all the rocks and roots.

The boy had a good grip, all right, keeping hold on him while they fell, a strong little sucker, pretty much squeezing the breath out of his daddy before they came to a stop, and now hanging on like a leech and moaning.

Aw, hush up, now, hear? he said to the boy. You ain't the one got pissed on.

To his surprise, the boy quietened, though breathing heavy and squeezing him hard around the neck again, but then, clear as day, he said:

Piss on you?

You sure did, you little sucker. I ain't going to hold it against you, though.

He tried to raise himself up. It was rough going. They were bent over at an awkward angle in a kind of trough, the ground rising up steep on both sides, water still rushing around them.

Listen, he told the boy, let up on the old man's neck a little, okay? I ain't going to leave you here. We're going after your little brother.

The boy loosened his hold on Dudley's neck enough so that Dudley could pull himself up and grab hold of a root, but Singer Joe weighed too much and he still couldn't raise himself up.

Let go of me a minute, he told the boy.

Singer Joe squeezed harder.

Now, let go of me, boy, for just a minute. I told you I ain't going to leave you.

He tried to talk soft to the boy, not to frighten him.

Once I get myself up, he said, I'll pick you right up again.

Singer Joe kept squeezing.

All right, then. We'll just lay here and rot, I reckon.

Then he heard something. It was somebody singing and it wasn't so far away:

I heard the thunder roaring, roaring, roaring,
I heard the thunder roaring in that great day.
Take your wings in the morning, sound the jubilee.
Take your wings in the morning, to Jesus fly away.

He thought at first it must be O. T. But then the hymn was interrupted by a laugh, and he knew it was his uncles up there above him on the path, old U. S. and Crockett.

Hey, he shouted. Here I am.

Hannah Ruth and Pink reached the Elizabethton Pike in half the time of the trip up the mountain, and easily caught rides from there down to Bristol. From the bottom of the hill to Mary Street, her mother's house in the early evening light looked good to her, looked in fact like the little cabin home on the hill sung about in all the sentimental songs, though it wasn't really a cabin and she never felt at home there.

Mama was sitting on the front porch with a man next to her—Dudley, she imagined from a distance, having returned Singer Joe. Her heart felt eased. They were returned to calm, surely.

But Singer Joe wasn't there, and the man seated next to Mama was Cloyd Shope, the Bristol, Tennessee, sheriff. They were waving cardboard funeral-parlor fans in front of their faces. Both stood up as she and Pink approached.

Evening, Sheriff Shope said. Quite a little storm this morning, wadn't it.

He ain't come back, is he, Mama said to her. You ain't brung him back.

Sheriff Cloyd Shope clumped down the steps in shiny, high-heel cowboy boots. His pants were tucked into the top of his boots. In one hand he held a broad-brim gray Stetson, in the other the cardboard fan. Hiram came from around the side of the house, Little Lewis close behind.

Hannah Ruth, they said.

Pink took hold of her hand.

You all right, honey? Sheriff Shope asked her.

I'm fine, thank you, Hannah Ruth said, Pink clasping her hand gently, and she thought again of their time in the storm, the press of his body against hers.

I understand we got a missing child here, the sheriff said.

He's not missing, Hannah Ruth said. He's with his daddy.

The sheriff appeared not to hear her.

Taken in the middle of the night, he said, by a mysterious stranger.

It was his daddy, Hannah Ruth said.

I believe it was a hant, Hiram said.

The sheriff smiled, as if a hant was right in his line of work, altogether better than a daddy.

She tried to explain how it was Dudley who had come for Singer Joe, but as soon as she touched on why he might have needed to come in the middle of the night, she began to falter in her own belief. Pink wasn't much help. He stammered a few words about their talk with Dudley's mother. The woman seemed truthful, he said, but Hannah Ruth heard no conviction in his voice either.

He ain't never bringing that boy back, Mama said.

Well, ma'am, Cloyd Shope said. A daddy has certain rights in the eye of the law.

We ain't seen hide nor hair of our daddy in a coon's age, Little Lewis said.

I wished he'd come and get us, Hiram said. One day I'm going out to Texas. Yes, I am. I'll know him when I see him. Kindly tall. A big man. I recollect him well.

It was dark in the little hut, no lantern allowed for the sake of secrecy. A fire flickered under the still, but mostly below ground level so that you wouldn't likely see it. Uncle Crockett, sitting close enough so that his knee now and then rubbed up against Dudley's, smelled rank. Uncle U. S. had gone off to his sweetheart in Elizabethton. You could hear, when Uncle Crockett stopped talking, the steady breathing of Singer Joe, asleep on a pallet on the ground, his head pressed up against Dudley's foot as though it was a pillow.

The little fellow had hardly complained at all while Uncle Crockett and Uncle U. S. pulled them up from the mud-slick gully and back onto the deer path. Then he'd kept up with them for a goodly distance, hanging on to his daddy's hand, stepping briskly along as if he really did see his way ahead of him, so that Dudley began almost to believe in the healing. When he got tired, he didn't whine. He just stopped dead still. At first Dudley, sore all over from the fall and not caring to lift the boy onto his back, tugged at him, tried to get him moving again, but it was no use. He carried the boy most of the time.

Now, outside the hut somewhere, an owl hissed and yowled like a cat whose tail just got stepped on. Uncle Crockett handed the jar of whiskey to Dudley. It tasted fine.

Uncle Crockett professed to being weary. Blockading was hard work, he wanted Dudley to know. In the olden days, he said, why, it was your old daddy Millard holping, and Fremont, too, and U. S., and we made us a team. Your papa had a good eye for a bead, as good as ary a man I ever knew. Times he mought tilt that jar and eyeball the bead of the liquor, and he'd say, No, sir, it ain't right, it won't do, and set it back down, and then Fremont would take and add some lye to it—that gives it a right smart semblance of a bead, don't you know—and a smidgen of ginger and tobacky before we could make that popskull something we mought sell.

Hard work never hurt no one. No, sir.

Singer Joe was making little whistling sounds in his sleep.

But now Milly's gone, and there's Fremont, out in the woods, hunting for a dead man, shooting up everything that moves, and U. S. chasing after a girl in Elizabethton.

He paused to open another fruit jar. The whiskey was as good as any Dudley'd ever tasted, surely no popskull.

I'll tell you what, Uncle Crockett said. Damn fool prohibition will shut down all them big stilleries. We're going to have folks from ever town and city coming down here for their liquor. I'm telling you, it's a boom a-coming.

Dudley reached down and touched Singer Joe's head, ran his fingers through the thick head of hair. He would have the other boy here soon, the little one living up in the big house. He'd raise them boys up to love their papa, and he'd love them back.

If you jine up with us, boy, Uncle Crockett was saying, I guarantee you won't live to regret it. Keep the profits in the family, what I say. Damn sure can't trust no one else. Soon enough, this boy of yours'll be old enough to help out.

Dudley saw himself learning everything about the making of the whiskey and then, a good daddy, teaching his own boys. Singer Joe could do it, he was sure, and in time so could the other one.

Uncle Crockett handed him the fruit jar.

So what do you say, son.

Count me in, Dudley said.

28

Mama paced and threatened and fumed. A week had passed with no sight of Singer Joe, and Dudley still on the loose.

Any sign of him? she asked Hiram and Little Lewis, who had undertaken their own search.

No, ma'am, Hiram said sheepishly. But we brung you some huckleberries.

I ain't studying no cobbler, Mama said.

A few minutes later, Sheriff Cloyd Shope drove up in his Model-T, much to the delight of the boys, who asked if they might sit in it and were given cheerful permission. The sheriff came up to the porch panting and huffing as if he'd just walked ten miles uphill. Hannah Ruth gave up her chair to him and Mama was all over him with questions, most that he couldn't answer.

Yes, he said to one of the easy ones, he was certainly in touch with Sheriff Burl Bateman over on the Virginia side, though of course the deed was done in the state of Tennessee. Furthermore, he would remind them that he had some knowledge of the Criders—his daddy's third and current wife was Rosanelle Crinch, a cousin once-removed of Pearlie Crinch, Dudley's mama—and he pointed out that Criders had strange ways sometimes.

Pearlie Crinch? Mama said.

Yes, that is correct, he said. A fine woman. Upright and sanctified. Rued the day she ever let herself be courted by Millard Crider.

Everybody has got regrets, Mama said, and she looked over to Hannah Ruth and added, Or might ought to have them.

Hannah Ruth would not defend Dudley nor herself. Truth to tell, she thought Dudley might be worse than Mama even imagined, though in some ways better, too, but she wasn't about to say that to Mama.

I reckon we'll find him, the sheriff said. Ain't no crime been committed, far as I can see, though. A daddy with his son ain't grand larceny.

Shit, Mama said.

Beg pardon, ma'am?

I'll fotch him myself.

Surely, ma'am.

And Sheriff Cloyd Shope sat there, talking to Hiram about Jesse James, who was still alive, he wanted them to know, oh, yes, alive and living in the state of Tennessee under a false name, a storekeeper, devoted husband, and father.

I'll bet he still robs banks, Hiram said hopefully.

At night, Little Lewis added.

Dudley placed his chair in a clearing so that the sun might shine upon him. Time passed slowly at the stillhouse and he was feeling no pain. He had not forgotten about the other boy, but what was the hurry in going to get him. The corn was good and he had no particular duties save to be on the lookout for revenues while his uncles chased around far and near in order to satisfy, as they said, the demand for the product.

Singer Joe sat at his feet, staring off into the woods. Maybe he saw something, maybe not. Sometimes he stumbled over rocks in plain daylight, other times dodged them. Dudley was growing fond of the chap. Maybe he would just keep on taking care of him. He had a few ideas. He saw himself rocking the boy to sleep or else taking him into the woods and teaching him to watch out for snakes.

You see me, now? he asked the boy.

The boy nodded his head yes.

Well, then, Dudley said. How many fingers am I holding up?

Singer Joe didn't answer. Maybe he didn't count yet, though. He might could see some things.

You know what, Dudley told the boy. Once I was a little chap just your size. What do you think of that, huh.

Singer Joe began to make a humming noise that put Dudley in mind of Hannah Ruth: why, this child was her boy, after all. He, the father and husband, had something to do with it, surely, but she did all the work, and then look what he did, chasing off and leaving her.

Still, he was the boy's father. What was done was done, and now was right this minute and what might yet be done. The boy might be hungry. He had a piece of jerky in his pocket and took it out.

Here, he said.

Singer Joe looked him right in the eye and didn't raise a hand for that jerky.

Ain't you hungry, then?

Yes, the boy said. Hungry.

But he was shaking his head no, at the same time holding out his hand.

He placed the jerky in the boy's hand and Singer Joe took to licking and sucking at it like a licorice stick.

He don't care to see, Dudley thought. He prefers not to look around him.

The boy was sweet one minute and ornery the next. Uncle U. S. recommended a shot of whiskey, which couldn't hurt, Dudley thought, and Singer Joe not only spit it out, but also kicked Dudley in the shin, hard, and lit out for the trees.

He like to never found him. The boy had crawled under a big rock and wouldn't move a muscle. Dudley had to carry him screaming all the way back.

It tried a fellow's patience.

He decided it wouldn't do to carry him along on his mission after the other child. He'd have to leave the boy with Mama. Maybe she could do something with him.

Moonlight shone through the big window. It was a warm night, a storm in the air again. Amelia wanted to sleep, but kept thinking about Emmett. Every time she looked into his son's eyes, she seemed plunged into some memory of him, Emmett as a boy, happy, mischievous, sly— too sly for his own good.

Now she was seeing him the day he was to leave for Aunt Judith's in Knoxville, Mother adjusting his sailor's cap. He didn't want to go and flung the cap to the floor several times. Surely he was too young to be sent away from home, but Mother was at her wit's end, and he had such obvious talent, six years old and playing Mozart before he could read a note of music, just from having heard her, Amelia, laboriously practicing.

What had gone wrong? She was the older of the two. Shouldn't she have provided better guidance? Instead, she had resented him, envying him his freedom, his gallantry, his spirit of adventure. He had seemed to her a usurper—wanting to do everything she did, and doing it better.

Even now, precocious in dying.

Oh, why didn't he leave her alone. Alex was not Emmett, he would grow into his own self, and in the meantime wasn't he a blessing. She thought she might go to the nursery. She could slip in without waking him. She liked seeing him asleep in his crib. She wouldn't disturb him.

Then she was thinking about Hannah Ruth, how fine to have rescued her from the kitchen, before Emmett had found her. It had been a mistake to try to teach Hannah Ruth anything about music, no doubt, her singing so pure, but she didn't regret the love, the desire, the decline of desire.

She thought she heard a voice. Was it Emmett? Of course not. Then Alex cried out. She took a deep breath. She must not go to him. Alva would take care of him.

The house fell silent for a minute or two, and then she was hearing somebody on the stairs. Father, poor Father, awash in his grief, unable to sleep. He did that, paced the house night and day. The moon shone full through the window, making the room almost as light as morning. Why didn't it cool off? Her neck felt sweaty. Emmett, at least, was at rest.

Approaching the big white house, Dudley was guided by Jesus. Standing in the broad hallway with its oak floor shining even at night, he knew Jesus had abandoned him. He remembered meeting Amelia Holt's brother on these stairs and broke out into a cold sweat.

They say it's my child, Emmett Holt had said to him, ushering him right up to the door of the room where Amelia Holt sat with the baby. Opening the door, whispering, he added, But we know better, don't we. You and me know it's the devil's child.

Emmett Holt shot his brains out that very same day. Maybe he was already dead there on the staircase and this had been his hant not yet departed from the premises, staying behind to act as Dudley's guide. Well, but this time no hant appeared. He was on his own.

The silence of the house now recalled to him long hallways, ladies asleep in big beds, their pretty heads resting on satin pillows. It was like returning to something he'd lost, something he needed to find.

In a room at the foot of the stairs the drapes had been pulled back and the moon shone through the windows. When his eyes adjusted to the dark, he went to the mantel and looked over the pictures and knick-knacks. He might find a pretty for Singer Joe. He picked out a picture of a lady, kindly a ugly lady, by the moonlight, but in a gold frame that would fit in his pocket alongside his Barlow knife. A picture wouldn't do for a blind boy, but he kept it anyway and was looking over a glass doll when he heard somebody or something say, Take it. Take everything.

He set the doll carefully back down on the mantel and turned around, slowly so as not to appear to be a person who meant harm. The dark shape in the doorway became an old fellow in a white nightshirt, legs skinny as sticks.

Howdy, Dudley said.

It means nothing to me, the man said in a low, hoarse voice. Nothing. Take whatever suits your fancy.

Well, I—

Dudley didn't know exactly what he was meaning to say, but the man didn't give him a chance to see. He turned and left, just like that.

Wasn't this the damnedest place you ever saw.

He did not like the idea that his boy was here.

Out in the hallway, seeing no sign of the old gentleman, he began to climb the stairs. Then he heard an infant crying out and knew it was his child. It give him a pang in his heart, bud. He would take that child to his bosom and comfort him.

Listening to the footsteps on the stairway, Amelia wished she could help Father to sleep, to forget. Maybe he needed to escape the house altogether, like Mother. But he would never go, she was certain. What he missed, what he looked for, the soul he'd lost years ago, he was certain was right here in this house.

His footsteps drew near her door, then stopped, and she sat up in bed and waited for him to enter. Lord, the moon was bright.

But the door opened and it was not Father at all who stepped into her room. She knew even before she saw.

What do you want, she said.

He didn't say anything. The moonlight illuminated his face, his entire body. Oh, he was a handsome man, all right, her Hannah Ruth's Dudley. He was smiling and had his hands in his pockets.

Howdy, he said at last.

She eased down from the bed, slowly.

I know you, he said. He spoke softly, and she had the thought that it was a musical voice.

Yes, she said. We've met before.

She stepped toward him, aware that she wore the flimsiest of night-gowns and that he stared at her. Let him. It would distract him.

Well, now, he said, I come for my baby boy.

Your baby boy?

Yes, ma'am. I heard him crying.

I don't hear any crying, she said.

He looked around, appeared to listen. She almost felt sorry for him. Her sense of what she must do was clear, though. She began to move slowly toward her desk, not taking her eyes off him.

He's not your child, she told him. He's my brother's child.

Your brother? The one that's dead?

There is no other.

Naw, he said. That couldn't be.

Oh, yes, she said. It very well could be.

He stepped forward. A mistake. She stood at the desk.

I want you to go get that child, he said, still in that soft, lilting, musi-cal voice. Bring my baby boy to me here.

When she reached into the drawer, he saw, of course, saw and jumped at her, but she took quick aim and it was nothing to pull that trigger, easy, easy. She aimed at the center of him. A sweet moment, Lord have mercy. He clutched his loins and looked at her as if trying to place her, as if she were somebody he'd known would try something like this. He should have recognized her, his expression said, his betrayer, his assigned murderer.

And he said, Daddy—and fell, still lunging towards her, his hand thumping down upon her foot. She pulled her foot free and drew back. Shot his hand and shot him again, hitting him, she thought, low in his back. Raised the pistol and aimed for his head, inches away from her, the back of his head, a dark mass of hateful, unkempt hair gleaming in the bright moonlight, but he gave such a shriek that she jumped back, shot wild, hitting something on the other side of the room, one of her mother's precious crystal figurines on the mantel, a mirror, something glass.

Daddy! Daddy! he screamed.

Your daddy's not here, she told him.

29

Didn't I tell you we'd find him, Sheriff Shope said.

It was late in the afternoon. They sat on the porch, drinking coffee, Hannah Ruth, Mama, and Cloyd Shope. Pink had gone off to the cemetery to play his fiddle.

Might have never found him, Mama said, if that woman hadn't shot him. She was right to shoot him. I wisht he'd die.

Well, ma'am, he's about as close as a man can get, don't you know. Hit three times, once just in the hand, but another in kindly a delicate spot.

Will she go to jail? Hannah Ruth asked.

Amelia Holt? Why, her shadow ain't about to darken no jail cell, I reckon.

What will become of him? Hannah Ruth asked.

It won't go easy on him, the sheriff said. Breaking and entering. Then there's the blockading. Them uncles'll testify against him to save their skin. Five years, maybe ten.

A life's not long enough, Mama said.

It's for the judge to say, the sheriff said. This trial will likely be on the Virginia side, since that's where the breaking and entering occurred. Blockading's a federal offense, of course.

Took that boy right here, Mama said. This is Tennessee.

Yes, ma'am. Jurisdiction's a delicate matter, surely.

Is he in Virginia or Tennessee?

Who, ma'am?

My boy, of course.

Why, Tennessee, we reckon. Not so far from here, we figure.

I'm going with you to get him.

I done told you, ma'am. We can't allow no woman on a posse.

Posse. You don't need no posse to go after a blind boy.

No telling what we'll meet up with in them hollers.

I'm going with you, all the same.

Mama went inside. Hannah Ruth wanted to go with that posse, too. If Mama went, she'd go. It wouldn't be like the other time when Pink had come along and the storm broke over them. She would know her purpose and stick to it.

The sheriff gave a little sigh. Pink walked up, his white fiddle case dangling from his arm. He'd likely want to come along, too, but this time she'd not allow it.

I'm going, she told the sheriff. I got a duty.

Mama reappeared. She had put her walking boots on.

Let's not tarry, she said.

The sheriff took a deep breath and slapped his hands on his thighs.

Lordy, he said. You women beat all.

Walking that same route he had taken a week ago with Hannah Ruth, bringing up the rear of a group that included her and her mama, the sheriff, and a skinny deputy name of Newton Huskey, Pink felt the heat of the afternoon settle down into his neck and shoulders.

You shouldn't have come, she said, I don't want you to come, but there wasn't any meanness in her voice. He knew he had to come with her as soon as he understood what was going on and knew she wanted him along though saying otherwise. They rode as far as they could in the sheriff's Model-T, him and her and her mama scrunched into the backseat, and then she walked alongside him except when they had to pass single-file through the laurel slicks and up on the steep slopes where the path narrowed. He liked watching her walk, the way she swung her arms like she meant to get there, wherever it was she was going. Now and then she looked around. Oh, she knew he was back there, all right. Once she winked, and when the trail broadened suffi-ciently, she let him take hold of her hand.

He thought of Alvin and the missions they'd gone on together in

France. Alvin liked to hear himself talk. He got lonesome—they all did, sitting against those walls of damp dirt. Boys who had itched to get away from home spoke of their mamas and daddies in low, tender tones. Pink even had a warm thought or two about his daddy and brothers and sisters back in Freedom, Oklahoma. But mainly he thought about how he had run away from a dirt house and now was stuck in a muddy ditch.

Some nights you could hear the Huns whispering. The length of a cornfield separated you—twenty yards, maybe. On nighttime patrols, crawling under the barbed wire on the mud-slick ground, when the flares went up at the right time you could see their faces and they looked like good old boys, some of them youngsters with pimply faces and peach fuzz mustaches. Sometimes they rose up out of the mist, waving white handkerchiefs, and sauntered right up. They made known quickly, through broad gestures accompanied by many okays, their desire for a cigarette. When this happened, all the rules of war were suspended. They were given cigarettes and they smoked them on the spot, saying thank you in their heavy German accents, and then stepping back into the gloom, their boots squishing in the mud. They reminded Pink of men who worked in the mills, taking a quick break for a smoke, shooting the breeze.

Back in the muddy trenches, the men around Pink talked of what they'd left behind in the States, what they expected when they returned. Rats the size of baby hogs sometimes appeared, and owls moaned out in the damp, misty night.

He hadn't expected a woman like Hannah Ruth, who made him feel as if he'd live forever. Alvin, buddy, he thought, I ain't gonna let your sister get hurt.

About four in the afternoon they caught sight of the old logging camp, the row of empty, rotting houses with the ridges rising up on either side, some of the houses so covered over with ivy and sumac you almost didn't see them. The sheriff, leading the way, stopped so abruptly at the edge of the trees that Deputy Huskey ran into him.

The woman sat on the porch, husking corn, with the boy on a little stool alongside her, husking too. The late afternoon sun cut through the trees and made the rust on the tin roof of the house shine. A blue jay shrieked from the trees. Gnats were thick in the air. Greenbrier grew up all around the house where once a yard might have been.

The sheriff motioned them forward, and the posse moved out of the trees into the sunshine. The woman looked up instantly. So did the boy. The woman looked down again and didn't miss a beat ripping husks off of that corn, but the boy kept staring right ahead, his hands still. You'd swear he saw them.

Then Hannah Ruth's mama broke loose, went running straight for that boy, yelling out, Sweetheart, sweetheart, honey, I'm coming.

Hey, there, ma'am, the sheriff said. Wait just a minute. Halt.

She didn't even slow down.

The woman looked up again and the boy jumped up and tugged at her arm.

And then it was Hannah Ruth, chasing after her mama, running through the greenbrier, her red hair like fire in the sun.

Come on, boys, the sheriff said.

They didn't need him. It was like the war, the generals and majors and their ilk just in the way once the fighting started. Give the fellows in the front lines a say, they'd likely call it all off.

The women could've settled this on their own, you ask him. The image of his own mama came suddenly hard upon his mind, Mama bending over the stove in the dark of the soddy, everything about her saying to him, Get away, escape as soon as you can. It ain't no life here, son.

She said no such thing, of course. What she said was, I'd be beholden to you, son, if you'd take up that fiddle and play me a tune.

The sheriff and his deputy, crouching, began to inch forward. Pink wasn't going to have anything to do with such tomfoolery. He'd walk with head held high in Hannah Ruth's footsteps, through the thorny greenbrier. It wasn't no enemy out there in the bright sunshine.

There went Mama, lunging across the greenbrier as if it was nothing but thicker air, waving her arms like a crazy woman.

I'm the one should be running, Hannah Ruth thought. I'm the one should be crazy to go after her baby boy. Mama knew what to do, while she, Hannah Ruth, the rightful mother of that child, hung back, craving the touch of Pink Miracle. He shouldn't have come. Hadn't she told him not to come? Her mind should have been on her boy, not on this fiddler trailing along behind her.

They had walked right past the rock ledge where the two of them had taken refuge during the storm. Some refuge! He saw it, too. She knew he did, and the knowledge made her tremble with fear of herself and what she had done and what she might yet do in the name of love.

Now, in that moment of Mama's sudden charge, she hesitated only an instant and then she broke loose. Ran.

I'm your mama, boy. I'm coming.

From somewhere she heard a loud thwock, as if somebody swung an ax into a tree. In front of her, Mama fell down. The noise came again, echoing all across the hollow.

Mama!

She tried to pull Mama up. There was blood down the front of her dress.

Then somebody was on top of her, hugging her to the ground, it was Pink, she knew the smell of him, damn his soul.

Don't move, he said. Don't move a muscle, darlin.

He was heavy, bearing her down next to Mama, covering her body with his. She was aware of somebody shouting. It sounded like the voice said, Eedgit! Eedgit! There were thwocking noises coming from the other direction now, a bunch of them. The ground was damp against her cheek, the greenbrier thorns sharp on her arms.

She tried to pull free of Pink. She needed to draw close to Mama.

Get off of me, she said. Get off.

He didn't budge. His breath was warm against her neck, his hands strong around her wrists. She felt as though she would suffocate.

Mama, she called out.

Mama didn't answer.

Interlude:

Singer Joe

There was a time when he wanted to know. It was summer again, a hot August day. Maybe he was eleven years old, maybe twelve. Soon he would be shipped back to school, where Auntie Lewetta—at great sacrifice to herself, she always said—made it possible for him to be among children like himself.

He did not want to be among children like himself, but he had come to like the teachers, who taught him words you could touch. He was quick, they told him, and they let him sing, too, and taught him to play the piano, and let him pick at his guitar, said what talent, what potential.

They had birds at this place, birds you could hold in your hand.

Feel the bird's warmth, the wings, cup the head, gentle, gentle now, stroke it and it will sing.

Now imagine the human soul, his teachers said.

It was easy, that was what it was, easy to say what they wanted him to say and then when alone make the guitar sound the way he wanted it to and sing to its sound. He'd listened hard to a man that sung down on State Street, blind like himself, Auntie Lewetta said, and a sad sight to see standing there in front of the bank with his tin cup taped to the neck of his guitar, his long black trembly fingers, his toothless grin.

Sad to see, maybe, but to hear was another story, and Singer Joe listened and heard plenty.

That was the summer Auntie Lewetta took him down to a furniture

store on State Street and had him play his guitar and sing for a recording machine. A man from New York was there looking for recording
artists—they had seen posters all over town, saying bring your fiddles
and guitars and banjos on in, singers of ballads and old songs welcome
too. It was a pack of people, all right, rubbing up against him sweat-
slick, feet scraping and tapping, clearing their throats and whispering
while waiting to be called up before the machine.

Lordy, Auntie Lewetta said, where'd all these musicianers come
from?

He sang "See, See, Rider," one of the blind man's songs, and one of
Auntie Lewetta's hymns, "Shall We Gather at the River."

The man with the recording machine smelled like old apple cores
mixed with cigars.

Not bad, son, he said. Come back in a few years.

You bet. He had all the time in the world, didn't he.

He hung back in the hall afterward to hear a little of the next ones to
audition. It was a trio, two women and a man. They sang "The Poor
Orphan Child," which he'd heard at camp meetings and never cared to
sing.

Them's the Carters, Auntie Lewetta said. I took you to hear them
once at the schoolhouse. Can't sing a lick.

What he heard was the guitar. Whoever was playing that guitar knew
something he wanted to know.

Some weeks after that, Auntie Lewetta sat at the kitchen table. He
heard the sound of beans snapping, and she hummed an old hymn off-
key.

To stop her, he said, Tell me about my daddy.

When he sang, he sometimes thought about his daddy.

She said nothing at first, as usual. He expected her to leave the room.
But she didn't. She said:

Your daddy was a bad man. It was a shame your mama ever married
him. There's no accounting for it. She was young and had no judgment.
But she's shut of him now. Thank God for that.

Is he alive?

Oh, I wouldn't know. But he won't be bothering you no more. Don't
you worry about that, honey.

Was he a bother once?

He had begun to remember the man lifting him to his shoulders and carrying him somewhere. Where? There was water in the memory, the feel of cool water in his hands and on his head, the sound of it, all a-rushing, and then singing. The singing seemed to come from the water.

It was not a bad memory. It came back to him more often than he would have expected. He was sure it wasn't a dream.

The bad memories came later. He regretted the trouble he'd made for Auntie Lewetta, who was, he now reckoned, as good a woman as any he'd ever run across. An ungrateful wretch is what he was, wanting more than he had any right to hope for. He had the guitar, didn't he, and before he went off to school Uncle Hiram read to him out of history books, stories about wars, famous battles and generals, a lot of foolishness, ask him. Summers he listened to the reassuring roughness of tree bark, the brush and brambles at his feet, sticks snapping in two, signals that he was far enough out of town to be hidden, at the edge of the knobs, the birds singing like crazy, the air smelling good and clean.

Along came the girl. She had been watching him, she said, how he sang out at that camp meeting, her father passing the offering plate. It was when the coolness began to move through the trunks of the trees that rose up all around the big tent, rustling the leaves. What was there to see, he wondered. A blind boy in the woods, sometimes walking, sometimes sitting. He walked with his arms at his sides, swinging them, deliberately not groping in the air, taking great long strides, singing loudly. Sometimes he ran into a tree, tripped on a rock or root. Had she found him amusing? She assured him she was not laughing at him, though she admitted to a smile at times. She had come here for the same reason as he, to be away, to be someplace other than where she was supposed to be. Her daddy the deacon whipped her.

But you see? he asked her.

That's why I'm here, she said.

He didn't understand.

She couldn't explain. She grabbed his hand, pulled it to her face, then all down her body.

Glad to meet you, she said.

Likewise.

Auntie Lewetta took him to Nashville on the train, which he loved in spite of himself, the wonderful motion, the shaking and the swaying, the floor buzzing beneath his feet, the smell of women and the sound of their swishing garments, their shoe heels when they walked in the aisle, the clicking of the conductor's ticket punch, the steady roar of the engine, the whistle, the screech of brakes at the approach of a station, the voices likely to erupt at any time all around. Where you headed. Where you been. Small world, ain't it.

It wasn't. The world was, he realized, large and grand and he was glad, finally, to be out in it, in a vast network of rooms, hallways, stairs, of smells ever shifting, dust and dampness, sweat, old wood, books, especially the books, the huge books with words rising up to his finger-tips, making him think, at first, of the girl in the woods, paper as mean-ingful, suddenly, as skin, at once a matter of sense and mystery. He might have stayed and stayed, but of course the point was to ready him for departure, for a world in which he might make his way, no beggar for scraps, a citizen with rights like another. He had his guitar, always. His voice, the music his mother must have bestowed on him even as she was separating herself from him once and for all.

But he didn't think of her. He could honestly say he didn't give her a thought, his fingers moving ever more rapidly across the deliciously bumpy pages, words, images, sounds at his fingertips. He would have done as she had done, he was certain, had he rightly considered the matter. This is what his learning amounted to, his learning from the books he read—Aristotle, Spinoza, Montaigne, Pope, Dickens, Keats, Emerson, Thoreau—this and instincts he brought to his reading. You were in the world but you were not the world. You had to set out on your own. Blindness beset everybody, but those who saw, literally, sel-dom comprehended the fact.

He began to dream of her before the memories came, dreams of her voice, her touch (though he could not be sure he wasn't really thinking of his grandmother's touch, or even of Auntie Lewetta's), her smell, coming at him in the hallways of the Tennessee School for the Blind endlessly multiplied, twisted, deepened then risen, dreamsounds echo-ing, becoming the feel of her finger on his cheek, her hand on his shoul-der. Gone, she was gone in the dreams as she had gone from his waking life, for reasons beyond him at the time, gone as time itself went, without malice or meanness, gone and ever present, only hidden, safely hidden in her own heart. Merciful Mother, don't forget me.

He wanted to sing her into being, and sometimes maybe he did, ever once in a while.

Part Five:

Family

30

Oklahoma City, 1923

Pink had meant to stop over in Oklahoma City for a couple of days, then head down to Dallas. He couldn't entirely account for what had happened at the Arcadia Ballroom, first just him and Hannah Ruth, pretty much the same repertoire they'd had all across Tennessee and Arkansas, a mixture of fiddle tunes and old-timey songs, and then, at the end of a night he'd expected to be their last, the manager, a plump, bankerly sort of fellow, suggested that Pink might stay on and form a band. It would be a house band, with Hannah Ruth as the girl singer, and now that Oklahoma City had a radio station, they'd go to the studio once a week and broadcast their music. You couldn't hardly beat that with a stick.

So things were going along just fine. The radio station turned out to be in a fellow's basement, but people listened from all over—he knew, because they sent letters and postcards saying they wanted more of the same, some from as far away as Ft. Worth, Texas, and Wichita, Kansas. One fellow with a recording studio right there in Oklahoma City heard them and soon they had a phonograph record with "Texas Quickstep" (fiddle solo) on one side and "Where Is My Wandering Boy Tonight" (fiddle and vocal duet) on the other.

Oh, it was going just fine. And then at the end of a set, stepping off the stage, Pink saw a man coming towards him. There was something about the man—the tilt of his chin, the high glossy forehead, the decisive stride—that put him in mind of his father. He paused. He seemed to see Daddy closing in on him. *You there, Gideon Pinkney.* He hurried toward the door, but as he reached for the knob, a hand came down hard on his shoulder.

Gid, the man said, and Pink swung around.

He saw now—not his daddy's face, but his mama's eyes. It chilled him.

Gid, it's Ollard. I saw your name in the paper, Gid.

Ollard? Ollard?

The man laughed, his mouth twisting to one side, and Pink saw then the face of the little boy, his brother Ollard, chasing a hen, swinging a stick at it, how old would he have been, eight, I left when I was thirteen and so that would make him eight. Thirty now, by God.

Jesus, Ollard, he said. Where've you been?

Where've I been? Why, I reckon I stayed put. You're the one went away.

He ushered Ollard back into his dressing room. Hannah Ruth was polite, and Ollard bowed stiffly, said, Fine singing, ma'am.

She went away, saying she imagined the two of them had plenty to talk about.

The windowless room was hardly bigger than a closet. It had one folding chair, a dressing table with a mirror, above which hung a bare lightbulb. Scrunched up on the concrete floor like an old dog lay a much-worn throw rug of indistinguishable color. Playing in a ballroom with a dressing room was no little distinction, though, no matter the shabbiness, and Pink took some pride in inviting his little brother Ollard to sit down in the chair. He stepped out into the hall and fetched another for himself.

Well, well, brother, Ollard said.

When Pink sat down their knees touched. He apologized for the cramped quarters.

Brother, Ollard said, it wasn't much room in a soddy, either, as I recollect.

He laughed again. Pink laughed, too, though mainly out of politeness. The memory of the soddy didn't amuse him.

It is a wonder, Ollard said. Truly, it is a wonder.

What is a wonder, Pink said.

Why, a family, Ollard said. A family. How it splits and comes together. Ain't it amazing, Gid?

It mainly splits, has been my experience, Pink said.

Ha, ha. Yes, indeed. I don't doubt but what that has been your experience. Ha, ha. Yes, sir.

Maybe, Pink said, it has been different for you.

Oh, yes. Yes, it surely has been different for me.

Again he paused, grinning, and Pink felt himself getting a little irritated.

How has it been different for you, brother.

I am a barber, Ollard said, his tone solemn now, his expression grim. He stared at the wall, squinting at a calendar without a picture on it and three years out of date. At the top of the calendar, it read, "Keep-U-Neet Cleaners" and beneath, "We Hurry."

Barbering ain't exactly a glamorous life, Ollard said, but it is steady work. A man's hair keeps growing.

Where's your shop, Pink asked.

Oh, it ain't in one of your grand hotel lobbies. No, sir. It ain't in the Huckins or the Skirvin or the Colcord or any of them places. Fellow's got to feather some nests if he wants a chair in one of them shops.

Pink hadn't thought that a barber in a hotel had it any better or worse than another and said so.

The layman don't know much, Ollard said.

He smiled that peculiar smile that had traces of the little boy Ollard's smile but still was something else.

Reno Street, Ollard said. I got a shop on Reno Street. You know where Fred Jones Autos is at? Between Robinson and Harvey? I'm right across the street, next to Maystrick Groceries.

Pink not only knew where Reno Street was. It was where he and Hannah Ruth stayed, at Mrs. Annie Bloom's Furnished Rooms—just down the block from Fred Jones Autos. He remembered walking past the striped barber pole many times.

Course it ain't exactly my own shop, Ollard said. Old man Kemper, he hangs on. His people are up in Woods County. Maybe you remember Benton Kemper, over to Avard? Use to come to Papa's, he and his brother Childon. Come near ever Saturday night. Sometimes they'd go in to Freedom. Had a old Studebaker wagon, wheels painted yellow, squeaked like the devil.

Pink didn't remember anyone ever visiting his father at all, nor his father going into Freedom on Saturday nights. What would he find to do there?

Whatever did our daddy come to, Pink managed to ask, but Ollard went on talking about old man Alton Kemper and the barbering trade, which led him to comment on the caginess of Jews and the necessity of keeping the Negro in his place. Pink began to wish that the buzzer might sound, signifying the end of the break between sets.

You married? he managed to ask Ollard.

Not no more. She run off with somebody she liked better. A woman these days—

Sorry.

It was a long time ago. I got over it. Say, I reckon you're doing pretty good for yourself, ain't you.

It's been worse, Pink said.

I tell you, it's hard for a honest man to make a living. Some has got it easy, but the rest of us is lucky for a pot to piss in.

Ain't no bed of roses for nobody, Pink said.

You said a mouthful, Ollard said, pulling a cigar from his lapel pocket, offering it to Pink, who refused.

Sure? Ollard said.

Yep.

You probly a teetotaler, too, ain't you.

Not hardly.

You was always a good boy. Mama's little favorite.

He pronounced favorite "fay-vor-eet," drawing out each syllable, then licking on the cigar, eyeing Pink closely.

Why, say, he said. What become of your fingers, Gid?

Shot off or blown away. Don't rightly know.

In the war?

Pink nodded.

Tooth, too?

Naw, that was another time.

I didn't go to the war. Junior did. He come back, I understand, but where he went off to is anybody's guess.

Ollard looked at his unlit cigar as if he'd forgotten he was still holding it.

Maybe you smoke cigarettes, Ollard said.

Pink didn't. It wasn't a virtue. Never was tempted.

You see women smoking cigarettes these days, Ollard said as he lit up the cigar. Yes, sir. Flat out in public view. It ain't a manly habit noways, them little sticks, but a lady ain't got no business smoking. And then cutting their hair short like a man's and them short skirts. It's a changed world, brother, ever since the war, I'm telling you.

He took a suck off of the cigar, blew out a stream of smoke, then continued:

Our sisters ain't no exception, I reckon.

You know where they're at? Pink asked.

Ellen's in California, but Josephine's right here in OKC. Married to Eskell Forrest. Remember good old Eskell? Garfield Forrest's boy. Garfield that was the preacher. Old Eskell works in the packing plant, clubbing cattle over the head. Pays good money, I'll tell you.

Pink had no recollection of Eskell Forrest.

Any childern? he asked.

I reckon so. Ten, last I counted. Seven boys and three girls.

Ten? Little Josephine with ten childern? She had been a scrawny little thing when he left—seven years old. Could that be right. Little Josephine, a mother of ten, wife to a man that clubbed cattle over the head in Packingtown.

I'd be interested, he said to Ollard, trying to sound casual about it, to know what become of our father. Is he still up at Freedom? I reckon he's still alive.

All depends on what you mean by alive.

Well, is he breathing, eating, sleeping. Is he getting around, still able to work? Is he mean as ever?

You're a card, brother. I'm glad to see you've developed a sense of humor.

He paused.

And giving a damn about family, my Lord, I never thought—why, did you ever write our daddy a single line of your whereabouts? Ever inquire of him—over the span of these last couple of decades, let us say—how he might be or if it was a thing on this God's green earth you might do to be of help to him?

I didn't figure he'd care one way or the other.

Care? Care? Why, I saw him waste away. Yes, sir. First his beloved wife gone, and then his firstborn son run off. It like to killed him, Gid, when you lit out. I don't care if you lost your whole hand, brother, you could of been of some help.

I ain't defending myself.

Ain't no defense possible, you want my opinion, brother.

Well, Pink said, rising, it has been good seeing you again after all these years. He fairly pushed Ollard out. In the few minutes before the buzzer sounded, he sat there and thought of defenses he might have offered. But by the time it rang, he felt exhausted, defeated.

He found himself lost in the music of that last set more than once, lost in tunes he knew by heart. His throat felt dry, scratchy, his hands clumsy, sticky on the strings, and he kept sneaking glances out at the audience, looking for Ollard, without ever seeing him. People danced as dreamily as before, smoke hanging heavy in the ballroom and the smell of sweaty bodies, steamy perfume.

When the set was at last over, Pink moved through the crowd, receiving hollow compliments and slaps on the back. Ollard wasn't there. Nor was he outside.

With Hannah Ruth, walking back to Mrs. Bloom's Rooms along Reno Street a little later, he stopped to peer in through the window of Kemper's Barbershop. It was dark and he couldn't make out much, of course, just the two chairs.

In the morning he woke early after a restless sleep and got up without waking Hannah Ruth. He dressed quietly and went outside. It was warm already, would be a hot day. He walked past the shop again. It wasn't open, being Sunday morning, but he could see inside, behind the big chairs, the shelves of jars and bottles and tubes, hair tonics, grease, soap, scents, and above the shelves the mirrors, mirrors placed on the opposite wall as well. You'd see yourself coming and going, shocks of hair falling right and left onto the linoleum floor.

Lower them ears for me, would you, bud.

When he returned, Mrs. Bloom, seated in the lobby behind her big desk, her small frame lit up by a crooked neck lamp, looked at him as if he was a ghost.

Upstairs, Hannah Ruth still slept, a pretty sight, lying on her side facing the wall, the sheets thrown off of her, all curve and shadow against the stark bed. Such sweet, steady breathing. Breath itself, that was the thing, wasn't it. Keep to that beat long as you can, boy.

He wanted to slip back in bed with her, wake her softly with his touch. Truly, she was all the family he needed. As quietly as he could, he began to slip out of his clothes, but the floor squeaked and she jumped up, eyes wide open.

Honey, he said, seating himself on the edge of the bed. It's just me. Your poor fiddler.

I dreamed he was dead, she said.

Beg pardon.

I saw him clear as day, the sun streaming in on his corpse, just like it is right now into this room.

Well, say.

She began to cry, cupping her face in her hands. He climbed into the bed next to her, tried to comfort her. It had been a dream about the blind boy, he supposed, her Singer Joe. She dreamed about him often.

Why, honey, he said. That child's with your sister, like always, probably putting down a stack of hotcakes about this time.

Her sobbing let up a little. She was warm in his arms, fragile as a little girl, and fragrant as a fresh-cut bunch of roses.

It was Dudley, she said quietly. It was Dudley I dreamed of dead. But it's something else. It's something else I've got to tell you.

She started crying hard again. Oh, she didn't mean for it to happen, she said. She hoped he understood that. She was so sorry. They could do something about it, there was ways, it didn't have to happen, she was sure she could find somebody to help her do something about it, she could ask their landlady Mrs. Bloom or somebody—

Do something? he asked. And then it dawned on him. She was in a family way. She was going to have a baby. He was going to be a daddy.

She stiffened, pulled away from him, but he drew her back.

Listen here, he told her. It's nothing to do. It's okay, it's fine, oh, Jesus, honey.

We'll still have our music, she said. Nothing can take that away from us.

Now he was the one sobbing.

I'm the happiest man alive, he told her, and remembering this moment years later, he believed he had spoken the truth.

31

Here it came again, a baby ripping her apart, shoving its way out of her, and Hannah Ruth saw her mother's face in the moment before the coffin lid was closed. That is not my mama, she had thought, but now, with this latest painful thrust of life, she knew better.

She remembered tunes never yet sung, a music coursing through her even in this agony as if it meant to pursue her unto death. Would they ever stop?

It made no difference, really. She had shaped her voice, or tried to, to the instruction of Amelia Holt, and then along came Pink Miracle and his fiddle. If he listened to her, it was himself he heard, just as she heard her own voice in his fiddle.

But what was it, this other life pushing its way out of her? There was Singer Joe, then Alex, and surely that was enough. Lord God, deliver me.

Now she was seeing Dudley clear as day, Dudley forlorn and angry in a white hospital gown, his hands gripping the arms of a wheelchair, looking right into her eyes. Paralyzed from the waist down, the newspaper had said, he'd probably not walk again, but he was fit enough for prison, was still there, far as she knew.

Even if he got out, Dudley wouldn't find her this time. She was not Hannah Ruth anymore. She was Argenteen Dupree and living in California in a little house made out of mud—at least that's what Pink said, though others called it stucco—mud painted pink, he said, as if especially in his honor. He said it often. The chance of a lifetime, he also said of their engagements in the smoky dance halls and dumpy beer joints of Norwalk, Venice, Alhambra, Burbank, Downey, Pasadena.

The yard was even littler than the one her mother's house in Tennessee sat on, but it had a palm tree growing on it, tall and pretty, and flowers—you never saw the likes of the flowers. Mama would've marveled at the flowers.

It was Dudley's uncle that shot Mama, a crazy man. He wouldn't stop running and they chased him all through the woods, shooting and shouting until they shot him dead. He had been suspected of all manner of mischief in these parts, the sheriff said, laughing pleasantly. Likely he saw the badge flashing through the trees and thought we was revenues.

The image of Dudley passed, thank God, but then came Esther, beautiful Esther, dead of the Spanish flu, Esther who had cursed her in her dying breath. *Damn you to hell, Hannah Ruth. God damn you, sister.* What had she done to Esther?

Who else had hated her? Singer Joe? Likely Singer Joe would come to hate her. He was to have been her baby girl. She had been so certain of it, leaving Knoxville, the train rocking along through the mountain passes, the green valley of the Holston: she would bring forth a girl child. Dudley had given her a girl child.

Instead, he had given her a boy, a blind boy.

This one would be a boy, too, she was sure. A big boy, a rough boy, a bully, punching at her, tearing and gouging the life out of her. *Let me loose.*

Now she seemed to be in Knoxville, not with Dudley but Pink Miracle after they'd left Bristol that first year. She was at Amelia's Aunt Judith's, sitting in the middle of the long scarlet-colored, yellow-fringed divan, next to her the gleaming grand piano. Aunt Judith wore the same black silks in the style of twenty-five years ago, only slightly faded, and she smelled of the same soapish scent, and she wore her hair as always, the long thick braids twisted and secured atop her head.

Who did you say this was? Aunt Judith asked, staring at Pink, who stood there in the high-ceilinged room twiddling the brim of his hat.

Oh, she said, I beg your pardon. This is Pink Miracle.

Pink Miracle?

Yes, ma'am.

That's his name?

Yes, ma'am.

Pink nodded, grinned sheepishly.

Pinkney's the full name, he said. Mama's family name.

The mantel clock ticked loudly. The air closed in. Pink, looking at the big piano, suddenly said, I wonder can anybody play that thing.

Aunt Judith grinned and said:

I've played it all my life.

He's a fiddler, Hannah Ruth said, as if that explained everything.

Fiddler, Aunt Judith said. I've known a few fiddlers in my time. Do you bear your fiddle with you, Mr. Miracle?

Yes, ma'am.

He needed no encouragement to retrieve it from the hallway, where it sat inconspicuous next to her trunk—Dudley's old footlocker, which she had redeemed from the Telford House, donating its contents to the Salvation Army.

How that fiddle did shine! He must have polished it daily, a hundred strokes, as a woman brushed her hair.

You start, he said.

Aunt Judith began to play, her fingers as if separate beings set adrift in the depths of music, and Pink, after listening about half a minute, began to stroke the length of his bow.

She never heard the like, before nor since.

Well, Aunt Judith said when they stopped (even stopping at the same time, as if they'd rehearsed it). Who would have thought Bach could sound like that.

Aunt Judith put them up for a couple of music-filled days, and then Pink was itching to move on. In Nashville, after two weeks in a dingy hotel, looking for places to play, they ran out of money. It wouldn't be the first time.

It's okay, Pink always said. We'll get by somehow.

And they got by, Pink signing on in some factory or mill for a spell, and she hiring herself out as a lady's maid, for you do many things you'd not care to do if you want to eat, as this child, this rude child bursting his way through her, would know soon enough.

Singer Joe, dear Singer Joe. Was your Auntie Lewetta a good mother for you?

From April into October, oh, my, they lived like gypsies, traipsing from one fiddlers' convention to the next, playing in schoolhouses, dance halls, opera houses, movie theaters, sleeping on a pallet beneath the broad starry sky out in some farmer's field or, if it rained (and it often did), in the hayloft of a barn.

Not such bad days at all, when you looked back on them. Lord give them back to her, anything but this moment, herself running across an open space, sawbriers cutting her ankles, her mama falling to the ground. Mama! Come back, Mama! But Pink lay on top of her and she could not bring Mama back, the thwacking sounds echoing all around, and this child, a boy child, for sure, Pink Miracle's baby, this one she promised she'd keep, the child of her loving Pink, this one she'd not leave behind, no, never, she promised, she'd swear it on Pink's beloved Chattanooga Strad, a good mother she'd be if only he'd get off her, let her breathe, let her, God have mercy, let her get to her mama, let her bring Mama back.

32

East Tennessee, 1925

Released from the Richmond penitentiary on a warm day in April, Dudley had been given a squeaky wheelchair, five dollars, an ill-fitting suit of clothes, and a pair of crutches. He was neither grateful nor contrite.

It was a year before feeling had come back in his hand, two fingers numb at the tips to this day, and the whole hand left crooked. For a long time his pecker pissed when it damn well pleased. The only way he would know was by the smell. Then he'd reach down and feel the wetness all over his pants. You think the boys in prison didn't razz him about that!

They said he'd never walk again, but he could get around on crutches when he had to, and he was strong in his arms from lifting bricks, still warm from the kiln, a job he was assigned because he could do it sitting down.

Not a soul met him when he got off the train. He had written Hannah Ruth from prison—at least twice—and the only answer he got was divorce papers, damn her hide. His boy that he had carried on his back in thunder and lightning was surely lost to him, reared up by some other daddy, and the other, the one called Alexander, he acknowledged might not have been his child after all.

O. T. once sent him a pamphlet entitled "The Wages of Sin," signed with his full name, Olden Times Crider, and his mama had written a letter once a year, on his birthday, asking was he saved yet? He wasn't. Maybe once he was, but no more.

In Johnson City, he caught a ride with a farmer that let him off at O. T.'s church, the steeple he had righted still straight but looking like an outhouse. The pigeons had come back, a mob of them muttering and pacing. He sat in his wheelchair beside the steps and yelled as loud as he could, but nobody came out.

Late in the afternoon he got a ride to Elizabethton and found O. T. easy enough, at the chili parlor he ran with Uncle Fremont's boy, Franklin. O. T. stood behind the counter, his back to the door, stirring a pot of beans. He looked heftier than Dudley remembered him. It was almost suppertime. Dudley hadn't eaten since morning. The beans smelled good.

Brother, he said.

O. T. turned around fast, dropping the spoon into the vat of beans, and looked at him as though he was a ghost.

Is that you, Dud?

Ain't no one else, brother.

While O. T. fished the spoon from the beans, he smiled, but it wasn't an honest smile. It looked as if he was afraid of something. Steam rose up from the pot of beans and the smell was strong and good.

Dudley wheeled himself closer to the counter.

Listen, he said, gimme some of them beans and then take me out to Mama's.

He pushed his wheelchair up as close to the counter as he could and laid a dollar bill down so as not to be beholden.

Nothing much had changed. O. T. preached on Sundays, and Mama read her Bible when not out gathering sang or galax. He had plenty of time to himself, and this was all right. Up at Richmond somebody was always around unless you were thrown in the hole.

Because there wasn't a thing else to do, he let O. T. take him to church. Up on the wagon bed with the folded-up wheelchair tied to the rail, he rode next to the wooden box that contained snakes for the service.

At church, a skinny fellow whanged on the guitar pretty good, but Mama sang the hymns so loud he could hardly hear himself think. The singing stopped and O. T. began to stomp about and shake his fist in the air. People went up to testify, O. T. laying his hands on their heads and urging them on.

The good part came when Cousin Franklin took out the box of snakes. O. T. unlatched the box, lifted up a couple of them, and they commenced to crawl around on his shoulders. Used to be, O. T. practiced with black snakes. These appeared to be copperheads.

Cousin Franklin grabbed a snake, and then a plump red-faced man came up and got one. The two of them paraded around, holding their snakes out for all to see. The skinny guitar player whanged away. It's a sign and a wonder, O. T. shouted from the front, the snake still crawling on his shoulder. People jumped up and some fell to the floor and rolled about, talking nonsense—God's tongue, O. T. said.

Well, maybe one of these days O. T. or Franklin would get bitten. It gave a fellow hope.

In the silence of the night, Dudley's head filled up with dark hallways, rooms, marble dresser tops and mirrors, the soft breathing of a sleeping woman, himself like a fellow she might dream up in a nightmare. Staying awake to keep from dreaming, he remembered Hannah Ruth's singing, so pretty it scared the daylights out of him. Then he tried to make his leg muscles work. He could lift the right leg about an inch, but he'd been able to do that for a couple of years. The other leg just hung there.

He dreamed of snakes. He would see them in the dark of a lady's room, the moonlight slashing through the window, the snake shaking its rattle, sidling across the floor. Trying to keep it from getting to her, he would reach for it, take its slick little head in his palm, and squeeze the daylights out of it.

Then, waking, he'd understand it was his pecker he was squeezing. It wasn't any pleasure, not a bit.

The next Sunday, Dudley told himself not even to think about letting one of those snakes crawl upon his shoulders. But when Franklin walked past him, a big rattler raising its head up, held out for all to see, its long finger of a body slithering around his arm, Dudley raised up his hands in spite of himself, and that snake lit upon his wrist and moved upwards.

Praise Jesus, Franklin said.

Stand up, brother, O. T. said. Stand up and get in line for the last judgment. Stand up and walk, praise the Lord.

I ain't going nowhere, he said.

The snake whispered something in his ear, but he couldn't understand what it was saying.

O. T. began to talk about a big camp meeting to be held in Bristol the following week. Plenty of sinners would be saved, he said, for this was a world-renowned preacher though a woman.

The box of snakes was underneath the porch, a cool and dry place. Some mornings O. T. fed them a mouse or two, trapped in Mama's root cellar, their necks broken.

Dudley could grab hold of one of the locust posts on the porch and ease himself down onto the ground. The first time, he didn't open the box up. He just watched through the screen window on the end of the box. The snakes lay twisted up together. One fellow kept looking him in the eye and sticking out his tongue. A soft scratching noise came from inside the box, and he opened the lid just a hair. Wouldn't you know it— one of them snakes came out, lickety-split, easing himself right up onto Dudley's shoulders. He closed the box so that the others wouldn't think they might get loose, too.

The sensation of the snake on his shoulders wasn't altogether unpleasant. It tickled a little.

I ain't brought you no mice, he said, so don't get your hopes up, boy.

With some effort, he raised himself up a little. The snake didn't mind.

Well, bud, here we are.

The snake inched its way across the back of his head, down his shoulders, into parts that had no feeling yet, and at last was on the ground. He rolled over then, away from the snake, slow and easy, a little at a time until he could reach his crutch. Using it, he was able, with a couple of nudges and gentle prods, to guide the snake back toward the lid of the box, then open the lid just enough so that the snake, if he had a mind to, might go back inside.

The snake went back in and the others stayed put.

O. T., having been bitten several times, neglected those snakes, Dudley believed. Franklin had also been bitten. They lived to tell about it, unlike some, but the poison laid them up for a while, forearms swollen big as bread loaves, great red and gray splotches and blisters all over them. Made you feel close to death, O. T. said cheerfully.

O for a thousand tongues to sing my great Redeemer's praise, Mama and O. T. sang from up on the buckboard. *Hear Him, ye deaf; his praise, ye dumb. Ye blind, behold your Savior come; and leap, ye lame, for joy.* While they sang, Dudley, seated on a pallet in the wagon bed, nestled the snake box onto his lap.

Howdy, bud, he whispered to the snake.

The woman evangelist, according to O. T., might not think to bring snakes, and so O. T. would take his just in case God needed them.

I reckon I can hold that box, Dudley said.

O. T. took that as a sign of hope.

In the wheelchair, the box of snakes held between his legs, Dudley propelled himself across the trodden grass, around the carriages and automobiles, toward the big tent. The ground was bumpy and rutted. Sweat broke out on his forehead and the back of his neck.

How you doing, fella, he said, not aloud, to the snake.

I'm doing just fine, he seemed to hear, considering I'm in a box.

I been feeling puny myself.

At least you ain't in no box.

Oh, yes, I am. Where is it I can go, answer me that.

You can go to Hell, boy. It is a spacious place. Your daddy's there and he wants to see you.

I don't care to see him again.

But he's your daddy and you ain't going to ever have no other.

It's no use talking about it, he said.

Inside the tent, he followed O. T. and Mama almost to the front. The two of them pushed their way onto a bench and left him in the aisle in his wheelchair. A huge, sweat-slickened man lay in front of him, huffing and puffing, curled up like a dog. Many others walked with canes or crutches or, like Dudley, rode in wheelchairs.

Up in front a lady dressed up all in white lifted her arms and blessed everybody. She was so pretty he expected to see wings on her shoulders, but there wasn't none. A piano began to play. Singing started. A lady in a blue dress thumped on a tambourine and a couple of fellows gathered around her, blowing on a horn and fiddling. Three men in black suits stood behind the lady in white, their arms folded across their chests, their chests all puffed out. They looked mad at somebody, kept looking all around as if they expected to be jumped. Then the lady hushed everybody up and began to talk.

She talked a good while. She flung out one scripture after another and raised her fist up and her hands began to swirl and flit around in front of her like bats at dusk. Everybody better get ready, she said, for judgment draweth nigh. When she stopped to catch her breath, it was quiet under that tent.

The men in the black suits stepped down into the aisles, one of them lunging towards Dudley. The big sweaty fellow in front of him stirred, and people began to murmur and moan. Come forth and be healed, the lady said. Let Jesus make you whole. Everybody began to sing and clap.

I am whole, he said to nobody in particular.

Sure, you are, the snake said. You and me, bud.

He let the snake out. It came slowly, slyly, and stayed there on his lap. He stroked it. It wasn't going nowhere.

Praise Jesus, O. T. said.

The wheelchair began to move. For a second he had the feeling it was Jesus pushing, but it was only O. T.

It's time, O. T. said, leaning down and shouting it into his ear as if he was deaf instead of crippled.

Up in a corner of the tent, a dark shape poised for a swooping descent. It had no business with him. Keep your distance, he told it, whatever you are. Go somewheres else.

But here it came and the snake, Lord help him, the snake was gone from his lap.

Hey, snake, he shouted. Where're you going, old buddy.

He realized he was standing. He was standing in the aisle, shoulder to shoulder with the sweaty man, the box of snakes fallen to the ground.

Sweet Jesus, O. T. said. Praise the Lord, others said.

Dudley's whole body shook. His snake, he saw, lay coiled at the foot of the angel.

I'm not going anywhere, he told himself. This old boy is staying put.

He began to walk.

This is where I stop, he said to everyone he passed by.

The angel woman leaned down and picked up the snake. She looked him, Dudley Crider, right in the eye and lifted up the snake and held it above her yellow hair.

Step right up, Mister, she said, and be healed.

He understood then. There was no place else to go. And, walking quickly, surely, he went there.

Coda:

Singer Joe and Alex

DALLAS, 1948

Singer Joe was doing all right, playing more jazz than blues these days. He had him an electric guitar, a good woman, and a dog named Dudley to see him from depot to depot and get him in and out of the hotels when the woman was elsewhere.

Once Charlie Christian—before he signed on with Benny Goodman—looked him up and traded licks with him, and Bob Wills came around, puffing cigar smoke, asking him to play this or that, but nothing came of it, and he didn't care to play with those Texas Playboys anyway, that country-boy jazz. That was Pink Miracle's music, not his, and good riddance.

He hadn't gone back to Bristol since the funeral of Auntie Lewetta ten years ago, and he for sure didn't care to see any brother, nor touch him, hear him. So when this man Alexander Holt came to his room one winter afternoon, saying I am your long-lost brother from Tennessee, it was nothing he needed to hear.

Touch me, the man said, touch me and see for yourself. Let me touch you.

He felt his hand clasped, a grip clammy but firm, and he yanked away.

Keep your hands to yourself, boy, he said. You got eyes. Look.

I've looked for the longest time.

This dog here's got teeth. All I've got to do is say the word.

It's a pretty dog.

I wouldn't know.

Doesn't look like he'd bite a soul.

He will if I tell him to. Don't rile him.

You sound like our mother, you know.

What do you know of her.

I've heard her recordings. You sound like her when you sing. My brother. My dear brother.

Shit, man.

It means something, all the same.

Nothing.

I always felt something was missing. You know what I mean? I mean, I had everything I could have wanted, but it wasn't enough—wasn't nearly enough.

What do you want from me.

Nothing. Everything.

Nothing's what you're gonna get.

It's all right. But maybe you can understand.

I don't understand shit.

You understand more than you know, brother. I've heard you sing.

Our mother—that's what you call her—our mother, as you call her, was no mother to me.

She gave you something all the same—a voice.

Heartache.

Heartache counts for something. Me, she gave away. Oh, but she was right to do it. What did I matter in the larger scheme of things?

Precious little, no doubt. As much as anybody.

You can't believe that. Your music tells me you don't believe that.

I believe what I see.

You're blind.

That's right. You understand something.

She gave you away, too. That's what I've always understood.

Left me behind, more like it. Blood raised me. My spinster auntie, Lewetta. She did her duty was all, while Mama sang to a fiddle.

If you could see me, you'd see how much alike we are. Anybody would see it. Brothers, they'd say. Those two men have to be brothers. We may have different daddies, but our mother left her mark on us.

Don't touch me. Keep your hands to yourself.

I wasn't going to touch you. I wasn't even reaching.

Don't even think about it.

It's how you see, isn't it—touching?

None of your damn business how I see.

I thought you'd be the one wanting to touch, see how my face is like yours. Our noses, Lord, our chins. I thought, I thought if I touched first, it would make it easier for you. I understand this must be very difficult for you—this meeting. Did you even know I was alive? I doubt it. I wouldn't be worth telling you about.

I knew about you, all right.

What did you know.

I knew some things. I heard about your father, for one thing. A rich man from a mansion on the hill.

Oh, yes. Rich. Emmett Holt cut off his pecker and blew his brains out in that mansion on the hill. Mother—Aunt Amelia, that is—told stories about him until she was blue in the face. Her daddy went crazy and her mama went west. I wonder how it was with my daddy Emmett and our mother Hannah Ruth. A brief moment of glory? Shall we say so?

Say what you want. My father was Dudley Crider. Nothing was expected of him, nothing delivered.

Oh, most blessed of souls! Listen. Auntie shot your papa—you must know that—shot Dudley Crider while he tried to kidnap me in the belief he was my true father. She told the story all her life. Imagine that. Someone should write a book. Or maybe a song, huh.

Not me, bub. You're barking up the wrong tree.

Tell me, then. Tell me what you know.

Yes, I'll tell you. Sure. You bet.

But how could he? How tell what could not be told. A life went on beyond words, even Dudley Crider's sad excuse for a life. You could not even tell your own life. How start on another's?

My father Dudley Crider, he said, killed himself on religion just as surely as your Holt father did with a pistol in his mouth. Snakebit. What does that tell you. Not a goddamn thing. He survived prison, got religion, began to walk again, claiming that he had been healed by Jesus, took to handling snakes in order to show the ferocity of his belief, and a

rattler bit him during a revival meeting in Nashville. He'd been bitten
before, but this time he dropped dead and there wasn't a cure for that. I
don't believe our mother would have grieved for a minute.

How'd you know all that?

I had an uncle name of Lewis. He took up the missionary trade with
daddy's brother O. T. for a while. Thought telling me the story would
open my eyes.

It didn't, though.

Most surely, it didn't.

Alexander Holt was quiet for a minute. The radiator clanked. The
dog gave a little yelp in his sleep. Singer Joe felt alone. Where was that
woman when you needed her? Off to Arkansas was what she said. Her
people lived in Arkansas. She hadn't seen them in ever so long. Did
he mind, really? No. Go on. He'd be all right. He could take care of
himself.

You never married? he asked Alexander Holt.

Naw. There's other fish to fry. Listen, brother. I don't believe our
mother ever loved, let alone grieved.

Singer Joe thought on that for a minute. It was worth thinking about.
Then he said:

I believe she would've loved her daughter. Maybe she was ready to
love by then.

Her daughter? Why, you should see her, brother, our half-sister
Rachel all decked out in cowgirl fringe, cowgirl boots, singing those
simpering duets with Pink Miracle, her proud papa. It's quite an act. A
kind of art, you might say. She'll make a movie star one of these days,
you just wait.

Singer Joe did not respond to that. What could he say. Of course he'd
heard Pink and Rachel and their band, the Oklahoma Plowboys. He'd
heard them on the radio and once in Oklahoma City he had gone to
hear them at the Trianon Ballroom. Her voice was nothing like his
mother's. It lacked conviction, depth, everything that mattered. He
would never seek her out any more than he would have chosen to meet
with this so-called brother, coming to him out of a darkness thicker and
deeper than anything he had ever known.

My mother, this would-be brother said in his soft womanish voice.
That is, the woman I knew as my mother, was your Hannah Ruth's . . .

dear companion. For some time—oh, she told me this, I couldn't say why—they were intimate. Does that shock you, brother?

I'm not shocked by anything I hear about her.

My mother—let me call Auntie Amelia Mother—took me to California to Hannah Ruth's grave. I was ten years old and accustomed to visiting my poor dead daddy's grave, once a year without fail, and so I was not particularly thrilled to come all the way to California to put flowers on the tombstone of a mama I'd never even seen alive. I remember mainly the long train ride, the swaying and the clicking and the long passage across land without trees. I wish I had been more alert. Mother might have shed tears on the grave. She might have kissed the marker. I was not paying attention. I remember her saying—but this might have been another time—what an amazing voice had been silenced.

I can hear her, Singer Joe said, I can listen to her phonograph records anytime I want. It's enough. It tells me all I want to know.

Oh, yes. Yes. Listening to that voice, I believe I hear how she broke my mama's heart. Have you heard it, too, that power, that seductiveness, that, that, *cruelty*?

I don't know what you mean.

It's pure desire, brother. Desire without end.

I hear something else.

Long live the desirable dead! Alex said. Let their voices ring.

They will, they will, whether we listen or not.

Alex didn't argue the point. Maybe he hadn't heard. His quickened breath in the sudden silence was, Singer Joe thought, almost like a woman's voice, the whisper of some lost sister, the utterance in that overheated little room of something familiar and dark.

That was when he had her again with him, now and always, the renegade mother and the dead grandmother and the aunt who had stayed and stayed, a trio bound into one soul, as sure as breath. The warmth of her hand seemed poised to touch him. He sang in order to keep the stillness of her presence, the fragrance of her hair as she leaned down to lift him up. He sang and heard her singing with him. He reached for her hand.

Have mercy. Let us sing.

The air was fast with death. The December sky moaned, then shrieked, then resumed moaning. The sky back in Tennessee had a different sound, after all, the summer sky especially, always summer in his memory, evenings out on the front porch, the rocker creaking, the air cooling, signifying the coming dark. Pink Miracle's fiddle sounded like that sky sometimes when Mama sang and something in him sang with her. Oh, he remembered it, all right, first and best memory, when he'd discovered his voice in his mama's song, and the fiddle hummed, warm and unwavering, holding and releasing all them that heard to this earth, this trembling, this everloving skin. On the porch, Little Lewis and Hiram put a ball into his hand, guided his arm. *This way.*

Little Lewis, Reverend Lewis Bayless, came to see him now and then, asking was he saved. Chloe, in Atlanta, last he heard, was on her fourth husband. Master Sergeant Hiram Bayless, thirty-nine years old, was killed at Normandy. Bristol was far away.

This was Texas now, where he lived. The wind blew dust against the windowpane. It seemed, sometimes, the end of the earth. A good place for music. He meant to stay.

When he reached for his brother, his fingers alighted softly upon an eye. A soft, moist, warm curving into bone, cave, vein. Sweet heaven, there could be nothing like it. The eyelid fluttered like a little wing.

See? Alex said.

Yes, he said. Lord God have mercy, I see.

Acknowledgments

The author is grateful for the support and friendship of colleagues past and present at Bucknell, especially Karl Patten, John Wheatcroft, John Rickard, Martha Holland, Shara McCallum, Ann Gray, Cynthia Hogue, Saundra Morris, Harry Garvin, Eugenia Gerdes, Michael Payne, Gary Sojka, and Dennis Baumwoll. Members of the Buck Mountain Band—Dan Peck, Jesse Lovell, Carl Kirby, and Amy Boucher—have been sources of inspiration, edification, and joy. Special thanks to Dave and Jan Pearson for longstanding kindness.

The following books (and, in some cases, films) helped the author to imagine the lives of the characters in this novel, as well as the times and places in which they lived their imaginary lives: Les Blank, Cece Conway, Alice Gerrard, and Maureen Gosling, *Sprout Wings and Fly* (a documentary film about Tommy Jarrell); Jean A. Boyd, *The Jazz of the Southwest: An Oral History of Western Swing*; Mary A. Bufwack and Robert K. Oermann, *Finding Her Voice: The Saga of Women in Country Music*; Christopher Camuto, *Another Country*; Al Clayton, *In Jesus' Name* (a documentary film about Pentecostal snakehandlers); William Ferris, *Blues from the Delta*; Chet Flippo, *Your Cheatin' Heart*; Alan B. Govenar and Jay F. Brakefield, *Deep Ellum and Central Track: Where the Black and White Worlds of Dallas Converged*; Dorothy Horstman, *Sing Your Heart Out, Country Boy*; Judith Clayton Isenhour, *Knoxville: A Pictorial History*; Marquis James, *The Cherokee Strip: An Oklahoma Boyhood*; Joe Klein, *Woody Guthrie: A Life*; Bill C. Malone, *Singing Cowboys and Musical Mountaineers: Southern Culture and the Roots of Country Music*; Margaret McKee and Fred Chisenhall, *Beale Black and Blue*; Gerald Milnes, *Play of the Fiddle*; Kinney Rorrer, *Rambling Blues: The Life and Songs of Charlie Poole;* William Savage, *Singing Cowboys and All that Jazz*; Roy P. Stewart, *Born Grown: An Oklahoma City History*; Marian Thede, *The Fiddle Book*; Charles R. Townsend, *San Antonio Rose: The Life and Music of Bob Wills*; Charles Reagan Wilson and William Ferris,

Encyclopedia of Southern Culture; Charles Wolfe, *The Devil's Box* and *Tennessee Strings.*

In addition, the author is indebted to recordings by early to mid-twentieth century musicians such as the Bogtrotters, Fiddlin' John Carson and Moonshine Kate, the Carter Family, Charlie Christian, the East Texas Serenaders, Patsy Cline, Elizabeth Cotton, G. B. Grayson and Henry Whitter, Ed Haley, Billie Holiday, John Lee Hooker, Tommy Jarrell, Skip James, Robert Johnson, Patsy Montana, Charlie Parker, Charlie Poole, Riley Puckett, Eck Robertson, Jimmie Rodgers, the Skillet Lickers, Arthur Smith, Bessie Smith, Bob Wills and the Texas Playboys. Thanks as well to Mike Seeger and the New Lost City Ramblers for kindling the 1960s revival of old-time music, continuing to this day.